D0065380

Cursing Columbus

Cursing Columbus

Eve Tal

Cinco Puntos Press El Paso

FIRST EDITION
10 9 8 7 6 5 4 3 2 1

Library of Congress Cataloging-in-Publication Data

Tal, Eve, 1947-
  Cursing Columbus / by Eve Tal. -- 1st ed.
     p. cm.
  Summary: In 1908, fourteen-year-old Raizel, who has lived in New York City for three years, and her brother Lemmel, newly-arrived, respond very differently to the challenges of living as Ukrainian Jews in the Lower East Side as Raizel works toward fitting in and getting ahead, while Lemmel joins a gang and lives on the streets.
   ISBN 978-1-933693-59-0 (alk. paper)
   [1. Immigrants—New York (State)—New York—Fiction. 2. Conduct of life—Fiction. 3. Jews—New York (State)—New York—Fiction. 4. Ukrainian Americans—Fiction. 5. Family life—New York (State)—New York—Fiction. 6. New York (N.Y.)—History—1898-1951—Fiction.] I. Title.

PZ7.T14138Cur 2009
[Fic]--dc22

                                2009015834

Thanks to poet Elinor Nauen for her read of *Cursing Columbus*
Cover painting by Susan Klahr acrylic and oil on pastel board
Photograph of Eve Tal by Tal Bedrack
Book and cover design by JB Bryan / La Alameda Press

In Memory of my Parents
Hannah and Irving Goldberg—

Love grows even after loss

Contents

An American Dream 11

1 ⊷ Family Reunion 13

2 ⊷ School Days 21

3 ⊷ American Beginnings 29

4 ⊷ Holiday Preparations 38

5 ⊷ Unhappy New Year 44

6 ⊷ News 53

7 ⊷ A Curse on Columbus 64

8 ⊷ The Contest 71

9 ⊷ Approaching Manhood 78

10 ⊷ A Lost Boy 87

11 ⊷ The Boarder 98

12 ⊷ Out of the Cold 110

13 ⊷ At the Theatre 118

14 ⊷ Back to School 124

15 ⊷ A Night Out 134

16 ⊷ To The Rescue 146

17 ⊷ The Letter 155

18 ⊷ The Gang's Plan 163

19 ⊷ My Brother's Keeper 170

20 ⊷ The Newspaper 177

21 ⊷ An Isle of Tears 187

22 ⊷ The Sacrifice 196

23 ⊷ Love and Marriage 206

24 ⟻ ON TRIAL 215

25 ⟻ NOTHING BUT THE TRUTH 221

26 ⟻ IN THE WILDERNESS 227

27 ⟻ THE PROMISED LAND 235

　　　　Afterword 245

　　　　Glossary 247

An American Dream

RAIZEL

Do dreams come true?

My dream was always the same: I was back in Jibatov, the little town in Russia where I was born. The whole family was sitting around the Sabbath table: Mama, Papa, baby Hannah and my brothers Lemmel and Shloyme. I was telling a story about America where the streets were paved with gold and roast chickens roosted in the trees. Everyone wanted to go to America and, suddenly, Papa and I were on board ship sailing farther and farther away from the Old Country and my family. I saw the Statue of Liberty towering over the harbor of New York. She raised her hand high above her head.

Was she waving to me?

No, her hand was raised to stop us. I looked around for Papa. I was all alone by the wide ocean.

Then I woke up and remembered:

In 1905, Papa and I arrived at Ellis Island. Papa had been sick for the entire voyage. We were rejected and deported back to Europe. On board the return ship, I became friends with Mr. Goldenberg, a wealthy businessman, and his blind mother. Mrs. Goldenberg and I told each other stories and she became like a grandmother to me. Together, we helped Papa make the hard choice of exchanging the traditions of his Orthodox religion for entrance into America. We even changed our family name from "Balaban" to "Altman." With Mr. Goldenberg's help, we returned on a second crossing.

For three years now, we had been living as boarders on the Lower East Side of New York. Papa worked from dawn to night in a sweatshop earning money to bring over the rest of the family, while I worked after school. I had tried to find my friends Reuben and Susan from the first crossing, but they had disappeared into the teeming masses of the city.

When I arrived in America, I couldn't read or write. Now I dreamed of going to college and becoming a teacher. But most of all, I dreamed of the day our family would be together again. Tomorrow, it would finally happen.

Do dreams come true?

Or does the answer depend on what you choose to dream?

I
Family Reunion

LEMMEL

We walked out of the Immigration Station on Ellis Island carrying our bundles. I recognized Papa and Raizel right away. Papa seemed surprised at how tall I was.

Mama and Raizel cried. Hannah wailed. Shloyme giggled.

Finally Raizel stopped crying. "Did you see the Statue of Liberty?" she asked.

"I saw it!" Shloyme yelled.

"Can we go visit the Lady?" Hannah asked her usual four-year-old questions.

"One day we'll go on a little boat. Would you like that?" Raizel tried to hug Hannah, who started wailing again.

"Never mind," Mama said. "She does not remember you. Since we left Jibatov, she cries when strangers touch her."

We took a ferryboat to the mainland. The late summer breeze stank of dead fish and garbage. Papa disappeared into the crowd and returned with two carriages. We loaded our bundles onto one and climbed onto the other. Papa held out his hand to help Mama and suddenly hugged her.

"Binyumin, people will see!" But Mama looked pleased.

Raizel plopped down next to me. "Lemmel, I can't believe how much you've grown. Tell me about the boat. Did you get seasick? Shloyme, did you know that almost three million people live in New York? Look, there's City Hall and the Courthouse! And there's…"

I stopped listening. Girls talked too much. New York had so many people and buildings, all crammed next to each other. Where were the trees and fields?

The buildings were huge. That one with the pointy roof and cross on top was much bigger than the church at home. I thought of the Christian boys back in my village. They didn't scare me. I could beat anyone my age, and older.

Crowds of men and women rushed along the sidewalks and swarmed across the streets like ants. Why was everyone in a hurry? A policeman stood in the middle of the street waving his arms and blowing a whistle like a wind-up toy.

Now the streets filled up with people who looked familiar. Bearded men wearing black hats and long coats struggled under huge bundles. Women lugged baskets of potatoes and onions. Boys chased boys. Girls pushed baby carriages.

Everyone was yelling in Yiddish. This must be—what did Raizel call it?—the Lower East Side where the Jews lived. Where we lived. The wagon could barely get by all the pushcarts. We turned down a narrow street. And still another.

"This is it: Goerck Street," Raizel said. "And here's our house, our very own house!"

We stopped in front of a four-story brick building. It looked dirty and run-down, just like the one next to it. Broken cobblestones pitted the street. The front stoop sagged in the middle. And what a stink!

"The East River is just a couple of blocks away." Papa apologized. "In the winter they say you hardly smell it at all."

Our apartment was on the top floor. I carried bundles up and down the stairs while Raizel waited below to make sure no one stole anything. The first landing smelled like cabbage. The second smelled spicy. The third smelled like old pee. On our landing there were four apartments. A woman with long black hair and a big belly stared at me. Two little kids with snotty noses peaked out from behind her.

I was sweating when I finished. August was hotter here than back home. In the kitchen everyone was sitting around a wobbly wooden table drinking lemonade. I gulped down two glasses and looked around.

"Where are the windows?"

They were busy talking so I went into the dark back room. There was barely space for the bed. A tiny window peered into an air shaft. The kitchen had no windows at all unless you counted the fake one opening into the front room. It had an enamel sink and rusty stove. The third room was bigger and two windows faced the street. I looked for the river but there were too many buildings, some taller than ours. This room had two beds and a lopsided bookcase. So we would all sleep together again, like we had back home. Shloyme, the human butterball, was sure to wind up on the floor!

"Binyumin, it is wonderful!" Mama exclaimed. "To think I have my own indoor sink. I won't have to go to the river to wash clothes."

Papa and Raizel burst out laughing.

"Mama, you can't wash clothes in the filthy East River!" Raizel said. "You do the washing in the backyard. I'll show you."

"Is that where I can pee?" Shloyme asked.

"No, there's a toilet on the landing. We share it with the other families on this floor. Come, I'll take you and Hannah." Raizel reached out to Hannah, who buried her face in Mama's lap. At least she didn't wail.

"So you like it?" Papa asked Mama.

"Oh yes. Imagine, an inside toilet and my own sink! The apartment is very clean and cozy."

"That is because Raizel is such a hard worker." Papa beamed. "When we have more money, we will find something bigger. Money is tight now."

Mama put her hand on Papa's arm. "Binyumin, it is perfect. A little fixing up and soon it will feel just like home."

This place *home*? How could home be a dark stinky hole with no fields and no trees and people everywhere you looked?

Had they all gone crazy?

RAIZEL

While Mama and the little ones rested, I prepared Friday night dinner. I wanted their first Sabbath dinner in America to be perfect.

The chicken was roasting in the stove when Mama stepped out of the backroom tucking her long hair inside a kerchief. Mama's hair had been black when we left Jibatov three years ago. Now it was threaded with white.

"You are not going to synagogue?" she asked Papa.

"Haveleh, I wrote you I don't go to shul anymore." Papa studied his hands.

"I thought you meant during the week, because of work. You always go to shul on Sabbath eve."

"Not in America." Papa sounded annoyed. "Here things are different. You will get used to it."

Mama shook her head. "Raizel, the chicken smells overdone!"

I rushed to the oven. Mama was right. The skin was already dark brown. I pulled it out along with the potatoes.

"Raizel, where are the Sabbath candles?" Mama asked.

I avoided Mama's eyes. "We have no candlesticks."

"I brought our brass candlesticks from home." Mama rummaged in a bundle in the corner. "And here is our Sabbath tablecloth."

I spread the tablecloth. The kitchen suddenly looked festive. "But we have no candles, Mama."

"What kind of Jews have you become? Your Bobbe, may she rest in peace, always said 'if a link is broken, the whole chain breaks.' So borrow two candles from the neighbors."

"Mama, our neighbors aren't Jewish. They're Italian Catholic."

Mama sat down heavily. "Italian? They don't even speak Yiddish? Where am I? What kind of place is this America?"

"Haveleh, everything will be all right." Papa rested his hands on Mama's shoulders. "You are just tired. You will feel better in the morning."

Mama looked up. Tears were running down her face. "But Binyumin, even on the boat to America I lit the Sabbath candles."

"I'll go ask the downstairs neighbors. They're Jewish." I scooted out the door. By the time I came back with two slightly used candles, Mama had set the table and everyone was sitting around it waiting for me. Everyone except Lemmel.

LEMMEL

Raizel was right. Judging by the brown scum on the river, it was no place for laundry. Where did that huge bridge lead? Was the other side New York, too?

I could see fish in the water. Dead fish. In the Polota River back home, the water was clean and clear. I loved swimming in the summer and lying in the furry ferns along the bank.

Like that time I ran away from home. I thought I would walk along the river all the way to Lubov and never come back. I was sure no one had seen me break Rebbe Shmuel's stick in school, but that snitch Pessel went and told on me. So I walked and walked until I finally got so hungry I turned back for home. Mama would never have known what happened if I hadn't fallen asleep alongside the river. I got home late at night and Mama knew all about my breaking the stick. But I'll never forget how beautiful it was along the river with the stars scattered like handfuls of sugar in the night sky.

Mama was so worried she forgot to whip me, not that she whipped very hard. No supper, though. And every time I peeked out the bedroom door, she was sitting in front of the cupboard. I thought my stomach would turn into a raisin. I think she sat there all night.

Uh oh. What were those boys yelling?

"Nah nah nah" to you, too.

Hey! That hurt.

Why were they throwing rocks at me? I didn't do nothing to them.

They could run fast, but not as fast as me.

There, I lost them.

Better not be late for Friday night supper. Strange. Papa said he didn't go to shul anymore. Maybe he wouldn't make me have a bar mitzvah.

Wish it hadn't gotten dark so fast.

"Please, where is Goerck Street?" Hey, why didn't you answer me? Guess she didn't understand Yiddish.

"Vere Goerck?" Don't look at me so funny. That's what they taught me to say on the boat.

No problem, I'd just head back to the river and retrace my steps. Let's see, the river must be there. Or was it over that way? The dark was confusing…

"Lem—mel!"

Someone was calling my name.

"Lemmel, where have you been?" Raizel ran up, her braids flapping. "Papa and I have been yelling up and down the streets for hours. Why didn't you answer?"

"I didn't hear you until now."

"But we're blocks from home, way over on Delancy Street and Suffolk."

"I got lost. These guys started throwing rocks and chasing me."

"Oh you poor thing. I should have warned you about the Irish gangs. I was afraid to move here, but we couldn't find a place cheap enough uptown. Don't tell Mama about the rocks. She's upset enough already."

Of course, I wouldn't tell Mama. I never told her about the fights in Jibatov unless I got hit in the face. She never believed I fell down. Mama was no fool.

Cursing Columbus

Shloyme and Hannah were fast asleep when we returned to the apartment. Mama had turned off the gaslights and we ate in the flickering light of the Sabbath candles. Mama kept looking at Papa and shaking her head. She barely nibbled the dry chicken and cold potatoes.

In bed with Shloyme, I couldn't fall asleep. It was hot and people were talking on the roof.

"Raizel, are you asleep?"

"How can I be asleep if I'm standing at the window? They say it's hot enough to fry an egg on the pavement this August."

"Raizel, how long did it take you to learn English?"

"I learned a bit from the Goldenbergs on the boat back to Europe, and then from the ship's cook. At first everyone laughed at my accent. At school they put me in a special class. We had to practice saying 'th' over and over again."

"Da."

"Th. Touch your front teeth lightly with your tongue."

"Ta."

"Better. After a couple of months they transferred me into a regular class."

"What about. . .reading?"

"Reading was easy. I don't remember how long it took me."

"I don't want to go to school. I want to work." I'd hated school ever since I was a little kid. Raizel used to be jealous that I went to school and she didn't.

"You have to go to school until you're fourteen. It's the law here."

"A year?" Too long.

"School here isn't like back home in Jibatov. The boys get to make things in carpentry class and play outside in the school yard. I bet you'll like it."

I had my doubts.

Raizel made a funny sound.

"You crying?"

"No. . . it's just that I've been waiting so long for you all to come and nothing worked out like I planned. Mama was mad at Papa for not going to synagogue and I burnt the chicken and Hannah was afraid of me and you disappeared and. . .I thought we would be so happy together after all these years apart." She sniffed and got into bed next to Hannah.

"G'night." I nudged Shloyme to the edge of the bed. Raizel hadn't changed. She always cried about nothing.

2
School Days

RAIZEL

"Mama, did you make the sandwiches?" A few weeks had passed since the homecoming and I was braiding my hair for the first day of school. "Shloyme, drink your milk. Lemmel, hurry up, we haven't got all day!"

"I can't help it if I had to wait for the bathroom. That girl, what's her name, was in there for hours." Lemmel plopped down at the table.

I nibbled a thick slice of bread and butter as Lemmel ate another, and still another. "Come on, we'll be late!" Lemmel continued eating. The freckles on his pale skin glared at me. Lemmel didn't care if he never got to school.

"Raizel, I'm ready." Shloyme's dark brown hair was brushed in a neat part. We had bought his white shirt and knee pants last week in the market. "I have my pencil case and my notebooks." He looked so serious, I wanted to hug him.

Lemmel pushed back his chair and stood up with a groan.

"Raizel, hold Shloyme by the hand all the way to school. And be there to pick him up when school is out, he shouldn't have to walk home alone. And come straight home after school so we can go to the store."

"Mama, I have to go to the library. My books will be overdue."

"Always with her head in a book, that one. You went last week and we need to buy food. Be good, boys, and listen to Raizel." Mama gave Shloyme a hug and Lemmel a worried look.

My books weren't really overdue. I read them too fast. But now I wouldn't be able to pick out new ones. The family had been here for weeks and I still had to go everywhere with Mama. She was afraid of getting lost. She was afraid of losing Hannah. She was afraid a horse would run Hannah over. No wonder Hannah was scared of everything!

"Now remember, Shloyme, in school your name is Samuel. And yours is Louis," I called over my shoulder to Lemmel.

"Why do I have to change my name?"

"Because 'Shloyme' isn't an American name. We're in America now, right?" Shloyme nodded happily.

We pushed our way through the crowds on Rivington Street and crossed Clinton. Once Lemmel ran across the street to talk to a boy I didn't know. He wore a cap pulled down over his eyes and his clothes looked new.

"Who was that?" I asked Lemmel when he sauntered back across the street.

"A guy I know named Harry."

"He doesn't go to school?"

"Nah, his mother's a widow and doesn't make him go to school. He runs errands and stuff." Lemmel tossed a lock of hair out of his eyes. He was the only one in the family with red hair. Even though I was almost a year older, he was taller than me.

"Here we are." Shloyme hung on my hand as we climbed the stone stairs to P.S. 160.

"Raizel, where will you wait for me after school?"

"I'll meet you at the bottom of the stairs." We entered the principal's office. "I've come to register my brothers for school," I said.

Miss Warren, the sharp-nosed secretary, glanced at us through her glasses and nodded to a row of chairs. "Mr. McGraw is in assembly. Sit down and be quiet."

A few minutes later Mr. McGraw strode into the office wiping his face with a white handkerchief. Mr. McGraw was always in a hurry.

I remembered when Papa had registered me at school the week after we arrived. Papa didn't know any English and was still looking for a job. He had been surprised when he learned that I had to go to school. There had been no school for girls in Jibatov. The people we boarded with told him the truant officers would come for me if I didn't go to school, so he reluctantly agreed. Then I had answered Mr. McGraw's questions as best I could in the little English I knew. When he asked me my American name, I didn't know what he meant. "'Raizel' isn't an American name," he repeated slowly. "You need an American name. Now what will it be? Rose? Rachel? Regina?" I had to give up my name? It made no sense. When I didn't answer, he picked up his pen and wrote something in strong black letters. "Rose. You are now called Rose Altman."

Now when Mr. McGraw asked for Shloyme and Lemmel's American names, I didn't hesitate. "Samuel Altman and Louis Altman," I said.

"Your brothers will go into Miss O'Brien's special English class. It's in 3C." He nodded at me and turned to Lemmel and Shloyme, who had been standing behind my chair. "Welcome to P.S. 160," he said and began shuffling through a pile of papers on his desk.

I led them down the corridor and up the stairs to the third floor. "Here's your classroom."

"I have to be in a class with Shloyme? He's only a baby!"

"I am not a baby!" Shloyme looked about to cry.

"Shhh, no talking in the halls! It's only until you learn enough English to go into a regular class. Miss O'Brien is nice. She was my first teacher. And remember, no speaking Yiddish, even to Shloyme. You're only allowed to speak English in school."

"No talking. No Yiddish. This place has too many rules."

I ignored Lemmel and opened the heavy wooden door. There must have been over forty kids of different ages in the classroom, all greenhorns, but there were still a few empty seats. "Good morning, Miss O'Brien, I've just come from Mr. McGraw's office. These are my brothers Samuel and Louis Altman."

Miss O'Brien had bright blue eyes and a big smile. "Good morning, Rose. I hear nice things about you from your teachers." She took the registration papers from me. "Thank you, dear. You can go to your class now. I'll take care of your brothers." I squeezed Shloyme's hand and led him to an empty seat in the front row. Lemmel chose a seat in the back next to a window.

LEMMEL

"My nam iz Lou. I go to P.S. Von Seex Zeero." I had been in school over a week now.

"Very good, but your name is Louis," said Miss O'Brien.

"Lou. I vant name Lou." Louis was a sissy name. All the guys said so.

"Don't talk back to your teacher. Now, Fanny, I want you to check that everyone's hands and nails are clean. Class, say 'clean hands.'"

"Ca-lean hands."

Everyday the same stupid thing. A girl wearing a yellow hair ribbon walked around inspecting our hands. Back front. Back front. I was last.

"Miss O'Brien, Louis is dirty hands."

"Louis *has* dirty hands. Louis, I have given you a bad mark. Now go to the lavatory and wash your hands. And come right back to class."

Finally. The door clicked shut behind me. I showed the hall monitor my pass and headed for the lavatory. Miss O'Brien still hadn't caught on. Everyday I left home with clean hands and arrived in school with dirty hands. Sometimes I rubbed dirt on my face. You had to be tricky. If I was lucky, I'd miss the reading lesson.

I joined the guys in the lavatory on the first floor. Hardly anyone went in there except the little kids and they wouldn't tell if they knew what was good for them!

"Hey Louie, howya doin? Gotta smoke?"

"Nah. No money."

"Here greenie, have one." Manny handed me a cigarette.

I sat in the stall, inhaling the acrid smoke. At first it had burned my throat but I got used to it fast. I needed to find a way to make money like the other guys.

It was always about money. In Jibatov we never had enough money, but at least we didn't have to pay rent. On the days I didn't go to cheder, I earned a few kopeks chopping wood and running errands at the tavern. Sometimes Boris let me take care of the horses. I loved those big strong brutes. I would do that for free. I almost cried when we had to sell our horse, Bunchik, after Papa left. I still missed him. The horses here were pitiful. Last week there was a dead horse in the street, just lying there. He had pink foam around his mouth and his hide was covered with bloody sores. Everybody walked around him. He lay there for days until they carted him away.

There was one good thing about school in America. When you got out, you still had time to play. In Jibatov we had to study after dark, especially when I was studying for my bar mitzvah. After Rebbe Shmuel threw me out for talking back to him, that was the best time. Mama was expecting the tickets to America and decided there was no point in looking for another teacher. I told her I would work and I did. I took care of the horses and brought her the money I earned. She was pleased, I could tell. We needed money for the crossing.

So why wouldn't they let me work here instead of going to school? I hated school. Reading English was worse than Hebrew. There were letters with straight lines and letters with circles. I couldn't tell them apart and they jumped around on the page.

Shloyme finished learning all his letters last week. Miss O'Brien started him on the first reader today. I hated it when my little brother was smarter than me.

Who needed to read, anyway? I could make money on the street. Harry had loads of money. Nice clothes too, with no patches. And new shoes.

"Louie, move it, the teach!"

I threw the butt in the toilet and flushed. The teacher looked at my hall pass suspiciously, but let me go back to class. Miss O'Brien was writing numbers on the blackboard when I slipped in. If I could just do the sums in my head, I'd be all right. Please don't make me go up to the board. I hated when they laughed at me. Even Shloyme laughed.

"I have found a teacher for Lemmel," Papa said when he came home that night.

"Papa, I already have a teacher. In school."

Papa smiled a tired smile at me. "This is a teacher for your bar mitzvah. He will come four days a week and prepare you. I told him you went to cheder." He turned to Mama. "He said that cheder boys learn fast, not like American boys. So it will not cost very much, just a few pennies a week."

"Papa, we can't afford it." I tried again. "How will we pay the rent? I don't need a bar mitzvah in America."

"What does a bar mitzvah have to do with America?" Mama asked. "Of course you will have a bar mitzvah. Every Jewish boy has a bar mitzvah."

"Calm down, Haveleh. Lemmel is a good boy." Papa touched my arm. "He knows how important a bar mitzvah is to his mother, don't you, son?"

I took a deep breath and nodded. "Yes, Papa."

But it wasn't fair. If I had to come home for lessons, I wouldn't have time after school to hang out with the gang. Just when they were beginning to think I was okay. When I first met them I thought they were tough. But they weren't so tough. I could beat them all, except Harry.

Cursing Columbus

We sat down to supper. The borscht tasted almost like home.

"Mama, there's no meat in my soup." Shloyme put down his spoon.

"Meat is expensive. We can't eat meat everyday," Papa said. "What do you think this is, America?" He laughed an unfunny laugh.

"Were there more layoffs at work, Papa?" Raizel looked worried.

"Too many. The newspapers say we are in a recession. That means people don't buy as many new clothes. Fewer new clothes, fewer orders, and then fewer workers."

"What will be, Binyumin?" Mama put an extra boiled potato in Shloyme's soup.

"This too will pass." Papa coughed his dry rattling cough.

"Papa, tonight you must study English." Raizel was teaching Papa to read.

"Your Papa is too tired. He has a cough and needs to rest," Mama said getting up from the table.

Behind her back, Raizel and Papa exchanged looks.

After supper, Mama put Hannah to bed. Raizel sat between Shloyme and Papa at the kitchen table. She listened to Shloyme read from the first reader. Then Mama put a cup of tea in front of Papa and took Shloyme to bed. Raizel wrote sentences for Papa, who read them slowly. He read better than Shloyme, but not much.

"You are out of practice, Papa. We haven't been working enough since the family came."

"I have too much on my mind now. It is hard to concentrate." Papa coughed and took a sip of tea.

"But you need to read if you want to find a better job. You know that, Papa."

Mama sat down. "You work too hard, Binyumin. You will make yourself sick."

"Everyone works hard here. What do you think this is, America?" Papa didn't bother to laugh at his joke this time.

"But why in the garment factory?" Mama continued. "I see what it is like. All day pressing with a hot iron. The air there never moves and is full of lint and dust. That is why you cough."

"It is not so bad. The first factory I worked in was a real sweatshop. The boss made us eat lunch at our work place and docked us money if we went to the bathroom."

"But why a presser? It is too hard for you."

"Because it is more money than sewing. I am not a cutter, I should be so lucky. What do I know about making suits? And it is better than peddling."

"You should have seen Papa carrying pots and pans when we first arrived," Raizel said. "He could barely walk up the stairs."

"Better I didn't see. *Oy*, my scholar, what will become of you?" Mama rocked back and forth. "My husband cuts his beard and to shul he doesn't go. For this we came to America?"

I stared at my arithmetic problems. The white spaces between the numbers criss-crossed the page. Silently I agreed with Mama.

3
American Beginnings

RAIZEL

"Raizel, take Shloyme and Hannah downstairs to play," Mama called from the kitchen.

"But Mama, I'm writing an essay about Columbus."

"What is this Columbus?" Mama peered through the window wiping the sweat off her face. A pot of vegetable soup bubbled a spicy fragrance through the apartment.

"Christopher Columbus discovered America in 1492. Miss Norman is going to enter the best essay in a citywide contest, 'Columbus, An American Hero.' So, please, Mama, I have to finish."

"Finish after dinner. Hannah has been inside all day."

"But Mama…"

"No buts. Helping your mama is more important than some dead Columbus."

I sighed and put my paper and pencil away.

"Go to the store and buy milk for the little ones." Mama handed me three cents.

"Can I have a penny for candy?" Shloyme asked.

Mama shook her head. "Not today."

"Puh-leeze, Mama." Shloyme gazed up at Mama like a cherub. "I got an 'A' on my spelling test today. And Miss O'Brien said I had the cleanest nails in the class."

"They say the stingy rich man is the worst pauper. I guess one penny won't put us in the poor house." Mama placed a penny in his outstretched hand. "Don't forget to share the candy with Hannah."

"Candy, candy, candy," Hannah sang as she skipped along the street next to me. She no longer clung to my hand like she did the first weeks, but she wouldn't play downstairs alone like the other little girls, either. I had stopped working after school at Mr. Abrahamson's store in order to watch her, even though he still let me work there on Sundays. "What would I do without my blooming Rose?" he asked, chucking me under the chin.

Worst of all, I never had time to go to the library anymore. It was too far for Hannah to walk. Sometimes my friend Sarah lent me her books if she finished them quickly enough, but lately she had been reading *Little Women*, which was so thick that even Sarah couldn't finish it in one week.

"Give me your hand," I said to Hannah. There were too many saloons on Goerck Street, and too many women in thick make-up and thin clothes standing outside them. And tough boys. The people here were poorer than on the streets Papa and I had lived on before.

"Those people are funny." Hannah pointed at a woman with five children sitting on a bed in the middle of the sidewalk. "They should sleep in their house."

"They can't because they were evicted," Shloyme said.

"Hush, they'll hear you." I shuddered. Every day families were thrown into the streets because they couldn't pay their rent. "There's no mercy on Goerck Street," people said. The woman on the bed held a baby in her lap and thrust out her hand to passersby. Like us, no one seemed to have any money to give her.

"Hey, there's Lemmel!" Shloyme called.

"Lemmel, don't forget your bar mitzvah lesson!" I shouted as Lemmel raced past. Mama would be furious if he missed his lesson again. The Rebbe made her pay even if Lemmel didn't show up. "He costs me another pupil," he would say, stroking his long white beard. Lemmel complained he smelled like garlic and pinched his arm every time he made a mistake. Lemmel must have made lots of mistakes because his arms were covered with black and blue marks.

"How is Lemmel doing in school?" I asked Shloyme.

Shloyme stared at the broken sidewalk. "Fine," he whispered.

"Did he tell you not to tell Mama?" I asked. Shloyme nodded. "Well, I'm not Mama so you can tell me."

"He can speak English good, better than me. But every time he reads, Miss O'Brien bites her lip and the other kids laugh like crazy."

"I hope you don't laugh."

"Not any more." Shloyme rubbed his arm.

Every time I offered to help Lemmel with his homework he shook his head and covered his paper. But I could see he was having trouble. Shloyme was almost through the first reader and Lemmel hadn't even started.

"What kind of candy do you want?" I asked Hannah when we reached the store.

"Chocolate babies," Hannah said, pointing to the tiny dark figures.

"I want hard candy. No, peppermint sticks. Wait, maybe I'll try those yellow ones over there." As usual Shloyme couldn't make up his mind.

"That's candy corn. It's soft and chewy."

Shloyme nodded, his eyes shining.

"Give me a half penny of chocolate babies and a half penny of candy corn," I told the lady behind the counter. "Separate bags, please."

"Big spender," she muttered and scooped up the candy.

"Have you seen Lemmel?" Mama asked when we came home with the milk. "He missed his bar mitzvah lesson again."

"He had to stay after school for extra help," Shloyme said, too quickly. "I forgot to tell you."

"That boy will be the death of me. Does he think we are made of money? How will he be ready for his bar mitzvah?"

I called Shloyme into the front room out of Mama's hearing. "Why did you lie to Mama?"

"Lemmel said it isn't lying. It's just not telling the truth. He gave me a penny to buy candy all for myself."

"You know Mama always says 'a half-truth is a whole lie.' It's a lie just like in the story about George Washington, the father of our country, and the cherry tree."

"Tell me the story, Raizel!" Shloyme had been begging me for stories ever since he arrived. I had almost forgotten the stories I used to tell him. In America I was always busy with school and work and girlfriends. No one wanted to hear stories about the Old Country. "I'll tell you the story, but you have to promise not to lie to Mama, even if Lemmel tells you to. And you have to give the penny to Mama. Every penny counts in the Altman family."

"Raizel, puh-leeze." Shloyme looked at me with eyes that could melt chocolate. But I wasn't Mama. The penny and the truth were safely in her hands before I sat down to tell him the familiar story.

LEMMEL

"So Lemmel, it is an honor to have your company tonight," Mama said as I walked in the door.

I washed my hands at the sink. "I'm sorry I'm late. Shloyme was supposed to tell you. Miss O'Brien said I need extra help."

If he had forgotten, I would take back the penny and give him something he wouldn't forget! Raizel and Shloyme were staring at their plates. A bad sign.

"Don't lie to me!" Mama spat the words through her teeth. "And don't you dare use Shloyme to cover your lies. What are you, some kind of gangster?"

I slid into my chair and picked up a fork. Potatoes again.

Mama grabbed the fork from my hand. "Go into the front room and do your homework. When Papa comes home, you are going to get a beating you won't forget!"

How did Mama expect me to do my homework on an empty stomach? I opened the book and tried to concentrate. The words swirled in front of my eyes.

"Wake up, you lazy good-for-nothing!" Mama was shaking my shoulder. "Papa is home."

Papa didn't look angry like Mama. He looked tired. "What is this I hear about skipping your bar mitzvah lesson? And making Shloyme lie for you?"

"Papa, the Rebbe is a terrible teacher. I can't learn from him."

"The Rebbe says he never had such a lazy pupil."

Lazy. Why did all my teachers call me lazy? I worked just as hard as everyone else, even harder. It wasn't my fault that the letters jumped around all the time. "Papa, I don't need a bar mitzvah when you don't even go to pray anymore."

Papa let out his breath slowly. "I was bar mitzvahed, and my father was bar mitzvahed, and his father and his father before him. And every son of mine will also be bar mitzvahed. That is how Jews enter manhood and accept responsibility. Even though I choose not to go to shul, I am still a Jew and so are you. Do you understand?"

I nodded my head.

"So you will come home to your lessons and study hard and in two months we will hold your bar mitzvah."

"Two months? Papa, I can't be ready in two months!"

"Two months. You have been studying in the cheder since you were four years old. Two months is enough time. And I will make a deal with you, as they say in America."

"What kind of deal?"

"I will tell the Rebbe not to pinch you. I see those marks on your arms. And I won't beat you either, even though your mama will be angry with me. But you must promise to study hard and be ready for your bar mitzvah in two months."

I stared at the floor. I wouldn't be ready in two months. I wouldn't be ready in a year. No matter how hard I worked, I wouldn't be able to read a passage from the Torah.

Because I couldn't read.

"I promise, Papa."

What else could I do?

RAIZEL

"Rose Altman, I knew you would win." Sarah squeezed my hand. We were walking home from school with Shloyme tagging along behind us.

"I haven't won yet."

"But you will. Your essay on Columbus was wonderful!"

Miss Norman thought so, too. She said it was the best in the school and had sent it to the city-wide contest. "I really liked your essay, too."

"Oh, it was good, but yours was. . .original, that's the word. Won't your Mama be proud?"

I skirted a pile of horse manure and checked that Shloyme was watching where he walked. "She's not like your mama. She doesn't care how well I do in school, only how much I help her around the house. You're lucky you don't have to watch your little sisters."

"That's because they watch each other. When they were really little, my older sister had to watch them. There are some advantages to being a middle child."

"I guess there are advantages to being the eldest, too. I got to go with Papa to America. I never would have met the Goldenbergs if I had stayed behind."

"Did you get an answer to your last letter?"

"Yesterday. Mr. Goldenberg wrote that his mother was too ill to write, but that my letter made her happy." Mrs. Goldenberg had been so helpful when we were rejected at Ellis Island. We had told each other stories on the crossing back and she had even invited me to stay with her in Belgium.

"And you never would have met Reuben." Sarah winked.

"Shhh!" I glanced back at Shloyme. He was kicking a can and paying no attention to our conversation. In the beginning he couldn't understand when we spoke English. It was like having a secret language. But everyday he understood more and more. I couldn't take any chances. Sarah was the only one who knew about Reuben. Not that there was much to know. "But I haven't seen him or his sister Susan since the first crossing."

"You might. He's probably living in New York. You could be strolling in the park and suddenly. . .it would be so romantic to meet him again!"

"Sarah!" I could feel myself blushing. Reuben had given me his address before he left the boat with his family. But by the time we got to New York after our double crossing, the letter I sent him came back marked 'No forwarding address.' I never saw Reuben or Susan again.

"Hi, Rose, wanna play?" Lucia was sitting on the front stoop of our building with her little brother and sister. They both had runny noses, as usual.

"I have to see if Mama needs help. How come you're home so early?" Lucia was in the grade below me at school.

"The baby's sick. Mama made me stay home to help her."

"Did you take him to the doctor at the charity clinic?" Like Mama, Lucia's mother hadn't learned English yet.

"Nah, we don't have money for medicine."

Mama was bent over the stove with her back to me when we walked in. "Guess what, Mama? Miss Norman sent my essay to the city-wide contest! Isn't that wonderful?"

Mama straightened her back and turned around. "Oy, what an aching back I have. Better I should be cooking at our stove back home. I need you to run to the market and buy the meat for tomorrow."

The aroma of honey cake filled my nostrils and sweetened the hurt of Mama's indifference to my news. A memory surfaced of Bobbe cutting me a slice of the still warm cake when I was little. "Shhh, your mama shouldn't see." We had licked the crumbs from our fingers and smiled at our secret.

"It smells delicious, Mama. But why do I need to go all the way to the market? I can take Hannah and Shloyme with me to the corner store." And have time do my homework.

"Raizel Balaban, don't you remember? Tomorrow is the evening of Rosh Hashanah!"

The Jewish New Year! I had forgotten all about it. We hadn't celebrated the Jewish holidays, except for Passover, since coming to America.

"Of course I remember, Mama." At least I did now. "What do you need?"

"A fresh piece of brisket, six onions, two carrots, and half a kilo of apples. No, make that a kilo. If I have time, I'll bake strudel."

I remembered Mama's strudel. Crisp and flaky, it tasted like something the angels ate in heaven.

"And tomorrow you will watch Hannah and help me cook."

"Tomorrow? I have a history test. I can't stay home from school."

Mama's face turned so red I thought she would burst into flames. "I am sick and tired of hearing about school this and homework that! What is so important about school for a girl anyway?"

"Mama, I love school. I want to study and. . ."

"You love *school*? Your husband and family you should love! A girl must know how to cook and clean and take care of her husband and children. History, she doesn't need."

"But it's the law in America. I have to go to school until I'm fourteen." I regretted the words as soon as I had said them.

"So what is the big problem? In a few months you will be fourteen and will not have to go to school anymore. You can work in a store and help me around the house like a good daughter. That will be more useful than your history tests!"

"Please Mama, I don't want to work in a store or a factory like Papa. My dream is to be a teacher."

"From golden dreams you wake hungry. When I was your age I had one dream only—that my father would find a kind hard-working husband for me, he should be a scholar, too, G-d willing. And my dream came true."

"But this is America, Mama. In America things are different."

"In this home, things are not different. Now, enough! Take the money and go to the market. And make sure you get a piece of meat with plenty of fat, it should be nice and tender the way your papa likes it."

I grabbed the money and the market basket and stormed out the door, almost bumping into Lucia's mother. She was holding the baby in her arms and talking loudly to a woman I recognized from the floor below us. "Bambino, bambino," she was crying.

"I have to go to the market," I called to Lucia as I ran down the steps.

If Mama made me quit school, how would I fulfill my dream of going to college and becoming a teacher?

4
Holiday Preparations

RAIZEL

The market was a long walk across Grand Street to Orchard. Usually Mama sent me only on Friday afternoons, with instructions to buy the freshest fish and a plucked chicken for the Friday meal. During the week we bought at the corner grocery store or at one of the pushcarts down the block. But for the more expensive items, I could save money on Orchard Street, and saving money meant we would have more to eat during the week. Lemmel could finish half a loaf of bread at a sitting!

Mama didn't understand about school. How could she? In our little town in the Ukraine, girls grew up, helped their mamas, married the boy their parents chose for them and had children of their own. They barely saw their future husband before the wedding. Either the marriage broker chose him or their parents. In either case, the girl had almost no say in the matter. And if she didn't like him? She was doomed to spend the rest of her life with a man she despised. I had known women like that back in Jibatov. Their children choked on their sour anger. I was grateful that Mama and Papa loved each other. Even though they had grown up in different towns and only met once before the wedding, Mama said their love grew as quickly as an oak sprout and with roots just as deep.

But was that what I wanted? A few years of working in an uptown department store followed by marriage to a factory worker? Then the rest of my life raising babies and cooking and cleaning and doing laundry day in and day out? With nothing to look forward to except a bigger apartment if my husband worked hard and didn't get laid off?

No, thank you! In America I could go to college and become a teacher! I could dress in ruffled shirtwaists, pile my hair on top of my head and teach children history, English and arithmetic. They would call me "Miss Altman" and after school I would go home to my neat apartment on a clean street and read all the books I wanted with no one to disturb me.

I packed my dreams away as I approached the pushcarts on Orchard Street. I would buy the fruit and vegetables last, I decided, after I saw how much money was left.

Papa wasn't the problem. After a few weeks working in a sweatshop, he had grasped that the only way to get ahead was to become an American. That's when he asked me to teach him English. Papa understood that staying in school was the way to get ahead. But Mama didn't, and at home Mama made the decisions.

How could I convince Mama to let me stay in school?

I was thinking so hard that I collided with a woman carrying a basket of potatoes.

"I'm sorry," I said stooping to pick them up.

"Noodle head! In bed you dream, not on the sidewalk!" she cursed in Yiddish. People stared and I felt my face burn. Handing her the last dirty potato, I headed for the butcher shop past the fish market.

Ugh, how I hated the smell of fish. I was careful not to step in the glistening piles of fish scales. The woman I usually bought the carp from for gefilte fish called out to me, but I didn't answer. She always tried to bully me into buying yesterday's fish. She never would have dared with Mama, but the vendors all thought they could make an extra penny on me. And they probably did.

"I want a fat piece of brisket," I said to the man behind the butcher counter.

"For how many people?"

"Five." Mama always said not to count Hannah because between Hannah and me we ate only for one. "No wait, seven." Mama was inviting the young couple from the next building. They had just come over on the boat and she felt sorry for them.

"This piece will cost you sixty cents. See the nice fat marbling? Very tender."

"Too much. I want something cheaper."

The butcher sighed. "Always they want the cheaper. And then they complain because the meat was tough. All right, girlie, you can have this piece for fifty cents or this one for forty-five cents. But your mama will be sorry you did not take the better cut, believe me."

I didn't believe him. Mama was such a good cook she could make shoe leather taste good. Her parents had owned an inn and she had grown up in the kitchen. "Forty cents."

"Forty-five and not one cent cheaper."

I turned to leave.

"Forty-three and that is my final price."

I counted out the money. The butcher looked pleased. He had probably planned on going down to thirty-five. Would I never learn?

I passed an old woman holding a stick full of thick chewy pretzels. Next to her a man was selling sweet potatoes hot out of the oven. The aroma set my stomach growling. I had been too upset to grab a slice of bread and butter at home. I counted the pennies I had left. Better not.

At the apple stand, I was glad I hadn't succumbed. The price of apples had shot up since last week, even though it was apple season.

"These *gonifs* always raise the prices before a holiday," grumbled the woman next to me. I picked out ten apples and was waiting in line to weigh them when I heard the man at the next stand.

"Apples half-price! Cheap and tasty. Half-price today!"

I dumped my apples back in the cart, earning a curse from the apple lady. The half-price apples were half-rotten, but since Mama was making apple strudel, she could cut away the rotten parts. I looked for apples with only a slight bruise or two.

"Nu, you have to handle all my beautiful apples?"

"Your beautiful apples are rotten."

"If they are rotten, why do you want to buy them?" He laughed through broken teeth.

"I will pay you for the good parts, not the rotten," I said, and offered him two cents less then he was asking.

"Such a little lady and already a cheap Charlie." But he was smiling good-naturedly. "You can have them for two cents less and may you have a healthy new year." He weighed the apples and poured them into my basket. Then he reached under a pile and pulled out a firm red apple. "And this one is for you, may some meat grow on your skinny bones."

I thanked him and took a bite of the apple. My basket was heavy, but my feet felt light. I had bought everything Mama needed and still had ten cents change. And an apple to munch, besides.

Six blocks later my basket seemed to have gained weight. Pain shot up my arm and into my shoulder. I spotted a familiar head of red hair among a group of boys playing one o'cat on a side street.

"Lemmel, come help me," I called.

"Can't. I'm in the middle of a game." He threw down his stick and chip of wood and ran up to me. "Can I have an apple?"

"Only if you help me carry the basket."

"Naww, they're all rotten anyway. Carry them yourself." He grabbed an apple and skipped away.

"Hey, give that back!" I was so mad I could have smacked him. He played while I worked. Why did boys have all the fun? I switched the heavy basket to my right arm and struggled on home.

LEMMEL

"Hey Louie, stop jawing with your sister and get back in the game."

Why did Raizel have to yell at me in front of the gang? I would have helped her if she had waited until I finished batting. The game was almost over and the guys were counting on me. I set the cat on the ground and struck it with my stick. Good one! I made it to second base.

"Joey, Joey, hit that cat!" Kid thought he was a big shot. He couldn't hit a piece of wood if…uh oh, it was sailing right for the second story window.

"Run, guys!"

I dashed down the alley followed by Joey and Harry. We were laughing so hard we could barely stand.

"Did you see how the cat went straight though the window?" I leaned against the fence trying to catch my breath.

"That lady sure was mad!"

"She should be happy I didn't break her damn window!" Joey stuck his nose in the air.

"You should be happy she didn't break your damn neck!" said Harry. We doubled over with laughter.

"If we could play on a ballfield instead of the street, it wouldn't happen." Harry was always talking about getting a ballfield. He said he saw them uptown. I had never seen one. But then I had never been uptown.

"What we gonna do on Wednesday?" Joey asked.

"What's Wednesday?" I knew Harry didn't go to school, but Joey did.

"Rosh Hashanah. We get to stay home from school."

"I got to work." Harry sighed. "Them Irish don't know about Jewish holidays. Maybe I could skip out early."

"My mama will make me go to school," I said.

"Nah, she won't. Everyone stays home on a Jewish holiday. The teachers don't mind."

"Really? Then we can play all day?"

"All you think about is playing. Let's get some money."

Cursing Columbus

"Okay." I could use money. "How? Pitching pennies?"

Harry and Joey laughed. "Should we teach the greenie?" Joey asked.

"Teach me what?"

"How to get money fast." Harry slipped his hand into Joey's pocket. Joey grabbed his wrist. "Too slow. You need practice."

"You mean stealing? Pickpocketing?" I had heard the guys at school talking about it.

"Them that got gives to them that don't." Joey grinned. "And I sure don't got."

"Come on, Louie, you a chicken or something? Buck, buck, buck!"

"I'm no chicken."

"Okay, now listen good." Harry gave the orders. "Meet me at noon at the El stop over on Rivington. We'll go uptown where the rich people live. Wear your best clothes."

All the way home, I practiced thrusting my hand in and out of my empty pockets.

They wouldn't be empty long.

5
Unhappy New Year

RAIZEL

I stepped back to admire the white linen tablecloth and the brass candlesticks I had polished until they glowed. The table was too small for eight people, but we would manage somehow. All day I had been helping Mama prepare the chicken soup, farfel, and strudel. I had run to the corner store each time Mama remembered that she needed something. There hadn't been a minute to regret the missed history test.

Afterwards, I had given Hannah and Shloyme a bath in the big tin laundry tub. Mama and I had gone to the public baths on Allen Street. Papa was there now and would be home any minute.

And then there was Lemmel.

"Where is that boy?" Mama grumbled. "I told him to come right home after school. Shloyme has been home for hours." Shloyme knew the way well enough to walk home alone now.

The door opened with a bang and Lemmel ran in. "I'm sorry I'm late, Mama. I brought you flowers for the holiday table." He thrust a bouquet of flowers into Mama's hands.

Mama's eyes widened. "Where did you get these?"

"I ran errands for the flower store down the block. There were a lot of deliveries for the holiday. They gave me these when I finished." Lemmel sounded pleased.

"They are beautiful." Mama touched a pink petal.

"We always had flowers at home and here in the city there is no place to pick fresh flowers so. . ."

"Yes, yes." Mama turned back to the stove. "Raizel, put these in water. Lemmel, wash up and put on your clean shirt. There is no time for a bath."

I filled an empty milk bottle with water and set the flowers on the table. Sometimes Lemmel surprised me. Who would have thought he cared about flowers?

"Good *yontif*, good *yontif!*" Papa walked in followed by Shayna and Mendel, the young couple who lived in the next building. They had married just before leaving for America.

"I brought you a nice potato kugel, you should have something to eat tomorrow on the holiday." Shayna was short and plump with red rosy cheeks and a tinkley laugh.

"Thank you." Mama gave Shayna a hug. "Now everyone come sit down. Dinner is ready."

Papa looked at the table with a big smile on his face. "I have been dreaming of this moment for three years." He kissed Mama on the cheek. "We are all together for the holidays, just like back home."

"It would be like home if you would go to shul," Mama said, covering her head with a square of lace. She and Papa had had an argument about that last night. Papa had promised to take Mama and the rest of the family to shul tomorrow. I noticed he hadn't promised to go himself. "Baruch Ata Adonai, Elohanu, Melech HaOlam. . ." Mama recited the blessing over the holiday candles.

Mendel blessed the wine and Papa blessed the bread.

"Where did you get these beautiful flowers?" Shayna admired the bouquet.

"The florist gave them to Lemmel for helping with the holiday deliveries, he should only work so hard at his bar mitzvah lessons," Mama said.

Lemmel hung his head. For a moment I felt sorry for him. He had tried so hard to please Mama.

"The soup is delicious," Mendel said. "It tastes just like my mother's. Not too much salt."

"Mendel says I put too much salt," Shayna said. "But that's the way I like it." She smiled at her husband. "Now I have some good news. I am going to have a baby!"

"Mazel tov!" Mama hugged Shayna.

So that's why Shayna seemed plumper than usual.

"Mazel tov!" Papa shook Mendel's hand. Mendel didn't look as happy as Shayna.

"Mendel thinks it is too soon to have a baby." Shayna shot him a worried look.

"I don't make enough money to support a wife and baby. And who knows if the job will last? There are layoffs all the time."

"By me, too." Papa sighed. "The boss said there will be more layoffs after the holidays."

"Enough of this talk!" Mama set the brisket on the table and cut it into thick slices. "It is the beginning of a New Year and Shayna is going to have a baby. We should be happy!"

"I haven't eaten meat like this since we left home." Mendel speared a chunk.

"He means we haven't eaten meat at all," Shayna said with such good humor that everyone laughed.

Just then there was a knock on the door and Lucia walked in. Her eyes widened when she saw the dishes heaped with food. "I am sorry to bother you. It is your holiday, yes?"

"Yes," I answered. "It's our new year."

"Mama sent me. She wants to borrow three spoonfuls of sugar for our sick baby. For sugar water."

I translated to Mama who got up and took out the sugar jar. She filled Lucia's cup to the brim.

"Thank you," Lucia said. Her eyes lingered a moment on the meat before she left, closing the door quietly behind her.

"Their baby has the croup," I said. "He's been sick for days."

"Croup, shmoop." Mama shook her head. "I heard his mama walking him in the hall yesterday. He has diphtheria."

"My little sister died of diphtheria," Shayna said softly.

We ate in silence for a few minutes. Then Mama remembered that it was a holiday and began to talk about food and shopping and holidays in the past. Soon we were all laughing and everything was just like I remembered it back home when we celebrated the holidays with Uncle Nahum and his family.

I was just about to clear the table when the door burst open.

"The baby! He's choking. Mama doesn't know what to do!" Lucia cried.

Both Mama and Shayna pushed back their chairs. "No, Shayna, stay here," Mama said. "In your condition, you do not touch sick babies. Raizel, come with me, I should be able to talk to them."

Lucia's apartment was more crowded than ours. She had six brothers and sisters, not counting the baby, and her grandparents lived with them. Where everyone slept, I had never figured out. The grandmother, Lucia's mother, and two neighbors were wailing *bambino, bambino*. Lucia's mother looked at Mama with hopeless eyes.

"Let me see the baby." Mama held out her arms. The baby's neck was swollen and his skin had a blue tinge. I turned my head away. "He's not dead," Mama said, resting her hand on the baby's chest. "Raizel, bring me a piece of flannel and vinegar."

Mama mixed the vinegar in water and dripped it down the baby's throat. Suddenly he choked and coughed. "Raizel, tell them to heat pots of water on the stove. We need lots of steam in the room to help the baby breath. Then go back to the family. I will stay here."

"What is happening?" Papa asked when I returned.

"The baby is alive, but just barely." I sank into a chair. Then I remembered that everyone had finished eating so I began clearing the table.

We sat sipping tea and nibbling on the crispy apple strudel. No one spoke. Only moments before the room had bubbled with holiday happiness. Now it felt like the holiday had been draped in a shroud.

LEMMEL

I was waiting for the guys at noon near the El stop. Luckily no one had asked me where I was going. Mama was asleep after being up all night. Raizel was reading and crying. The baby had died early in the morning. Papa took Shloyme and Hannah "to get some fresh air," he said.

Didn't he know there was no fresh air in this city?

"How 'ya doing?" Joey appeared wearing a new pair of pants. Back home we got new clothes for the holiday, but here there was no money. Plus we had to buy clothes when we arrived so we wouldn't look like greenhorns. I did shine my shoes, however.

"Okay. Where's Harry?"

"Doing one last errand and then skipping out. Got money for the El?"

"Yep." The florist had given me a nickel for helping him. Plus the flowers, of course.

When Harry arrived, we climbed up the steps to the El train. I tried to look bored even though I'd never been on one before. We each paid a nickel and stepped out on the platform. If we didn't get some money, I would have to walk home.

The noise was deafening. We didn't even try to talk. How could people live next to the El? Even though it was a holiday, I could see them bending over their sewing through the open windows.

"Come on." Harry punched my shoulder. We got off the train and pushed our way through the crowds to the street. Outside it looked like another country. The streets were wide and clean with no rubbish lining the sidewalks. The women wore fancy hats with veils and flowers. None of the men wore the long black coats and beards of the East Side. And the stores! They had sparkling glass windows crowded with pretty things. Wouldn't Hannah love that doll with curly yellow hair?

"Come on, greenhorn." Joey pulled my arm. "Stop gawking at everything."

"What I got to do?"

"See that big store entrance?" Harry pointed. Ladies wearing flowered dresses were walking in and out of a set of glass doors. They carried brightly wrapped packages. Some held little boys or girls by the hand.

"Yeah, I see it."

"Well, Joey is going to stand there looking in the window. You run by and knock him down. He starts screaming and crying. When a crowd gathers, I graft em."

"Where do we meet?" asked Joey.

Harry looked around. "Two blocks down you turn right. See the man selling chestnuts? At the end of the block there's a park. Louie sits on a bench looking innocent. You join him and I'll meet you there. Got it?"

I thrust my hands in pockets to keep from shaking. What if someone in the crowd grabbed me? What if a policeman chased me? I would pretend I didn't understand English.

"Louie, move it." Harry shoved me. Joey was across the street pretending to look at a display of fancy hats in the window. I crossed over. Then I walked quickly down the street. When I got close to Joey, I began to run. I knocked him down hard.

"Owww!" he wailed. "My leg!"

I kept on running until I reached the chestnut man. Before I turned the corner I looked back. A crowd had collected around Joey. I turned the corner and walked slowly down the block, whistling.

I waited in the park a long time. Ladies wearing white aprons were watching little kids play on the swings. There were a few skinny trees, their leaves turning yellow. I scuffed through fallen leaves remembering the huge pine forests back home. The needles were so thick they swallowed the sound of your feet.

What if Harry and Joey didn't come for me? What if they got caught stealing? It was like a game with them. Joey's father was a foreman in a clothing factory. Harry delivered messages for the Irish boss who ran the elections. He said he could get me a job if I wanted one, but I thought he was just bragging.

Just then Joey strolled into the park. He was eating an ice cream cone.

"Wanna a bite?"

He was okay, Joey. "Where's Harry? Did he get caught?"

"Nah, not him. He knows his stuff. He had a good teacher."

"What kind of teacher?"

"Hey, guys." Harry sauntered up with a big smile on his face. "Let's get a cuppa coffee." We followed him into a diner and sat down at a table.

"How much did you get?" Joey whispered loudly.

"Shhhh."

A waitress in a starched white apron looked down at us suspiciously. "What'll it be, boys?"

"Three coffees and doughnuts."

When the waitress had gone, Harry leaned across the table. "Guess how much."

"Five bucks?"

Harry shook his head.

"Six? Come on, tell us already!"

Harry smiled. "Hold your horses. It went like clockwork. I pick out this lady wearing a coat with big pockets. She stands there watching the poor little boy crying on the sidewalk. I reach in my hand and. . . jackpot!"

Cursing Columbus

"Nu, how much, already?" Joey practically bounced out of his seat.

"Twenty-five bucks! That's ten for me, ten for you and five for Louie."

"How come I get only five?" Twenty-five dollars was more than Papa earned in a week. Two weeks.

"'Cause you had the easy part. And besides, you're green," Harry explained. "I didn't make five bucks my first time. And hey, the coffee's on me."

I poured in sugar and cream and took a sip of the watery liquid. I liked the doughnut better. I was still licking sugar off my fingers when we got up to leave.

"Hey, why you leaving money on the table?" I pointed to the nickel.

"Greenhorn. That's for the waitress, she shouldn't think we're a bunch of cheapskates."

"What 'cha gonna do with your money?" Joey asked.

"Give some to my mama for the rent, maybe buy a new shirt. And use it to make more," Harry said.

"Don't gamble it all away." Joey winked at me. Harry loved to pitch pennies. "I'm gonna buy shiny new boots for the winter. Last year my feet were freezing!" Joey jiggled his pockets.

"Boots sound good," I said as the El pulled in with a roar.

But I wasn't sure. Mama would notice. Same if I bought a new shirt. Even if I gave her the money for the rent, she would want to know where it came from. How come I could earn five dollars while going to school and taking bar mitzvah lessons? I had to spend it on stuff she wouldn't see.

Candy?

Naw, no one needed that much candy, not even Shloyme. Maybe I could save it, spend it little by little. I could make a hole in my straw mattress and hope Mama didn't find it.

Because she would beat me something awful if she knew I stole money. *Lemmel the thief*. Mama would tear her clothes and sit in mourning.

And Papa would be disappointed and sad. He worked from six in the morning until nine at night to support us. And then I went and stole. What was I, a thief or something? Naw, I didn't come to America to be a thief.

By the time the train pulled into our station, I had made up my mind. I wasn't going grafting anymore, no matter what Harry and Joey thought of me.

Lucia was standing in front of our building wearing a black shawl over her head. "For the baby's funeral," she said to the passersby, shaking a metal cup. I reached in my pocket for the five dollars.

As I trotted up the stairs, I felt suddenly lighter.

6
News

RAIZEL

My teacher, Miss Norman, greeted us with a smile. "Good morning, class. I hope those of you who didn't eat yesterday are feeling well."

Yesterday had been Yom Kippur, the Day of Atonement. Mama, Lemmel and I attended shul and fasted all day. Or at least Mama and I went to synagogue. Lemmel disappeared around noon. I saw him sneak back in as the cantor blew the ram's horn at the end of the service.

"I have good news for you," Miss Norman continued. "One of our pupils has been chosen to take part in the city-wide essay contest next month."

Everyone turned to stare at me. My face grew hot.

"Congratulations, Rose!" Miss Norman said. "Yours was one of five essays chosen from all over New York City. The *Columbus, An American Hero* contest will be held on Nov. 18th at Townsend Harris High School. I will be there, and your family is invited."

"Can we come too, Miss Norman?" Sarah asked.

"Each participant is allowed five personal guests. They can be family members or friends."

"Take me, Rose!" begged Sadie.

"And me, I'm your best friend!" Mamie waved at me.

"Me, too. I want to come!" All the girls leaned towards me and some of the boys, too.

"Class, that's enough!" Miss Norman clapped her hands. "Rose will invite whomever she pleases, and I don't want anyone pestering her. Rose, please stay after school so we can set up some practice time for reading your essay. Now, class, open your arithmetic books to page 44."

My mind fluttered around the details of the contest. What would I wear? I only had two shirtwaists and both were old. My skirt was all right. I had let down the hem this fall and the hemline didn't show. Wouldn't it be wonderful if I could buy a new dress? Perhaps Mama could make me one. Then I would only need to buy material and thread. I couldn't stand up in front of all those people in my worn, faded clothes.

All those people! My stomach clenched around my breakfast porridge. There would be hundreds of strangers. What if I were too frightened to speak?

"I can't do it," I said to Sarah during lunch break. We were sitting outside eating our sandwiches. "I ruined the class play last year with my stage fright."

"You didn't ruin the play. I told you no one noticed that you forgot your lines."

"You noticed."

Sarah took a bite of her liverwurst sandwich. "That's because I was your understudy, remember? No one in the audience noticed."

"But what if it happens again? I get butterflies in my stomach every time I recite before the class. And this will be a hall full of strangers! I can't do it."

"Honestly, Rose, you're the envy of every girl in the class. You'll get to spend extra time with Miss Norman and participate in the contest and maybe even win first prize. Twenty-five dollars! Imagine!"

Winning first prize would be lovely. With the money, Mama could buy curtains for the front room and extra chairs and all the things she wanted to make the apartment more comfortable. Or put the money in the bank for a rainy day.

LEMMEL

"Come on, Louie." Manny tugged my arm. "Let's cut out for the docks. It's too nice to spend the day inside."

That Manny couldn't sit still a minute. "Naw, the Irish gang will murder us if we show up there again. I had enough rocks yesterday." I rubbed my shoulder. Sitting in the women's section on the other side of a curtain, Mama hadn't seen me sneak out of shul—or sneak back in again.

"Let's collect the gang after school and pay them back!" Manny said.

"What'll we use for weapons?"

"Sticks. Stones. What we always use."

"Okay, spread the word to the gang. I'll talk to Harry."

"Aw, forget Harry. He's too busy making money."

Harry's boss had promoted him to personal runner. But he was still the gang leader even if they did listen to me when Harry wasn't around.

"So, you coming or what?" Manny cocked his head in the direction of the street.

"Not today." When I had cut school on Monday, Miss O'Brien threatened to suspend me if I did it again.

The bell rang. Manny followed me inside. Without me, he didn't dare leave.

"Settle down, class," said Miss O'Brien. "I've just heard some exciting news. The essay of a pupil in our school was chosen to participate in the city-wide essay contest! Yes, Ella?"

"Vat dis 'participate' mean, Miss O'Brien?"

"Participate means 'to take part.'" She wrote the word on the blackboard. "See the word 'part.' You participate in class. We participate in the auditorium. Say 'participate,' class."

"Participate," we all chorused like a cage of parrots.

"Good. And the pupil chosen is connected to our class. She is Rose Altman, the sister of Louis and Samuel."

Everyone looked at me, because Shloyme got moved into a regular class last week. So my smarty sister was chosen. Big deal.

"Now, class, let's talk about a holiday we will soon be celebrating. Does anyone know what it is called? No? The name of the holiday is Thanksgiving." She wrote it on the board in big letters. "What two words can we see in Thanksgiving? Louis?"

Without looking at the board, I answered "Tanks and giving."

"Th-anks. Put your tongue in front of your teeth and say it again."

"Thhhnks." I should have left with Manny.

"Yes, class. On Thanksgiving, we give thanks. Now I'm going to tell you the story about why we give thanks on Thanksgiving."

She droned on and on about people named pilgrims. The only interesting part was the Indians. Even back in Jibatov I had heard of Indians. But I hadn't seen any in America. Except wooden Indians in front of cigar stores and Indian heads on pennies.

"Miss O'Brien?" I raised my hand.

"Don't call out, Louis. What is your question?"

"Where the Indians today?"

"You mean where *are* the Indians who used to live here? They live out West now."

"Why they go?" I was disappointed. It would be fun to see Indians walking around the streets with their feathers and painted faces.

"Because there was no room for them here. Indians do not like living in the crowded city." Miss O'Brien looked annoyed. "Now let's get back to Thanksgiving. The pilgrims learned to eat many new foods from the Indians. There was turkey and corn and pumpkins and. . ." I kept thinking about Indians. Who cared what people ate hundreds of years ago?

"Why Indians?" Manny asked as we headed out of school at the end of the day.

"Because everyone says the Indians were fighters," I said. "They snuck up on people through the woods and attacked them. We can sneak up on the Irish gang."

"There ain't no woods here."

"But there are plenty of things to sneak behind."

Manny's eyes lit up. "Yeah. We can send out a scout to find them. Wait 'til I tell the guys!"

We galloped down the street whooping like we imagined Indians would.

"Lemmel, don't forget your bar mitzvah lesson!" Shloyme called.

"Ouch!" I swatted him on the head as I ran past.

One by one the guys squeezed into the empty shed behind the saloon where we met after school.

"Where's Joey?"

"He had to help his mama," Manny said. "His papa got laid off last week and they're doing piece work at home. We used to do that. It's no fun."

Too bad. I could use Joey. He wasn't a scairdy-cat like some of the guys, especially the younger ones. I explained my idea about the Indians.

"Indians! Yeah!"

"I wanna be chief!"

"No me, I'm the chief!"

"Louie's the chief 'cause it was his idea," Manny said. "And I'm the chief scout."

We planned a special meeting. The other guys called it a pow wow, and talked about building a fire and sending out scouts and dancing a war dance and before I noticed, it was dark and though I didn't mean to, I had missed my bar mitzvah lesson. Again.

RAIZEL

Mama and Papa were sitting at the kitchen table when I walked in.

"I'm sorry I'm late, Mama, I had to stay after school to talk to Miss Norman. And guess what? My essay on Columbus was chosen for the city essay contest. Isn't that wonderful?" I grabbed Hannah and danced around the room.

"Raizel, stop bounding around like a wild rabbit and be quiet. Can't you see your papa is upset?"

My bones froze. "Why are you home so early, Papa?" Before he could open his mouth, I knew the answer.

"The boss let me go. There isn't enough work for everyone." Papa stared into his tea.

"Did he say when there will be work again?"

Papa shook his head. "Who knows?"

"You should have gone to shul, yesterday," Mama said. "A little prayer couldn't hurt."

"I am proud that you are in the contest," Papa said. He didn't sound proud. He got up, walked slowly into the bedroom, and closed the door.

"This contest, it will cost money?" asked Mama.

"No, but I need a new dress."

"Dresses cost money."

"Couldn't you make me a dress like you used to back home?"

"Fabric, thread, buttons, they don't cost money?"

Mama pushed Papa's half-empty glass of tea towards me. "No sense wasting a glass of tea. Who knows how much longer we will have money for tea? Or sugar."

Hannah took her thumb out of her mouth and burst into tears.

I rocked her back and forth on my lap. "Don't worry, Papa will find a new job."

A new dress was the least of our worries. There were so many people out of work these days.

I felt like crying, too.

For Papa. For the family. For myself.

"Did Papa have any luck today?" I asked Mama as I set the table for supper a week later. I already knew the answer. I could feel it in the house as soon as I opened the door. All our happiness at being together again had evaporated like puddles on a summer pavement.

Mama shook her head. "He will go back to peddling if he doesn't find work. To think of him outside in this freezing weather. *Oy veh.*"

It was cold. Icy winds stinging with grit blew down the November streets. By the time I got home, it was too dark to take Hannah outside to play. Mr. Abrahamson had given me back my old job at the store after school. For less money. "Things, they are bad." He apologized. "Too many people out of work. They go to the market for bargains."

I had seen them on the streets. Instead of men coming home from the factories, they lounged around street corners, talking excitedly to one another or staring into space. Women huddled against the wind clutching half empty baskets, tugging whining children past the candy story into the dark tenements. The stores looked empty. Only the saloon on the corner seemed busier than ever.

"Raizel, you tell her!" Shloyme stomped out of the front room, his face streaked with tears.

"Tell her what?"

"Mama won't let us celebrate Thanksgiving! Miss Ryan said that Americans celebrate Thanksgiving so I want to!" He banged his fist on the table.

"Stop that right now!" Mama looked puzzled. "What is this 'Thanksgiving' he keeps talking about?"

"It's an American holiday, Mama. It celebrates the first harvest the pilgrims had in America."

"Nu? And this is a big deal to cry about?" Mama wiped her hands on her apron.

"Everyone has a special dinner on Thanksgiving, Mama. School is closed."

"We do not celebrate these foreign holidays."

"Mama, you don't understand!" Shloyme yelled. "We are the foreigners. They call me 'greenhorn!' I want to be an American like everyone else."

Mama sighed. "And what do we eat to become Americans?"

"Turkey and sweet potatoes and corn and cranberry sauce and . . ." Shloyme jumped up and down with excitement.

"Turkey, I know. Potatoes we eat every day. Corn they feed to cows back home." Mama shook her head. "We don't have money for this Thanksgiving. It is a holiday for rich Americans."

"Maybe we could just buy a little piece of turkey," I suggested. "We could have it instead of chicken on Friday night. And sweet potatoes instead of white potatoes."

"What, you have gone crazy too?" Mama shouted. "When there is no money for chicken, there is no money for turkey! Or challah, or tzimmis. With luck we will have money for Sabbath candles. Enough! Children do not talk back to their parents, not in my house!"

Shloyme threw himself on his bed, his shoulders heaving with sobs.

"Don't cry, Shloyme. You can be American without celebrating Thanksgiving."

"No you can't! Miss Ryan said so."

"She didn't mean it like that."

Shloyme glared at me. "You said to do what the teacher said. How can I do what she says when Mama won't let me?"

"You don't become an American by eating turkey and sweet potatoes on Thanksgiving," I tried to explain. "Becoming American is a. . . process. Do you know what that means?"

Shloyme shook his head. At least he wasn't crying anymore.

"That means it takes a long time and involves things like speaking good English and learning American history and reading American books and learning to act like Americans do." And dressing like Americans. And living where Americans lived and not with thousands of other immigrants in the slums of the Lower East Side. Just thinking how long it would take us to become real Americans made me tired. And in the end, would we ever really be Americans?

"Miss Ryan said my English is getting better every day. And that my nails are clean. She said if we want to be good Americans, our hands have to be clean."

I wasn't sure I liked this Miss Ryan. Plenty of Americans had dirty hands. But she seemed to like Shloyme, and that was important.

"I have an idea! Even if you can't eat a real Thanksgiving dinner, you can draw one."

Shloyme thought about that for a moment. "Do you think Mama will let me hang the drawing on the wall?"

"We'll ask her."

"I'll draw the picture after supper." He smiled up at me.

After supper, I finished my schoolwork and waited for Papa. Since he hadn't been working, he had more time to improve his English.

"Papa, it is time for your lesson. Put the newspaper away." Papa always managed to find a Yiddish newspaper someplace.

"It says here in the *Forward* that the recession is getting worse. The rich uptown Jews are opening food kitchens on the Lower East Side." Papa folded the paper carefully.

"Heaven forbid! I did not come to America to beg for food. Back home I gave food to beggars." Mama sat down heavily at the table. The little ones were already in bed.

"These people are not beggars," Papa explained. "As soon as they get work, they won't need charity."

"I know, I know, but I have never taken charity in my life and do not want to start now." Mama rubbed her back.

"Papa, your lessons." I pushed the page in front of him. "Today we will begin learning the past tense."

"It is too late for lessons," Mama said. "I want you should read to me from the newspaper. Maybe there is a nice story, not about people taking charity?"

Most evenings Papa would read to Mama before they went to bed. But tonight he shook his head.

"Later, Haveleh. Raizel is right. It is important for me to improve my English."

Mama looked at her hands. They were red and swollen from doing the washing and scrubbing the floor. Mama kept our apartment spotless, even when dirt and grime blew in through the windows from the street. "Later I will be too tired. All the time I am tired these days."

Papa squeezed Mama's shoulder. "It is the move, with everything so new. You will get used to it. I will read you one thing from the *Bintel Brief*."

Mama smiled. She loved hearing the letters in the *Bintel Brief* section of the *Forward*. Wives wrote asking for advice about their husbands. Husbands wrote about their wives. Children wrote about their parents. Mama said it was almost like being back home in Jibatov where everyone knew everyone else's business.

"Dear Editor," Papa read. "I have been out of work for three weeks. My wife still has a job sewing ribbons on bonnets so we have enough to eat. But I am going crazy. The boss said the shop will reopen soon, but in the meantime, what can I do? I do not have the money to sit in a café drinking coffee all day long."

"We should have such problems." Mama sniffed. "Cafes. Ribbons on bonnets!"

"Shhh, listen to the answer. 'Dear Going Crazy: While it is hard to be out of work, you have been given a golden opportunity. You can use the free time to study and get ahead in the world. If you do not know English, go to the Educational Alliance and join an English class. If you already speak English, go to the library. It is warm in the library and they don't charge for sitting at a table like they do at the cafe. Fill your head with as much knowledge as possible. When you go back to work, you will work better and get ahead faster.'"

I clapped my hands. "Papa, that is exactly what I have been telling you!"

Mama sat up straighter. "Binyumin, what are you wasting time for? Start your lesson. And I hope you were listening," she called to Lemmel who was sitting in the corner copying something from a piece of paper. He looked up as Mama spoke.

"I'm doing my homework, Mama." His hands covered the paper on his lap.

"Come sit at the table, you shouldn't ruin your eyes," Mama said.

"I can concentrate better over here."

I wondered what Lemmel was copying. And why he didn't want anyone to see it.

7
A Curse on Columbus

LEMMEL

"Louis, come to the front of the class."

Uh oh.

"Did you write this composition about how we celebrate Thanksgiving?"

"Yes," I lied.

"I'm going to ask you one more time, Louis." Miss O'Brien leaned forward. Her breath smelled like cough medicine. "Did you write it? Tell me the truth. I won't punish you for telling me the truth."

"Yes, I wrote it."

Miss O'Brien shook her head. "Then I'm afraid I have to send you to the principal's office. You didn't write this composition. Your brother Samuel did."

"But. . ." If Shloyme told on me, I'd drop him off the roof. I'd tell Mama he doesn't share his candy with Hannah. I'd. . ."

"Let this be a lesson for everyone. I will not stand for cheating in my class. When I first read Louis' composition, I was pleasantly surprised. It was excellent. But I began to wonder how Louis had spelled so many words correctly."

"Because Louis can't spell!" Bernie blurted out.

"Quiet, class. So I went to Miss Ryan's class and asked to see Samuel's composition. And to my great sorrow, they were exactly the same. Except yours had more mistakes."

I couldn't meet her eyes. "I'm sorry, Miss O'Brien. I don't cheat again."

"It's too late for sorry. You need to learn a lesson. Take this note and go to the principal's office. You will not be allowed back into class without permission from the principal." She opened the door.

I grabbed my jacket and the note. I could use a smoke.

The boy's room on the first floor was empty. Where was Manny when I needed him? It was no fun in there alone.

Miss Warren was sitting in the outer office. She looked at my note and squeezed her lips together. "Sit there and be quiet."

I joined the line of boys and girls holding notes. One by one they went into Mr. McGraw's office and came out again. Finally I was the only one waiting. I got up to knock on the door.

"Sit down!" Miss Warren practically hissed. "You'll go in when I say so."

I sat down. I swung my legs. I scratched my arm. I watched Miss Warren pick up a page, open a file drawer, leaf through rows of files and slip the paper inside. Again and again. No wonder she was so sour. The clock overhead ticked loudly. The bell rang and I could hear kids out in the hall. Then it got quiet again. I took a deep breath and let it out loudly. Maybe she had forgotten I was here.

"Be quiet." She put another page away. "You may go in, now."

I knocked on the door.

"Come in." Mr. McGraw frowned when he saw me. He read the note.

"Well, Louis Altman, what do you have to say for yourself?"

"I'm sorry. I won't do it again."

"Well, sorry isn't good enough. You were sorry about fighting last week. Sorry about being out of class without a pass the week before. And now you're sorry about cheating from your little brother. Louis, sorry isn't a magic word."

I knew that. But grownups acted like it was.

"Miss O'Brien said she offered you extra help after school, but you never came. She said you haven't learned to read and write. Is that correct, Louis?"

"Yes."

"Speak up."

I looked him straight in the eyes. "I try to read. But the letters move and jump around."

Mr. McGraw threw back his head and laughed. He had a laugh like a donkey. "You are quite the funny man, aren't you, Louis? Next thing you'll be telling me that the letters dance an Irish jig!" I didn't know what a jig was but it didn't seem like a good idea to ask.

"I suggest you make up a better lie next time. Because I know your problem, Louis." He leaned across his desk. He couldn't lean far because his belly got in the way. "You are too lazy to learn to read, too lazy to write your own composition, and too lazy to get extra help. There is no place for lazy boys like you in P.S. 160." He wrote something on a note and handed it to me. "Take this note to your parents. Tell them that if they want their son to come back to school, they must make sure he does his work. You are suspended from school until you come back with your parents. Do—you—understand?" The words shot out like bullets.

"Miss Warren, Louis Altman is suspended from school. His parents will contact you for an appointment when he is ready to come back and do his work."

Miss Warren smiled, probably for the first time in years. "You will leave the school premises at once," she said. "Do not come back without your parents, not even to the playground, or I will call the police."

I folded the letter into tiny pieces and stuffed it in my pant's pocket. Outside rain was falling like it never planned to stop. I buttoned my jacket. If I went home, Mama would be furious. Papa would be disappointed. I knew Mr. McGraw wouldn't believe me about the letters. My teachers back home never believed me. Even Raizel thought I was making it up. I'd be stuck in Miss O'Brien's class for the rest of my life. Everyone would know how dumb I was.

I couldn't go home.

I pulled out my sandwich. Might as well eat it before it got wet. I sank down in the corner of the porch where the wind wouldn't hit me and took a bite. It rained all afternoon.

RAIZEL

"Don't make it too short, Mama." Mama was pinning up the hem on my new dress. Well, not exactly mine.

"Don't squirm, you want I should prick you?"

It was a lovely dress with pleats and lace trimming. Except for the length, it actually fit me. "Isn't it handsome, Mama? I'm so lucky that Henny agreed to lend it to me!" When I had told Sarah that Mama wouldn't buy me a new dress, she suggested her older sister's. "Mama made it for the play she was in, remember?" After Sarah explained how important it was, Henny had agreed! When the contest was over, I would let down the hem and return it to her. But for now it was the most beautiful dress I had ever worn.

"Ouch!"

"Stand still already! Why you are so fidgety about this silly contest, I do not understand."

Mama didn't understand about the contest, but she understood about the twenty-five dollar first prize. She was doing everything she could to help me win, except come to the ceremony.

"They will talk English all evening and I will not understand," she said when I begged her to come. "Besides, I have to stay with Hannah."

"Lemmel can stay with Hannah. That is, if he doesn't want to come. You don't, do you, Lemmel?"

"A curse on Columbus. Listening to an essay on Columbus is boring."

"I want to come, Raizel. And Lemmel shouldn't talk like that. Columbus discovered America in 1492." Shloyme puffed out his chest.

"Don't mind Lemmel," Papa said. "People say 'a curse on Columbus' because they have so many troubles in America, working so hard and such long hours for little money. They have to blame somebody, so they blame Columbus. *Klug tzu Columbus!*" We laughed at the familiar expression.

"Well, I don't care what they say, I want to hear Raizel. Can I, Mama? Puh-leeze."

"You can go with your Papa and Raizel," Mama told Shloyme.

"Yeah!" Shloyme jumped up and down. Soon the downstairs neighbors would be banging on the ceiling.

That meant I could invite three more people. Miss Norman was coming as my teacher. So I would invite Sarah, of course, and Henny, because it was her dress. For the fifth person I invited Lucia. She was so sad since her baby brother died, I hoped it would cheer her up.

Soon it was Monday, the day of the contest.

"I'm so nervous I can hardly breathe," I said to Sarah as we walked home together.

"You know your essay by heart. And so do I!" Sarah laughed. "Good thing I'll be hearing the other essays for the first time."

"But what if I stutter? Or mispronounce a word? Everyone will laugh at me for being a greenhorn."

"Rose Altman, don't you know that you'll be wearing a magic dress?"

"Dresses can't be magic," Shloyme said.

"Didn't you ever hear of Cinderella?" Sarah asked.

"No. Tell me about her," Shloyme demanded.

"Some other time. Raizel will be wearing the magic dress my sister wore in *Little Women*." She turned to me. "Did she forget her lines? Or mispronounce words?"

I shook my head.

"So when you're wearing her dress, you won't either."

"Raizel has a magic dress!" Shloyme shouted to Hannah as we walked into the house.

Hannah stuck out her lower lip.

"This one has been crying all day. She is driving me crazy." Mama set three glasses of milk on the table for us.

I stooped down to Hannah's height. "We have to travel a long way uptown and it will be very late when we come home. Besides, Mama needs someone to take care of her. She doesn't like to stay home alone, right, Mama?"

"Right, *meydele*." Mama picked up my cue. "I need Hannah to keep me company."

"Will you bring me a surprise?" Hannah rubbed away her tears.

"I'll try."

"Oh, I almost forgot. Lucia was looking for you. Sarah, have some bread and butter, you shouldn't be hungry for the contest. And hurry up, Raizel, I want to do your hair."

Lucia's little brother answered my knock. "Shhh, Mama's sleeping," he whispered.

Lucia was sitting at the table reading the little ones a story. The room was dark and nothing was cooking on the stove.

"Is your mama sick?"

"No, she stays in bed all day since the baby died." Lucia looked angry. "Papa won't give me the money for train fare. He's so mean. I hate him!"

"I wish I could pay your fare." Mama had made a fuss about how much money we were spending. "I wish you could come."

"Me too. Good luck." She turned back to the book.

At home I was too excited to eat anything. Mama pinned my braids around my head. I felt so grownup!

Lemmel was sitting with Rebbe Kagan for his bar mitzvah lessons when we left. Lately he had been coming straight home for his lessons and even studying in the evening. With his bar mitzvah only two weeks away, I guessed he was working hard to make up for lost time.

I only hoped it would help.

8
The Contest

RAIZEL

On the way uptown, Henny kept us laughing with her imitations of the people on the train. Papa's lips twitched, but he managed to keep a straight face.

"Just look at all those people!" Sarah exclaimed as we walked into the auditorium. "Uh, I mean, there aren't as many people as I thought." She squeezed my hand.

I walked toward the stage. Miss Norman waved and beckoned to the seat next to her.

"You look lovely, Rose. What a beautiful dress!"

"Thank you." I didn't tell her it wasn't mine. "I like your necklace."

Miss Norman touched her cameo. "It was my mother's."

Miss Norman had green eyes and very white teeth, but her wavy chestnut hair was streaked with silver strands. We all thought she was beautiful and wondered if some dark romantic secret had kept her from marrying.

"You're the third speaker, after that girl with the blond curls." Miss Norman pointed to a girl at the end of the row. The girl looked vaguely familiar. Did I know her from somewhere? "Don't be nervous. Just pretend we're back in the classroom practicing during lunch break."

I took a deep breath. I remembered to let it out when a tall man approached the lectern on the stage.

"Good evening, ladies and gentlemen and children," he said in a deep voice that boomed into the hall. "Good evening to the superintendent of schools, the members of the Board of Education and to his honor, the Mayor of the City of New York. Welcome to the *Columbus, an American Hero* Contest."

The mayor himself was here!

The tall man was followed by several other speakers. They all talked about the same thing: the importance of establishing a national holiday called Columbus Day.

"How much longer?" I whispered to Miss Norman.

She touched her finger to her lips.

"And now I ask our first contestant to read his essay. Will William O'Reilly please come to the stage?"

There was a round of applause mixed with some loud hoots. A tall boy with rosy cheeks and slicked-down hair strode up on stage.

"My essay is entitled 'Why Christopher Columbus was a True American Hero,'" he announced loudly. "'Why Christopher Columbus was a True American Hero,' by William O'Reilly. Christopher Columbus was a true American hero. He was a bigger hero than George Washington and should be called the father of our country. He was a true American hero because he was so brave. In Columbus' time, people thought the earth was flat. They thought that if they sailed west they would fall off the ends of the earth, if a sea monster did not eat them first. Columbus did not believe this..."

I listened as he went on and on about how brave Columbus was and all the dangers he had to face. Everyone clapped when he finished. Only one more speaker to go. My stomach felt like a wadded handkerchief.

"Thank you, William. Now I would like to call Susan Feinstein to the stage." At the sound of her name, I sat up straight. The girl with blond hair curled into ringlets skipped up the steps. She was wearing shiny patent leather shoes and a pink dress studded with bows. "My essay is entitled, 'Christopher Columbus, A Hero to Admire.' We do not know much about the circumstances of Christopher Columbus' birth, but we know he did not come from a wealthy family. All his life he had to work hard to earn his living. He was born in Genoa, Italy and went to sea at an early age. . ."

The essay was well written and interesting, but I couldn't follow the words. In fact I could barely breathe—because I had just recognized Susan, my friend from our first crossing, and Reuben's sister!

"Rose, turn around and keep your eyes on the speaker," Miss Norman whispered. "It will be your turn next."

Reuben wasn't sitting in the row behind us, but he had to be here. And he would see me when I got up on stage. Hundreds of people, the mayor—and Reuben, too.

It was too much.

"Rose, smell this."

I inhaled something sharp from a tiny glass bottle. The room came back into focus.

"Thank heavens for my smelling salts. I've never seen such a case of stage fright, child. Have you eaten today?"

Vaguely I remembered having a bite of bread for breakfast, but I had been too excited to eat anything since. I shook my head.

"Quick, suck on this." Miss Norman popped a butterscotch candy into my mouth.

"Shhh." The woman sitting next to us was watching Susan with rapt attention.

"And so, Christopher Columbus was more than a daring explorer, more than a consummate captain, he was a man who rose above his humble origins to become a hero admired and respected by people all over the world." Susan smiled at the audience and curtsied slightly to acknowledge the wave of applause.

"Rose, spit out the candy and take a deep breath." Miss Norman held out her handkerchief. "You are going to be wonderful."

"Will Rose Altman, the next speaker, please come to the stage."

I stood up. For a moment the room spun around. Then I pinched myself, breathed out sharply, and walked up the stairs to the stage. Without looking at the audience, I smoothed out my essay. "My essay is entitled. . . ," I raised my voice slightly, remembering Miss Norman and our practice sessions, "'If Columbus Had Not Discovered America.'" There was a vague sound like bees waking up. I glanced at the audience. The people in the first row were smiling at me. I looked back down.

"If Columbus had not discovered America, if none of the explorers who followed him had had the courage to make the journey westward into the unknown, what would our lives be like today?

"First, let us imagine our great city of New York. Where the tall buildings of the financial district stand, there would be wigwams of the native Indians. Instead of paved streets, the island of Manhattan would be crisscrossed by footpaths. All along the eastern coast would be villages of Indians hunters and fisherman.

"And what of Europe?" I went on to tell of the English, Irish, German, Italian and Russian immigrants, the Swedes and Finns, the Spanish and Portuguese who would have remained behind. "The Puritans would never have found religious freedom. The Irish would have starved in the great Potato Famine. The Germans, Italians, Swedes and Russians would still be living in terrible poverty in their home countries. The immigrants were not the rich and the prosperous, but those who had nothing to lose." I spoke briefly of Papa and the immigrant Jews who had escaped from the murderous pogroms and economic oppression of Russia.

I forgot that people were watching me. I let my words and ideas sweep me far away where no one could laugh at Raizel, the greenhorn. "And so we must weigh the good against the bad, the advantages against the disadvantages. The conclusion is clear. . ." My voice rang out. "If

Columbus had not discovered America, we would not be this great nation of freedom and justice for all that we are today!"

A thunder of applause shook me awake. I blinked at the audience and remembered to smile. It was over and I could leave the stage. I walked down the steps, careful not to trip or stumble. I sank into my seat and felt my bones turn to water.

"Rose, that was fantastic! Just listen to the audience. I am so proud of you!" Miss Norman hugged me.

"Very nice, my dear," said the woman next to me. "Very original."

I didn't hear the next two speakers. Sarah told me afterwards that they were as boring as the first boy and how many times could you listen to the obstacles Columbus overcame and what a hero he was?

"And now, while our judges confer, I'm going to tell you a little about the Columbus Day committee and its work," said a gray-haired man. The audience got noisier and noisier as he spoke.

"Ah, the judges have given me the sign. Madame Chairman, would you please read the results?"

"It is quite late, and tomorrow is a school day. . ." a slim woman began. The audience groaned. "So with no more preliminaries, the first prize winner in the *Columbus, An American Hero* contest is. . .Susan Feinstein for her fine essay 'Christopher Columbus, A Hero to Admire.' Susan is the winner of our first prize of twenty-five dollars. She will have her picture in the newspaper tomorrow along with the mayor and the superintendent of schools. Susan, please come up on stage." There was a round of applause. Miss Norman put her hand over mine.

"We are also presenting a special honorable mention award to Rose Altman for her highly original essay 'If Columbus had Not Discovered America.' Rose will receive a consolation prize of ten dollars."

There was another round of applause mixed with boos and shouts of *Unfair! She should have won!* I hunched down in my seat, my face burning.

"Raizel, you were wonderful!" Sarah hugged me. "You should have won first prize."

"I am very proud of my American daughter," Papa said with a big smile on his face.

"As well you should be, Mr. Altman." Miss Norman gathered up her coat. "Rose wrote an excellent essay even if she didn't win first prize."

"It's not fair!" Shloyme stamped his foot. "Raizel should have won."

"I agree," said a deep voice. I looked up to see the same curly brown hair, warm brown eyes and wide smile that I remembered from the ocean crossing. But I didn't recognize the broad shoulders and the shadow of a mustache peeking from his upper lip. The face was both familiar and strange, but it was definitely Reuben. "How are you, Raizel? I wasn't sure it was you when I heard your new name, but as soon as you began to speak, I was certain. You did a terrific job."

"Thank you." I could feel my face burning. Sarah's mouth hung open as she looked from me to Reuben and back. I remembered my manners. "Reuben, this is my friend Sarah and my brother Shloyme, and you remember my Papa."

"Yes, of course." Reuben shook hands with Papa. And Shloyme.

"Mr. Balaban, what a pleasant surprise!" Reuben's mother turned from the stage where Susan was posing with the mayor. "I've often wondered how you and Raizel had fared."

"You never wrote us," Reuben said.

"I did, but it was after a long time and the letter came back."

"Yes, we have moved around." He looked at his mother. "And will again." His voice sounded bitter.

"Reuben, it will be for the best." Mrs. Feinstein was wearing a feather hat and elegant coat. "Well, I'm going to collect Susan. We have to be getting home." As she turned, I noticed her coat was worn in the seat.

"Where do you live?" Reuben asked.

"On Goerck Street in the Lower East Side. And you?"

"Up in Harlem, not far from here. We're moving soon. My father's business failed. He decided to try his luck in Denver, Colorado. We're going to join him."

I had finally found Reuben and he was leaving again. But I didn't have time just then to feel sad.

"Look, Susan," Mrs. Feinstein was saying. "Here's your friend Raizel from the boat. Isn't this a nice coincidence?"

Susan's cheeks were flushed and her eyes sparkling. "Mama, my picture will be in the paper tomorrow! Can we send it to Father? Oh, I'm so excited! Everyone said I would win first prize."

"Congratulations, Susan," I said.

"Your essay was nice, Raizel. I'm glad you won a consolation prize."

"Isn't she sweet?" Sarah whispered.

"Say goodbye, darling. Reuben, come along. It was lovely meeting you all again." Mrs. Feinstein turned to go.

"Wait, I want to hear what's been happening to you," Reuben said. "If I manage to get off work early on Sunday, I'll come to visit."

I told him our address.

"Come, children, we have a long ride home," Papa said.

A blast of cold air hit my face as we left the auditorium. I was starving. Well, in an hour or so we would be home. Even though I hadn't won the contest, it had been a wonderful night, the most wonderful night of my life!

9
Approaching Manhood

LEMMEL

"No, *dummkof*!" Rebbe Kagan swiped my head. I ducked and he almost fell off the chair.

"Mama! Mama!" Hannah skittered into the back room like a frightened sparrow.

"What seems to be the problem, Rebbe Kagan?" Mama emerged rubbing her stomach.

"Never do I have such an impossible pupil. He makes mistakes on purpose!" Rebbe Kagan's horse face got redder and redder.

"Lemmel, your bar mitzvah is only five days away. Please try harder."

"I am trying, Mama." I was. Since I got suspended from school, I'd been home for my lessons everyday and even studied at night. I figured I'd tell them about the suspension after my bar mitzvah, when they'd be too happy to get mad at me.

"This you call trying? A donkey could do better than this! I should charge double price for teaching this *dummkof*!"

"Rebbe, calm down. Would you like a cup of tea and a piece of my special mandelbrot?" Mama asked.

Rebbe Kagan didn't hesitate a moment. "The mandelbrot I take for the road. I am late for my next pupil. What a delight! A joy to teach!" Mama tucked a slice of toasted cake studded with almonds into his coat pocket as he walked out the door.

"Me, too, Mama." Hannah stretched out her hand.

Mama measured the remaining cake with her eyes and broke off half a piece for Hannah. She gave me the other half.

"Mmmm, delicious. It tastes just like back home."

Mama ate a crumb. "So you miss home, too?"

"I miss the trees and the river and the forest. Here everything is crowded and dirty."

"I miss the family and my friends. Here I am alone with neighbors who speak only Italian. And Papa is all day looking for work and doesn't go to shul anymore. Who knew America would be like this?"

"Mama, maybe we can go back home?"

Mama shook her head. "Your papa likes it here. So do Raizel and Shloyme. And we do not have the money for passage home. No, we are in America now, for better or for worse."

I sighed. Hannah climbed into Mama's lap. The daylight seeped away as we sat in silence, each thinking of the Old Country and what we had left behind.

Later that evening, Papa burst into the apartment with a smile on his face.

"Haveleh, guess what?"

"You have found a job?" Mama was stirring a pot of soup.

"I wish. No, the landsmanshaft have gotten together to help with the bar mitzvah."

I looked up. I felt like someone had opened a window in January.

"First, they arranged for Lemmel to read his Torah portion at the Grand Street shul. Then, they took up a collection so that we will be able to provide refreshments as befitting my eldest son." Papa poured a handful of coins into Mama's palm.

"Wonderful!" Mama hugged Papa who hugged Hannah. They all beamed at me.

"Papa, who are these landsleit?" Raizel asked. "Do I know them?"

"You know a few. They are men who came from Jibatov or the surrounding villages. We have formed a self-help society to buy cemetery plots and medical services. I am on the organizing committee."

"Papa, I don't want you to go to all this trouble," I said. They were spending too much money on this bar mitzvah. What if . . . ?

Mama ignored me. "We will invite our friends to the *landsmanshaft* room after the service. Let's see, I will make knishes and at least three kinds of cake. Raizel, you will stay home from school to help me."

"Mama, no!"

"I cannot do all the work alone and Shayna is too pregnant to stand on her legs. It won't hurt you to miss a day of school. After all, you'll be finishing when you turn fourteen."

Raizel looked like she was about to cry. She told me she wanted to be a teacher. I hate teachers!

"What does Rebbe Kagan say?" Papa looked worried. "Is Lemmel ready?"

"That man is always fuming over something or other." Mama met my eyes.

"Lemmel, you feel ready, don't you?"

"I feel ready with my Yiddish talk, Papa. It's the Hebrew Torah portion that I have trouble with."

"Well, you have five days to learn it. My *landsleit* will all be there. If you put me to shame, I don't know what I'll do!"

"I won't put you to shame, Papa." I promised.

Another promise I knew I couldn't keep.

RAIZEL

I waited for Reuben all day Sunday. I wore my nicer blouse and put my hair up so I would look older. Mama noticed, but she didn't say anything. She was tired from all the bar mitzvah preparations. I hoped she wasn't getting sick.

And in the end, Reuben didn't come.

"Well, he didn't promise," said Sarah the next day. "He said he would try."

"I know. But that doesn't mean I can't be disappointed."

"So maybe he'll come next Sunday," Sarah suggested.

"But he's moving away." I bit into my hard-boiled egg sandwich and sighed. Since the contest I had felt like a deflated balloon. My ten-dollar prize had helped with the rent money, but with Papa out of work, the rent, food and bar mitzvah preparations were eating up the little savings we had.

More and more I worried about having to leave school. Mama didn't understand how important school was. Papa said she needed time to adjust to the American ways. When she was growing up, girls didn't go to school. I had thought Papa was on my side.

Until he lost his job.

"It will only be for a short time," he explained as we walked to Seward Park on Saturday. "You can start again after I find a job. Renting the apartment costs more than being a boarder and there are extra mouths to feed."

"But Papa, if I leave school I'll miss my class work and won't be promoted. I'll have to start the year all over again!"

"I know, *meydele*. It will be hard, but I can't see another solution."

I pushed Hannah on the swing. She squealed with delight. "Higher, Raizel, higher!"

"And if we never have the money for me to go back to school?" I tried to keep the tears out of my voice.

"Then you will work like other girls your age."

Work. I could work in a garment factory, spending long hours over a sewing machine breathing fabric dust. Or I could get a job in an up-town department store where I would wear pretty clothes, but the pay was terrible, no more than five dollars a week. I could wind up selling ladies' corsets until I married an assistant store manager or clerk out of despair. No, I would take a stenography course at night and learn typing and shorthand. A secretary's hours were a little shorter, and maybe, just maybe, I could complete my high school diploma in night school, even though it would take years and years of work and study. And no time for fun.

Angrily I brushed away my tears. It wasn't fair. All my life I had dreamed of going to school and here in America, where it was possible, I had to stop.

"Papa, you push me," Hannah demanded. "Raizel is a crybaby."

Papa took over. "Raizel, that is the fate of the eldest. I, too, stopped my studies to support my brothers and sisters after my father died. Your sacrifice will help Lemmel, Shloyme and Hannah. You want your brothers and sister to get an education, don't you?"

Of course I did. I would be proud of them. But it hurt so much to give up my dream.

I had found a way to help us out of our troubles before. Perhaps I could find one again.

But how?

I could smell Mama's baking as I passed the second-floor landing. There was laughter coming from our apartment. When was the last time I had heard Mama laugh?

A cloud of aromas engulfed me: burnt sugar, jam, cinnamon, yeast dough rising. Mama's fingers were flying as she rolled the rugalach cookies. Next to her sat Lucia's mother, her thin cheeks flushed from the heat of the oven.

"Raizel, look!" Mama's arm swept the room. Every surface was covered with platters of cookies and cakes. "Maria came over this morning,"

Mama explained. "She said she followed her nose. We've been working all day and look how much we made!"

I spied Hannah and Lucia's little brother and sister playing under a tent made of a sheet.

"That's wonderful, Mama. And Miss Norman said I can help you tomorrow."

"I won't need you, *meydele*. Maria does more in an hour than you do all day."

The dough seemed to shape itself under Maria's fingers. I was glad I could go to school tomorrow, but, at the same time, I had enjoyed cooking with Mama for the New Year. It had been almost like being back in Jibatov. I missed that closeness.

"I need you to go shopping." Mama wiped the sweat from her face with a floury arm. "We need a bag of flour and a kilo of potatoes for the knishes. Get some kasha too and half a kilo of ground meat, the cheapest kind, we should all be healthy, and. . ."

"Wait, mama! I can't remember all that without writing it down!"

Mama cocked her head at me. "Go to the market, it will cost less than the corner store, are you writing? We need two bottles of sweet Kiddush wine, the *landsleit* shouldn't think we are cheap, and a bottle of schnapps, no two. . ."

"Mama, I can't carry all that!"

""My mama say take the baby carriage to carry," said Roberto, who was about Hannah's age.

Mama smiled at Maria. "Tank you."

"And don't be long," she called as I headed out the door. "I want you should make soup for dinner and peel the potatoes for tomorrow."

I sighed. I wouldn't miss school, but clearly I was going to spend half the night helping Mama in the kitchen.

LEMMEL

"Hey, Louie, we meetin' tomorrow morning?" Joey was always the last to leave these days since his papa disappeared. He said his mama cried about how they'd be thrown out on the street. The charities gave them rent money last month.

"Naw, I got my bar mitzvah tomorrow."

"I forgot. Bet you'll have good stuff to eat." Joey looked hungry.

Maybe I could bring leftovers to the gang. We could have a picnic.

Yeah, some picnic.

It was cold in the shed. I pulled up the collar of my winter jacket. When Papa bought it from the second-hand peddler on Hester Street I thought it was the warmest coat I had ever had. But December in New York was cold, almost as cold as Jibatov. My hands were freezing. Maybe I should be a chestnut seller. Their hands were always warm from the coals.

Today I helped in the market with the Friday afternoon rush and made fifteen cents.

I could hear mamas calling their kids to supper. It was time to go home.

I didn't want to go home.

Tomorrow I would go with Papa to the shul on Grand Street. I would stand at the pulpit in front of all those people and read from the Torah scroll.

I couldn't do it.

Those crooked little letters would dance and jump around. I would try to capture them with my eyes, make them stay still on the parchment. I would stutter and make mistakes. At first the room would be silent. Then everyone would start whispering. And then they would laugh.

Everyone except Papa.

Cursing Columbus

His shoulders would slump. His face would turn the color of sour milk. Papa would know. Everyone would know.

Lemmel can't read. Lemmel was the biggest dummy who ever lived.

Lemmel was like the idiot boy with the big head in Jibatov. He had drooled and giggled when people talked to him. He went barefoot even in the winter. His mama bought him shoes and he threw them away. The other boys and I made fun of him. But sometimes I let him help me brush the horses. I wondered what he was doing now. I wished I were back in Jibatov.

I rubbed the tears out of my eyes. I tried to think of something to stop my bar mitzvah from happening.

Pretend I'm sick?

They would only postpone it to another time.

Pretend I'd gone blind?

Stupid.

Burn down the shul?

Dangerous.

Run away?

Too cold. I had no place to run to.

I had no choice. I had to tell Papa the truth and ask him to call off the bar mitzvah. After they'd spent so much money on Rebbe Kagan, that smelly horse face, may he drown in his own piss! Bought new clothes. Prepared the food. And taken charity from the *landsleit*.

They would be furious. Mama would cry. Papa would punish me.

They'd never forgive me.

And they didn't even know I'd been suspended from school.

It was dark in the shed now. The wind attacked me through the holes in the roof. My stomach was raging for supper.

I needed to go home.

It was all their fault. They had forced me to have a bar mitzvah. I had told them not to spend that money. They wouldn't listen. They never listened to me.

Ever since I was little my teachers had been beating me and pinching me and calling me names in front of the other boys. *Stupid! Good-for-nothing! Donkey-head!* It never stopped.

I used to come home crying. Mama wouldn't listen. She called me lazy, said the teachers were right, that I should work harder. And when I skipped school, she dragged me back through the streets by my ear.

I hated them.

If only I were in Jibatov. I would run away into the woods. Find a family of woodcutters to live with. I was strong. I could cut wood and take care of the horses. Healthy horses, not these bag-of-bones city horses full of sores.

Why did they make me come here? Why did they make me go to school when I wanted to work? Why did they make me have this bar mitzvah ?

They didn't love me. They only loved Raizel and Shloyme and Hannah. Well, I didn't love them either!

I wasn't crying anymore. I felt like a flame was burning inside me, sending sparks into my arms and legs, into my brain, setting everything on fire. I had fifteen cents in my pocket. I wouldn't go hungry.

I knew what I needed to do.

10
A Lost Boy

RAIZEL

Papa wandered out of the bedroom rubbing his eyes. "Is Lemmel here?"

Mama shook her head. "When I get my hands on that boy, I'm going to shake him so hard his teeth will fall out." Mama sounded mad, but she wasn't. She was worried sick.

When Lemmel hadn't come home last night, Papa and I went looking for him. We went to his friend Joey's house and then to more friends. We came back cold and tired and without Lemmel.

"I saw him. Last night." Shloyme stumbled into the kitchen. He hated getting up early on Saturday.

"Where did you see him?" I asked. "In your dreams?"

"In bed. He pushed me and lifted the mattress."

"Did he say anything?" Papa asked.

"He said 'Shhhh. Go back to sleep.'"

Shloyme wasn't dreaming.

"How did he sneak into the house last night without my hearing?" Mama had dark circles under her eyes. "I never closed my eyes all night."

"His new long pants are missing," I reported. "And my blue scarf is gone."

"See, I knew it," Papa said, taking a slurp of hot coffee. "He is going to meet me at shul." He put down the empty cup and reached for his coat. "I'll see you later."

The house seemed to wake up. Mama dressed Hannah. Shloyme went into the hall to use the toilet, and I set bread and hot milk on the table.

I was running up and down the stairs loading platters of food into the neighbor's old baby carriage when Papa returned to the apartment. One look at his face told me that Lemmel hadn't been waiting for him.

"You waited outside?" Mama asked. "And looked inside?" She sat down at the table.

"The service is half over." Papa stood in the middle of the room, his shoulders slumping.

"Why didn't Lemmel come to his bar mitzvah?" asked Shloyme.

Something made me reach for the onion basket and search for the purse where Mama hid the coins she hoarded for rent money. She took the money Papa and I brought her, put a few coins in her pocket for food, and stuffed the rest into the purse to save for rent. My fingers touched the cracked leather.

"How much?" Mama whispered.

I shook the contents into my palm. "Three dollars and forty cents. How much was in there?"

"Over eight dollars." Mama whispered. "The rent is due next week."

"Lemmel took the rent money? My *son* took the rent money? Why?"

"Oh Papa, don't you understand?" I couldn't hold back any longer. "Lemmel ran away. He's never coming home again!"

Reuben's visit on Sunday did little to cheer me up.

We were sitting on our front stoop. It was too cold to sit outside but this was the only place we could be alone. I had been dreaming about his visit for weeks, and now that he was finally here, I almost

Cursing Columbus

didn't care. Mama had been lying in bed all day. Papa sat at the kitchen table with his head in his hands, sighing.

"You looked for him all over the neighborhood?" Reuben's cheeks were red from the cold, but his brown eyes were warm with concern.

"Of course. We looked all day Saturday. His gang looked too. Nobody has seen him since Friday." Or so they said. There was one boy named Harry whom I suspected was lying, but I couldn't get anything out of him.

"Today I had to work, but Papa went looking with Shloyme. Not a trace."

Reuben had appeared just as I finished work. All day I had been selling Mama's rugalach and cakes and knishes in Mr. Abrahamson's store. He was letting us keep the profits and I had a pocketful of coins to give to Mama.

"Perhaps you should go to the police," Reuben said slowly.

"Why should we go to the police?" We hadn't told anyone about Lemmel taking the rent money. Papa was too ashamed.

"They might help find him. But there are thousands of runaway children in New York City. I don't think there's much they can do."

I shook my head doubtfully. Papa didn't like the police. They reminded him of the police in Russia. The police there never helped the Jews. "I'm sorry I'm only talking about our troubles. I want to hear what you've been doing." I hadn't seen Reuben for years, and all I could talk about was Lemmel! Because that's all I could think about.

"Don't worry, I understand." Reuben pulled me off the stoop. I felt like a joint of frozen meat. "Is there a coffee shop around here?"

"On Goerck Street? Not likely." I had never been in a coffee shop. We walked towards the river, the icy wind hammering at our faces. "How are your mother and Susan?"

"Susan is too full of herself since she won the contest. Which you definitely should have won."

"Thank you." The contest seemed long ago.

"The problem is my father. When we first got to America, he had a job working as a fur cutter. Then he decided to open his own business. I thought he was taking too much of a risk. He would have been better off saving more money. But you can't tell my father anything." Reuben clapped his hands together to warm them.

"He found a partner, rented a workshop, invested in furs, made his first sales—and then his partner disappeared with the furs and the money and he was left with the debts."

"How awful!"

"We had to sell the house and move into a tiny apartment. Mother sold her furs and jewels to pay the debts. I took a job after school and on weekends working at the Educational Alliance."

"And your papa?" I was afraid to ask. Had Reuben's father deserted the family? It happened in other families when things went bad.

"He went crazy for a while. He got his old job back and then got fired. Then one day he came home and told us he was moving to Denver, Colorado."

"Why so far?"

"That's what mother asked. He decided that the only way to change his luck was to move as far from New York as possible. He went to the IRO and asked for help. He didn't tell us until it was decided and then he bullied my mother into signing a consent form."

"What is the IRO? I've never heard of it."

"Neither had I. The Industrial Removal Office was set up by a group of wealthy Jews who believe that Jewish immigrants will have a better chance of becoming part of American society and getting ahead if they spread out across America rather than crowding together in places like the Lower East Side where everybody is so poor."

"That makes sense."

"I'm not saying it doesn't make sense." Reuben walked faster. "They help men get jobs in other cities, lend them money for their train fare, and make sure there are other Jews waiting to help them in their new homes. Then when they make enough money, they send for their families."

"Is your father there now?" That's why Mr. Feinstein hadn't come to see Susan.

"He's been in Denver for almost a year. At first he had a terrible job in a bottling plant, but someone helped him get a job as a fur cutter. Next month we're all moving to Denver."

"How can you move in the middle of the school year?"

"That's what makes me so mad!" Reuben's eyes blazed.

"What d-do you want to d-do?" My teeth were chattering from the cold.

"I want to attend City College and become a doctor. In another year I finish high school. I go to Townsend Harris." He paused. The name rang a bell.

"That's the high school for smart boys, isn't it? Where they had the Columbus contest."

Reuben looked pleased. "I'm doing a four-year high school course in three years. Mother agreed to wait until I finish the term in mid-January. Then we move."

"I'm sorry." I touched his jacket sleeve.

"Father wrote there are good schools in Denver. But there are no free universities like there are in New York. We won't have the money for me to go to college, let alone become a doctor." He looked out over the East River, glistening black in the winter light. "Guess I'll have to become a cowboy."

I giggled. "You know how to ride a horse, I presume?"

"Not yet, but I'll learn. Maybe I'll join a rodeo. That would serve my father right."

"I have to leave school, too. I'll be fourteen next week."

"You seem older."

I flushed. Did he mean it as a compliment? "Unless Papa finds work, I'll have to get a job. Papa said it's only temporary, but who knows?"

"What a shame! I remember how much you wanted to go to school. When I saw you at the contest, I was so happy for you."

"I want to be a teacher, if I can finish school. . ."

We huddled by the riverside. The sky turned strawberry pink and faded to gray behind the wooly clouds. It hadn't snowed yet this winter. Our shoulders touched.

"I have to be going," Reuben said.

"Come home with me and have a cup of hot tea first."

"Your parents won't mind? I would like to warm up."

We burst shivering into the apartment. Papa, Shloyme and Hannah were sitting at the table. Shloyme was reading to Hannah from his second reader. She followed his finger as it moved along the words. I'd bet she'd know how to read before she went to school.

"Papa, look who came to visit. I'm going to make Reuben a cup of tea before he goes back uptown."

"Come in and warm up, Reuben." Papa looked worried. "Your mama's been sleeping all afternoon. I hope she isn't getting sick."

"I know you. You're Reuben from the Columbus contest." Shloyme cocked his head. "What are you doing here?"

"Visiting your sister."

Shloyme seemed satisfied with the answer.

"And this must be the lovely Hannah. You have big green eyes just like your sister Raizel."

Hannah dived for Papa's lap and peered at Reuben between her fingers.

"She's shy. It took her a month to get used to me." The kettle was boiling. "Would you like some tea, Papa?"

I set three glasses of tea on the table along with a plate of cookies that I hadn't been able to sell.

"Mmmm, these are delicious." Reuben bit into one of Mama's crispy cookies. Shloyme and Hannah stretched out their hands and all the cookies disappeared.

"Papa, Reuben thinks it might help to go to the police to report Lemmel's disappearance."

"The police I do not like. What do they care about one Jewish boy?"

"It's their job to care, Mr. Balaban—I mean, Mr. Altman. But there are thousands of homeless boys in New York City."

"Lemmel is not homeless." Mama stepped out of her room, her face puffy. "He can come home any time he wants."

"I'm sorry. I didn't mean anything by it." Reuben looked uncomfortable.

"Mama, have a cup of tea and meet Reuben. And look how much money I made in the store selling your cookies!" I poured a handful of coins on the table.

"I'll count them, Mama." Shloyme's mouth moved silently. "Two dollars and fifty three cents."

"Barely enough to cover the cost of ingredients. Oh well, every bit helps." Mama dabbed at her eyes with her apron.

Reuben stood up. "I have to be going. Thank you for the tea and cookies. It was nice to meet you, Mrs. Altman."

I walked down the stairs with him. "I'm sorry about my mother's behavior. She's very upset about Lemmel."

"You don't have to apologize. I wish there was something I could do to help."

"Will I see you again before you leave?" I couldn't believe I had asked him that.

"I have exams at the end of the month so I'll be awfully busy. Perhaps after that. And I'll write you from Denver. Don't go moving on me, Rose Altman!"

He winked and disappeared down the dark street. I liked the way he said *Rose*. It sounded softer than Raizel. But I liked the way he said *Raizel* too. I walked slowly up the stairs, relishing the sweet feeling, almost tasting it on my lips.

I was just passing the second story landing when I had my brilliant idea.

LEMMEL

They didn't see me, I was sure of it. I had to be more careful. I was too near home.

I wondered who that boy was. Raizel had a boyfriend! If I said that to her face, she'd get all red and flustery. It would be fun to tease her.

It won't happen.

Last night was bad. The rats down here were awful. You'd think the cold would keep them quiet. But I'm out of the wind and the other kids let me sit next to their fire. They're tough: newsboys and boot blacks and saloon sweepers.

Wonder when Harry will show up. He promised to get me a contact. Said if I don't know someone they won't let me sell newspapers. A newspaper boy. I saw them all over the city. I never knew they slept in the streets.

Harry said they have special shelters for newsboys. He didn't know where. Anyway, I wasn't a newsboy yet.

Harry said he'd come today or tomorrow. Well, I had time. No school. No job. Not enough money. Time I had.

If only it weren't so cold.

RAIZEL

"Happy Birthday, Rosie." Sarah hugged me. My friends shouted "surprise" and handed me a package.

A present for me? We never gave presents. No one had extra money among my friends

"It's from all of us," Ruthie said. "Because we want you to remember us."

Cursing Columbus

I blinked away my tears. They all knew that this was my last week of school. And they knew about Lemmel. "You shouldn't have done it," I said, as I unwrapped the brown wrapping paper. Someone had drawn roses all over it, probably Molly.

"Oh, this is wonderful!" They had given me *Rose in Bloom*, by Louisa May Alcott. "It's just perfect. And I haven't read it yet!"

"That's what Sarah said."

"When I told the book seller that it was for your birthday and that your name was Rose, he let me have it for half price!"

I ran my hand over the worn cover. It felt good to own a book. "You'll all have to come and borrow it," I said. I hugged them each in turn.

"You'll be in school tomorrow, won't you, Rose?" Molly asked.

"Yes, Papa said I can finish the week." If my plan worked, I might be in school longer than a week.

Mama was putting supper on the table when I came home. "Mama, look at the birthday present my friends gave me!"

"That was nice of them. There's a letter on the table. Can you read it?"

"I asked Mama to bake a birthday cake, like the one in my book." Shloyme pointed at a fancy cake in his reader. "But she won't."

"We don't have money for cakes, this is not a wedding." In Jibatov we hadn't celebrated birthdays. It was another American custom that Mama had to get used to.

The letter was addressed to Mr. B. Altman from P.S. 160. We never got letters from school. I skimmed it quickly: "This is to inform you. . . Louis Altman. . .suspended. . .appointment with the principal. . .at your convenience."

"Mama, it's a letter from school. It says that Lemmel was suspended over a month ago!"

"What is this 'suspended?'" Mama asked.

"It means Lemmel did something bad," Shloyme explained. "Bad boys get suspended from school."

"And he never said a word!" Mama exclaimed.

Everyone was upset about Lemmel, too upset to enjoy the delicious meat soup Mama had made. We rarely ate meat these days, so I knew she wanted this to be a special day for me. I tried to hold on to my happiness at receiving a birthday present, but the news about Lemmel worried me. He hadn't run away just because of the bar mitzvah. It was worse than we thought.

After I had served tea, Papa cleared his throat.

"Today is Raizel's birthday and Mama has a surprise for you."

Mama's cheeks grew red.

"Did Papa find a job?" Shloyme asked.

Now that would have been a perfect birthday present.

"Not yet." Papa patted Shloyme's shoulder. "I will find one soon. The papers say this recession can't last forever."

"I want a surprise," Hannah said. "A red ribbon for my hair."

"If you know what it is, then it can't be a surprise," Shloyme said.

"Yes, it is. I want one!"

"Enough!" Papa said. "Let your Mama speak."

"I am going to have a baby," Mama said. Her eyes were shining. "An American baby!"

Suddenly I understood why Mama had been so tired lately. I had forgotten her pregnancy with Hannah.

"But I'm the baby!" Hannah wailed.

"Not anymore," Papa said. "Now you'll be the big girl."

Hannah wailed even louder.

"Babies don't eat regular food, do they?" asked Shloyme.

"Not for several months," Mama answered.

Shloyme looked relieved.

"When is the baby due?" I asked.

"In the early spring."

"But what were you thinking?" The words rushed out before I could stop them. "How are we going to support a baby? Babies need special clothes and a carriage. A baby will be another mouth to feed and. . . !"

Mama slapped my face.

"Raizel Balaban! Is that any way to talk?" Mama's voice shook with anger. "A baby is a blessing from G-d."

I couldn't stop the tears. Now I had no choice but to leave school. Even if Papa got a job, we would be too poor to support an extra mouth.

For a moment my eyes met Papa's and I knew that he understood what I was feeling. Then he looked away.

"Everything will be fine," he said too loudly. "Lemmel will come home. We will have a new baby. I will find a job. This is America, not Russia, remember."

I rubbed my cheek where Mama had slapped me. If only I could believe him.

II
The Boarder

LEMMEL

"Where were you?" I asked Harry. I was sitting at the edge of the dock. My feet were freezing. Harry had promised to come three days ago.

"Aw, cut your crap. I told you it would take time." He thrust a meat-loaf sandwich into my hands. "Got this for you."

I ate so fast I almost choked. "Thanks." I hadn't been eating much. I still had three dollars from the rent money and two dollars from under my mattress. I kept them inside my pants so no one could rob me when I was asleep. I kept the change I took from the sleeping drunks in the Bowery in my pocket. Tim, one of the boys who hung around the dock, had told me that if a thief found change, he wouldn't look any farther.

"Hey, slow down." Harry looked worried. "Do you need money?" He handed me a dollar. I took it. He had plenty more. "Where you're sleeping, it's okay?"

"Oh, great. Ten homeless kids, twenty drunken bums and thirty million rats. Just like home."

"Look, I could take you home with me, but my ma would tell your parents."

"It's all right. It's warmer under the pier than you think." Harry was trying his best for me.

"Listen, I got you a name. You go to the Herald building and look for a boy named Buck Charlie."

"How will I know him?"

"Everybody knows Charlie. He's eighteen, has brown hair and front teeth that stick out. You buy your papers from him and he gives you a spot."

"Why can't I buy papers from the newspaper?"

"They won't trust you 'cause they don't know you."

"But I got enough to pay in advance." Tim had said you could earn more money as an independent.

"Look, you want my help or not? If you don't buy from Buck Charlie, you'll have to fight for your spot. All the best spots are taken."

"So? I ain't afraid of a fight."

Harry put his hands on my shoulders. "Louie, take my advice. These guys are tough. Some of 'em been living on the streets since they were six years old. They'll come at you from behind with a stick and roll you into an alley where you'll freeze or bleed to death, whichever comes first. Start slow, make friends, work your way up. That's the way to get ahead on the streets."

"Aww, what do you know about living on the streets?" Harry went home to his nice warm apartment after work.

But I took his advice. I could always do something else if it didn't work out. I needed money before it got colder.

One of the drunks under the pier hadn't woken up this morning.

RAIZEL

"Mama, Papa, I need to talk to you about something important." We were sitting around the table after dinner. The little ones were in bed. Reuben's answer to the letter I wrote after his visit had arrived today.

"How much money did the cookies make last week, Raizel?" Mr. Abrahamson had asked Mama to supply her rugalach every Thursday so people could buy them for the Sabbath. She was also taking special orders for bar mitzvahs and weddings. Sometimes I helped her, but when she had a big order, she called Maria in and split the profits with her.

"Only $1.50. Mr. Abrahamson said people don't have money for frills these days."

Mama sighed. "So much work. My legs are still aching. But a dollar is a dollar."

"What did you want to tell us, Raizel?" Papa coughed into a hand-kerchief. He was helping with the milk delivery while the regular milk-man got over the flu. I hoped Papa wouldn't catch it.

"I have an idea how we can make enough money for the rent. . ." I began.

"We will have enough money when you quit school and find a job." Mama said. "Two weeks already you are fourteen and still going to school."

I had convinced Papa to let me finish December, but there was only one week to go.

"Haveleh, give Raizel a chance. What was your idea, *meydele*?"

"We take in a boarder. In fact, I have a boarder for us!"

"A boarder?" Mama looked suspicious. She was still mad at my out-burst about the baby. "Where can we put a boarder?"

"Mama, we have extra space now that Lemmel is. . .gone."

"Lemmel will come flying home with the first snow. Just wait and see." Mama crossed her arms on her chest.

"Who do you have in mind, Raizel?" asked Papa.

I explained how Reuben's family was leaving next month for Denver and how much Reuben wanted to finish school in New York. And his mother had agreed because she trusted Papa. They would pay for his room and board. They were coming over next weekend to discuss the terms.

"Raizel," Papa said gently. "Reuben cannot sleep in Lemmel's bed."

"Why not, Papa? I slept with other girls when we were boarders. Shloyme is a sound sleeper and he won't bother Reuben."

"Reuben cannot sleep in Shloyme's bed because of you. It would not be proper for you to sleep in the same room with a young man."

"So. . .he can sleep in the kitchen." I looked around quickly. "We can put a bed against the wall and keep it in the front room during the day."

"My son sleep in the kitchen?" Mrs. Feinstein cried when Papa told her that Sunday. She was sitting with her hat on her lap sipping a glass of tea. "Raizel wrote he would sleep in the bedroom."

"That is my fault, Mrs. Feinstein," Papa said. "I cannot permit my daughter to sleep in the same room with a young man."

"But Raizel is just a little girl!" Mrs. Feinstein looked amused.

"Raizel is fourteen already. Reuben is seventeen. It would not be proper." Mama spoke softly, but firmly. She was staring at Mrs. Feinstein's feather hat.

"The kitchen is fine, Mother. I don't go to bed early. Anyway, between my job at the Alliance and school, I'll hardly be here."

"Well. . ." Mrs. Feinstein looked at Reuben fondly. "I suppose it can't hurt for a few months. Just until you join us in Denver."

"That's settled then." Reuben grinned at me.

"You will give my son breakfast and supper," she continued. "A nutritious supper with meat at least three times a week."

"We don't eat meat for supper anymore." Shloyme was leaning against the doorway.

"I insist he eat meat. Winters in New York are not as cold as St. Petersburg, but they are cold enough. If my son gets sick without his mother to nurse him, I shall never forgive you, Mrs. Altman."

"Mother, please! I can take care of myself."

"Reuben, you are still a child. It breaks a mother's heart to leave you." She dabbed at her eyes.

Mama reached over and touched her arm. "Don't worry, Mrs. Feinstein. I have four children and one more on the way. I know what children need to eat and I will take good care of Reuben."

I breathed a sigh of relief. It was going to be all right.

"We will pay you six dollars a month for room and board. Reuben will pay three dollars from his earnings and we will send three dollars each month from Denver."

Mama was figuring quickly on her fingers. "I will need an extra fifty cents a week for the meat."

"Twenty-five cents a week. I cannot feed your whole family, just my son."

"That's seven dollars a month. I can manage with that." Mama smiled.

"Great! I'll bring my things over next week." Reuben kissed his mother on the cheek.

"So now we will have money for rent each month," I said after the Feinsteins had left.

"Yes," said Mama. "But we still have to eat, of course."

"Mr. Abrahamson pays me ten cents a day for working after school and fifty cents on Sunday," I said.

"And I earn a few dollars a month from odd jobs. And there are your cookies." Papa continued.

"We aren't spending as much on food as we did before. . .before Lemmel left," I added.

"All right already. You can stop with the hints. If we watch every penny, we will have enough money to live on." Mama gave me a half smile.

"Does that mean I can stay in school? Please, Mama, puh-leeese!"

"Stop talking like Shloyme. You can stay in school for now. But when the baby comes and Reuben leaves, it will be another story. We will need two salaries then."

"Oh thank you, Mama!" I threw my arms around her. I would finish the year and graduate from eighth grade!

Now I only had to worry about high school.

LEMMEL

"*Extra! Extra! Da Mayer Cunfesses!* Buy a paper, mister. Tanks."

Another penny. I had been here three hours and earned thirty-five cents. I still had sixty-five papers to sell. And it was costing me sixty cents to buy the papers. So if I sold all my papers, I earned. . .forty cents. Forty cents a day times six days a week. . .two dollars and forty cents. And I had to give Buck Charlie ten cents a week for this corner.

"*Extra! Extra! Horrible muhder in da Bowery!* Read all about it!"

Another cent. If I could sell all these papers by noon, Charlie would sell me another fifty.

My stomach was growling. It must be lunchtime. I had been up before sunrise to get to newspaper row before they gave out the papers.

"*Extra! Extra! Man wit' no head in Bowery alley!* Read all about it!"

Another cent. I wondered what a headless man looked like. Ugh.

"*Extra! Extra! Bloody body wit' no head!* Read all about it!"

Only twenty more papers and I could buy some more. Beef stew for dinner tonight. Mmmmm. Wished I had some now. Uh, oh. It was starting to rain. I had better get the papers inside a doorway.

"*Extra! Extra! Bloody headless body in Bowery alley!*"

No one stopped in the rain. Buck Charlie said they took papers back if you didn't sell them. I didn't like him. He had ugly black pimples and acted like he was the boss.

"Paper, mister?"

Hah! He was using it to keep off the rain. If only I could read the paper when there were no customers. Shloyme could read it.

I wondered if they were still mad at me. I hadn't planned to take the rent money. I took my money from under the mattress, but there was less than I remembered. I even thought about adding it to the rent money, leaving them a present so they wouldn't feel too bad. But then I had the rent money in my hand and kept it there. What if they got put out in the street? Then I could never find them again.

I wished I could go home to our miserable little apartment and get warm and eat Mama's cooking.

If only I hadn't stolen the rent money. I could never go home again.

RAIZEL

"Gut afternoon, Rose. Any news of your brother?"

Mr. Abrahamson's store looked darker and emptier than usual. Clouds smothered the rooftops and smelled like snow, clean and sharp.

"No, nothing." I hung my coat on a nail in the back room.

"How is your mama holding up?"

"Mama is sure he will come home when it snows."

"I hope so. Imagine a boy wandering around in this cold."

I tried not to imagine it. Lemmel was smart. He would manage. There were plenty of other homeless boys in the city.

"How's business, Mr. Abrahamson?"

"It's warmer then peddling."

Mr. Abrahamson had been a peddler when he first came to America. He had saved every penny to open a store. He and his wife were child-less. She helped him in the store until she got sick. That was why he hired me. That and the fact that he liked children.

"My mama needs half a pound of flour." A boy about Shloyme's age thrust out a penny.

"That's not enough money," I said giving him the flour. "You owe two cents."

"Mama said to write it up on the credit."

I glanced at Mr. Abrahamson, who nodded.

"Name?"

"Eisenberg, Freida."

I added two cents to the long list of family debts.

When the boy left, Mr. Abrahamson sighed. "Five children she has, and her good-for-nothing husband ran off with a seamstress from the Bronx. Two cents won't break me."

Whenever they could, Mr. Abrahamson's customers sent their children. He could never refuse a child.

Three children ran into the store, laughing and shoving each other. Their hair was sprinkled white.

"It's snowing, it's snowing!" they cried.

"Just what I needed." Mr. Abrahamson groaned.

Suddenly a picture of winter in Jibatov flashed into my mind. There the snow was clean and dry and covered the houses like a thick white blanket, tucking them in for the winter. The trees sparkled with snowy white powder in the sunshine. In New York, the snow clogged the streets, black with dirt, and you clambered over lumpy piles with frozen feet. But maybe Mama was right and the snow would bring Lemmel home.

After the children had gone, Mr. Abrahamson stood in the doorway warming his hands on a glass of tea. "It looks like a flurry. Maybe it won't pile up too bad." He turned to me. "Oy, I almost forgot. You know the man who collects fat for soap?"

I nodded. I was trying to read my history book in the dim light. Mr. Abrahamson didn't mind, as long as there were no customers.

"He said the Irishman who owns the soap company is looking for a good steady worker. Your papa can drive a wagon, yes?"

"He used to have a horse in Jibatov." *Bunchik.* We all loved him, especially Lemmel.

"Then he should go tomorrow and ask for a job." Mr. Abrahamson handed me a piece of paper.

"Thank you so much, Mr. Abrahamson!" I put the address carefully in my pocket. A few more customers dribbled in to buy half a loaf of bread, a few potatoes, a quarter pound of sugar. I put on my coat. Even with the stove it was chilly in the store.

"You can go home, Rosie. The snow is keeping the customers away. I'll close up soon, and go home to the wife, may she be healthy."

"What did the specialist say?"

"Not good, not good. He wrote a prescription for pain." Mr. Abrahamson let out a long sigh. "If only I could send her some place warm for the winter. The colder it gets, the worse she feels. Oh well, she'll feel better in the spring."

"I hope so," I said. Mama said Mrs. Abrahamson had the cancer and wouldn't live much longer. It must be sad for someone you love to be sick and not be able to help.

"Here, Rosie, take this to your Mama. It will only spoil overnight." He pushed half a loaf of bread into my hand.

"Thank you." I had learned it was useless to resist "spoiled" food. He always sent me home with a few potatoes, wilted carrots, or day-old bread. Mama bit her lip when I gave them to her, but I said it made Mr. Abrahamson feel good, so we shouldn't call it charity.

It was snowing hard by now. Mr. Abrahamson was wrong about a flurry.

"Where's Mama?" I asked Shloyme who was doing his homework at the kitchen table.

"Looking for Lemmel out the front window. Ever since the snow began she's been standing at the window."

"Mama, look what Mr. Abrahamson gave me."

"What will be with my poor baby? He'll freeze to death in the snow." Mama was hugging Hannah and crying.

"He'll be fine, Mama," I said with more confidence than I felt. "He probably has a job by now and a warm place to stay."

"Yes, yes, I'm sure you're right." Mama put Hannah down and dabbed at her eyes with her apron. "Tonight we eat soup and dumplings, we should have something to warm our insides in this snow. And I put a piece of meat in the soup for our boarder, his mother should be happy."

Reuben had moved in with us last week. Papa had found a low cabinet and mattress for him to sleep on. Mama rolled up the mattress during the day and kept it in the front room under our bed. Reuben usually got home late. He had a job after school at the Educational Alliance where he taught English and ran a boys' debating club.

After supper I told Papa about the job that Mr. Abrahamson had mentioned and gave him the address.

"What is this fat collector?" Mama asked.

"A man who goes around to restaurants and stores collecting left-over fat. He brings it to the soap factory. Each man has his own territory."

"How do you know this, Raizel?" Papa looked curious.

"The man who comes into Mr. Abrahamson's store once a week to collect fat likes to talk to me.

"Papa's English is getting better," I told Reuben that night. He was eating his supper while I finished my homework. The rest of the family had gone to bed.

"That's because he has a good teacher. Mmmm, this soup is good. Don't tell anyone, but your mama is a better cook than mine."

"Her family owned a tavern and she helped in the kitchen."

"In St. Petersburg we had a cook, but here in America Mother does the cooking. Even Susan is a better cook than she is!"

I told Reuben about the job possibility. "If Papa gets a regular job, then maybe I won't have to quit school."

"I hope not. You know, if things work out for my family in Denver, then I will stay here in New York and go to college and medical school. I don't plan on moving to Denver if I don't have to."

"I thought you promised your mother to join them."

"I think becoming a doctor is more important. Don't you agree?"

"I guess so." Something in Reuben's voice made me shiver. He sounded so coldly determined.

"I wish Lemmel had the sense to come home on a night like this. . ." I changed the subject.

"From what you tell me, he has sense. What he needs is courage."

"What do you mean?" Courage was something Columbus had when he sailed into the unknown. It was something Papa had when he left Jibatov for America. But Lemmel. . . ?

"Lemmel got suspended from school. He didn't come to his bar mitz-vah. He ran away from home."

He stole the rent money, I added silently.

"To come home now requires the courage to admit he was wrong. As hard as it is living on the streets, coming home must seem even harder."

"So you think he'll n-never come home?"

"I didn't mean to make you cry." Reuben put his hand on mine. "I'm a realist, the opposite of my parents. My father thinks he can get rich quick. My mother thinks she can live like a lady even though she's poor. I think illusions get in the way of success."

"Don't you have dreams?"

Reuben screwed up his forehead. "Realistic dreams. Don't laugh. My dream is to become a doctor. I know I'm smart enough. So I need to earn enough money to go to medical school."

"I see. My dream of becoming a teacher is also realistic. If I work hard enough, I can become one. But I have a friend who dreams of be-coming a famous actress. Yet when we put on a play in class, she forgets her lines and giggles instead. So that's an unrealistic dream."

Cursing Columbus

"But she can still enjoy going to the theatre. Life isn't all work and no play. Have you ever been to the theatre?"

I shook my head. We never had money for luxuries.

"Then I shall have to take you to a serious play for a serious girl."

I would love to go to the theatre with Reuben! But did boys like girls who were serious?

I left him doing his homework. The front room was freezing. That was the advantage of sleeping with Hannah. She had warmed up the bed by the time I got into it.

I thought of Lemmel outside in the snow. What if Reuben were right? What if Lemmel lacked the courage to come home? Was it possible that we would never, ever, see him again?

12
Out of the Cold

LEMMEL

People hurried too much in the snow to buy newspapers. Last week I made five dollars, but the way things had been going this week, I'd be lucky if I made three. Buck Charlie would be mad. Last week he gave me a better corner near the subway.

"Hey, Tough Louie, you finished for today?" Tim strolled up with his hands in his pockets.

"Yeah, I'm done." I checked my pocket. "Fifty-five cents. This snow is killing my business."

"Got enough for Newsboy Lodging?"

"Not if I want to eat. I'm starved. How much you make?"

Tim dragged me into a doorway. He pulled out a fistful of bills.

"Hey, you didn't get that sellin' papers! I wasn't born yesterday."

"I keep tellin' you there are more ways to earn money than sellin' newspapers." Tim wore a grin on his pimpled face. He'd been on the streets so long he could barely remember his home. And he never went to school. I told him he was lucky.

"Aww, I hate rollin' drunks," I said. "They get mad if they wake up." I still had a cut on my arm where a drunk slashed me. I was sure he was asleep.

"Drunks don't have this much cash. Even you know that." Tim looked pleased with himself.

"Okay, I give up. Where'd you get the dough?"

"I'll tell you while we eat. My treat."

Cursing Columbus

We left the business district and headed towards the cheap food joints in the Bowery. We ordered chowder and hash. The food was hot and heavy and sat in my stomach like a lead ball. I missed Mama's cooking, but my feet thawed for the first time all day.

"So where'd you get the money?"

"Shhh! Not so loud." Tim drank a glass of beer. I took a sip but I didn't like the bitter taste. "I got it in exchange for a gold pocket watch."

"So where'd you get the watch?" Tim was having fun drawing me on.

"Oh, a rich gentleman gave it to me."

"Sure, and I'm John Jacob Astor."

"Well, he might have given it to me, but he was too busy reading his paper to notice."

"You mean you sold him a paper *and* stole his watch?"

"Louie, I had you pegged for a smart guy. Don't you know that's what papers were for?"

I stared at Tim. He bought a stack of papers from Buck Charlie just like me. But he always seemed to have more money. He loved to gamble and go to the pictures. If I made enough money for a night at the Newsboy Lodging and supper, I was doing good.

"Okay, I'm game. How can I make more money by sellin' newspapers?"

"It's not the sellin' that makes the money. The sellin' acts like, you know, a disguise."

"What's 'disguise'?" Usually when I don't know a word in English, I pick up the meaning later. But this sounded important.

"I forget you're a greenhorn. It's like a costume. Because the mark thinks you're a newsie, he doesn't expect to have his pocket picked."

"I didn't leave home to become a pickpocket."

"Sure, you left home to become President of the United States! But in the meantime, you need money. You may be tough, Louie, but sleeping on the streets in the winter is suicide. You know what suicide is, don't ya?"

"Yeah, I know. Hey, where ya goin'?"

"I'm gonna do a little crap shooting, someplace I know where it's warm and you can get a whiskey for two cents. They don't let you in with no money." He gave me a long look.

I sat at the table until the waiter told me to order something or move on. By then it was late and I needed a place to sleep. Last night I slept at the Newsboy's Lodging House in a room full of other boys. They had a lot of rules, but it was clean and warm. Tonight I didn't have enough money, not if I wanted to buy papers in the morning. Cold nights and bad sales had eaten into my savings. Well, plenty of boys slept in the streets in the winter.

I headed back to Newspaper Row. A group of boys was huddled around a hot air grate.

"There ain't no room for you here, greenie."

The boys were younger then me, but there were six of them, so I moved on. I spotted a little kid I knew who used to sleep under the pier.

"Hey, Nickels, know any place warm to sleep?"

"Nah. Last night a janitor let me and some guys sleep in the furnace room, but tonight he kicked us out. Said we made a mess and he got in trouble."

"Let's go build a fire." I was getting really cold.

We collected some boxes in a back alley.

"Got a match?" I asked.

"Sure." Nickels pulled out a box of matches and we got a fire started. He offered me a cigarette. I couldn't stop thinking about what Tim had said.

"You ever do any pickpocketin'?"

"Some. I ain't fast enough."

That time I went grafting with Joey and Harry, Harry was quick. I wondered where he learned it. I remembered how bad I felt about stealing and how I gave all the money to Lucia for her brother's funeral.

Sucker. I could use that money now. It was going to be a long cold night.

RAIZEL

"Your papa got the job," Mama announced with a smile as I walked in the door after work. Hannah ran to show me her new red hair ribbon.

"Wonderful, Papa! Tell me all about it."

"I went to this old soap factory on East Broadway. A big man was sitting with his feet on the desk. I told him I came about a job. He looked me up and down and asked something in English. I could barely understand him, his Irish brogue was as thick as butter. I told him I had a horse and wagon back in Russia, that I know how to sell, and that I'm trusty. That is how you say it, no?"

I nodded.

"He started to laugh. Said he never hired a Jew before, that I looked like a scarecrow, and that a gust of wind would blow me over."

"Uh oh, that doesn't sound good."

"I was about to leave when he called me back. Asked if I could read and write English. I said I could, not so good, but I'm learning."

"Why did he ask?"

"I need to read the addresses. And keep records where I go, when, how much I collect, how much I pay for the fat. I have to write it down so I don't cheat him. I told him I'm an honest man, I don't cheat anybody, ever. He asked if I'm a family man and I told him about us. He liked hearing about family. His wife died and his sons live far away. We drank a glass of schnapps together and talked. I never talked so much English before. Then he put out his hand and said he never met a Jew he liked, but he likes me. He is going to give me a chance!"

"That's wonderful, Papa! Will the work be hard? What about the pay?"

"Questions, questions! Tomorrow I will have answers. Someone will teach me for a day or two and then I will get my own route."

"And your own horse, Papa? I want to see him!" Shloyme was sucking a gigantic lollipop. It looked like Papa had bought presents for everyone.

"I'll take you to see him just as soon as I can."

"Papa, you didn't answer me about the money."

"*Oy* Raizel, always you are so serious. Be happy for me."

There it was again. Why did everyone say I was serious?

"Your papa will be making less money than as a presser," Mama said. She closed her mouth in a thin line.

"But you forget the commission. In addition to my weekly salary, I earn a commission for every new customer I bring. And the Irishman promised to raise my salary if I do well."

"We can't live on promises," Mama said. "Why should you believe him?"

"He seems like an honest man. And Haveleh, what choice do I have? It is more than I can make with odd jobs." He put his arm around Mama's waist. "Your Mama is angry because I bought presents for everyone."

"Fool! Why are you wasting money?"

I noticed a shiny red-checkered oilcloth covering our old wooden table.

"Because I am happy, Haveleh! Because I finally have a job after two months! You would prefer I went to the saloon and drank a bottle of whiskey to celebrate?"

Mama burst out laughing. "One drink and they would have to carry you home, Binyumin. *Nu*, show Raizel what you bought her already."

I unwrapped the brown paper and pulled out a brand new blouse. The blue fabric was embroidered with tiny pink flowers. "It's beautiful, Papa. I haven't had new clothes since I don't remember when."

Cursing Columbus

"You deserve it," Papa said, kissing me on the forehead. "If you hadn't been so stubborn, I would never have learned to read and write English and I would never have gotten the job!"

I stroked the silky fabric with my finger. Now I would have something pretty to wear when I went to the theatre with Reuben. I hoped he hadn't forgotten his promise. I wanted to have some of this fun people were always talking about.

LEMMEL

"This is Tough Louie. This is *the* Dodge," Tim said by way of introduction and left.

The Dodge looked me over. He wasn't a kid anymore, but he wasn't old, either. He had curly brown hair, a long nose and a white v-shaped scar under his left eye. He was wearing a fancy wool suit with a gold stickpin in his tie. Before he opened his mouth, I could tell he was one of us, even though he carried himself differently, kind of proud and confident. He didn't look like Papa and the other Jews I knew who huddle into themselves, always scurrying along as if someone were chasing them.

"Tim explain about the deal?" he asked.

"You teach me and I give you fifty percent for a month, ten percent for two months. How long this gonna take?"

"Not so fast, kiddo." The Dodge threw back his head and laughed. "Sit down. Have a cuppa coffee. Warm your hands."

We were sitting in a first floor apartment on Ludlow Street. It didn't look like much from outside, but inside it was twice the size of our apartment, with nice shiny furniture and rugs on the floor. The Dodge handed me a cup of coffee and a sugar bun. I hadn't eaten all day, trying to save money for the Newsboy Lodging tonight. I figured one day I'd eat, one night I'd freeze. And vice versa. I had enough of freezing last night.

"Got a home?"

I shook my head.

"Parents?"

"What's it to you?" I didn't like all these questions.

"I take care of my boys." He leaned back in his chair and put his big feet up on the table. He was wearing shiny black shoes. His face was shiny, too. "So I'll tell you about me. I was born in the Old Country. My papa was a scholar. You don't believe me?"

"I believe you." What do I care if he's lying?

"He died when I was little. My mother remarried a drunk and a bully. He gave me this one night." He pointed at the v-shaped scar. "But he did one thing right. He took us to America. So when I was about your age, I left home. Too many beatings, not enough food. I sold newspapers, blackened shoes, all the usual. And like you, I realized it wasn't enough to live on. See this place?" He waved at the apartment. "It's a dump. I would move uptown, but my business is here in the neighborhood."

"What business?"

"Oh, I collect things, me and my guys. And people pay for my protection. Hear about those horses that got poisoned?"

It had happened in the fall. I had seen a dead horse with bloody foam in its mouth lying in the street. A man was sitting next to the horse with his head in his hands. Just sitting there on the sidewalk next to the dead horse.

"I like horses."

The Dodge threw back his head and laughed again. His face got red, except for the scar, and his belly shook. I wanted to punch him in his soft stomach for hurting those horses.

"You're a tough guy, Louie. I like that. Know why I'm tellin' you this?"

I shook my head.

"So you'll see the possibilities. Right now you're a poor dumb kid who doesn't know nothin'. You probably cry for your mama at night when no one's watching. All you can think about is your next meal and where you'll sleep tonight. Am I right?"

I glared at him.

"Okay, okay. The point is, I was like you, so don't get hot under the collar. I don't have to help you. I make enough dough. But I'm not self-ish. I like a bit of charity work, help the less fortunate. And if you learn fast and do good, who knows? The Dodge has plenty of friends."

And plenty of enemies, too, I'd bet.

13
At the Theatre

RAIZEL

"Raizel, where you going all dressed up?" Shloyme stuffed a slice of challah smeared with butter into his mouth. His cheeks bloomed from playing outside in the cold.

"To the theatre." I braided my hair into a single braid so I would look more grown-up. The face that looked back at me was thin, but my new blouse made me feel pretty.

"I'm going out," I called to Mama, who was resting in the back room. "I'll be home for supper."

"But I want to go outside and play!" Hannah wandered out of Mama's room.

"Take Hannah with you," Mama called sleepily.

"I can't." I took a deep breath. "I'm going to the theatre with Reuben."

"The theatre? On the Sabbath?" Mama was wide-awake now. "Why didn't you ask me before?"

"Reuben only told me this morning that he got student tickets. We can't go during the week because of school." *Please let me go, Mama, please.*

Mama walked out of the bedroom. She had a round stomach now. "What will be with this family? Papa no longer goes to shul. Lemmel runs away from home because of his bar mitzvah. And now you go to the theatre on the Shabbas. Your Bobbe would turn over in her grave."

Mama knew how to make me feel bad. I loved my grandmother very much. But she had died years ago in the Old Country and, though I would never forget her, I was living here and now in America.

"I'm sorry, Mama, but Reuben already bought the tickets. I'm meeting him at the theatre and he'll be worried if I don't come."

Mama shook her head again and sighed. "Hannaleh, Papa will be home soon and take you outside."

I breathed a sigh of relief and slipped out the door. Mama was changing. Only a few weeks ago she wouldn't have let me go to the theatre on the Sabbath.

The Thalia Theater in the Bowery looked like the picture of a Greek temple in my history book. Reuben was standing next to the far-left column as he had promised, talking to a girl with wavy blond hair.

"Raizel, this is Sally. She has a ticket, too."

Sally had blue eyes with long black lashes and rosy cheeks. Sally was pretty. No, she was beautiful. I felt a pang of jealousy.

"I love the theatre, don't you? I try to go once a week if I have the money." Sally giggled. "I even bought new shoes for the show." She raised her skirt to reveal a shiny pair of black patent leather pumps.

"Very nice." Reuben handed a uniformed man the tickets. We were swept into the crowd of people. I struggled to remain close to Reuben. Why had he brought Sally with him? Was she his girlfriend?

"This way. Up the stairs!" Reuben called over his shoulder. We pushed our way through families with children and clusters of single girls laughing and talking as they made their way into the great hall.

"We're up in seventh heaven! We won't be able to see a thing." Sally stripped off her coat and plopped into the chair next to Reuben. I sat down on his other side.

"You get what you pay for." Reuben laughed.

I couldn't take my eyes off the crowd. There were mothers with babies, young couples holding hands, girls in smart hats laughing and calling to one another, boys playing tag between the rows, and sedate men and women, some old enough to be my grandparents. Men selling nuts, soda water and even apples wandered up and down the aisles, just like a market.

"Peanuts?" Sally offered me a handful from her pocket. I shook my head. "Go on already." She pushed them into my hand. "Hey, there's Gertie. Yoo hoo!" Sally waved at a woman I couldn't see. "She works in an uptown shop. Just look at that fancy coat she has on. You wouldn't believe how she used to dress."

"Rose, did you have any trouble coming?" Reuben asked. Sally's chatter seemed to slide off him like rain off a duck.

"Mama wasn't happy about my going to the theatre on the Sabbath."

"I was afraid of that. What did you tell her?"

"That you had already bought the tickets."

"Terrific. So she'll be mad at me instead of you."

"I'm sorry. I didn't think of that."

"I'm just kidding, Rose. Don't take me so seriously."

Suddenly the noise faded. The lights in the theatre dimmed and the heavy red curtain began to rise. I leaned forward in my seat as the actors appeared.

People were still talking so much that I could barely hear a word on stage. Actors came and went, dressed in elaborate costumes. When a plump man with curly black hair strode on stage, the audience went wild, clapping and stamping their feet.

"Don't you just adore Boris?" Sally asked as if she were his close friend.

I kept trying to follow the story. Jacob loved Dina but Jacob was too poor to marry her and his mother was a noble woman but he didn't know she was his mother because she was living in disguise and . . .

"I don't understand what's happening," I said to Reuben during the first intermission. "Why did the noble lady abandon her son and why was that other actor being so mean to him and why. . . ?"

"Oh Rose, you are a baby!" Sally burst out laughing. "It's only a play. The important thing is the acting. I just adore Boris Thomashefsky, don't you? I once saw him sitting in a café and he was even handsomer off-stage." Sally sighed. "I would love to be an actress."

Reuben tried to explain the plot to me. "The play is called "The Jewish Heart." It dramatizes the Jacob and Esau story from the Bible. The character named Victor stands for Esau, and Jacob is Jacob, of course."

"How brilliant you are!" Sally fluttered her eyelashes at Reuben. "I never try to understand the plot. I come for the romance scenes and a good cry. They say the end is tragic. I can't wait!"

Reuben winked at me. I couldn't figure out whether he liked Sally or not. She didn't seem to be his girlfriend, but then why had he come with her? I settled back for the second act, determined to find something to like about the play, which up to now had seemed like nothing but a lot of foolishness.

"What did you think?" Reuben asked as we walked home. Sally, to my relief, had left us as to join her girlfriends.

"It was. . .interesting." I didn't want to hurt Reuben's feelings.

"I thought it was the biggest mess I've ever seen. I expected more from a theatre like the Thalia. I should have taken you to something serious by Jacob Gordin."

That word again. "I thought some of it was funny. Although the tragic parts were probably the funniest of all. Nobody acts like that in real life!"

"People don't go to the theatre to see real life."

"I see what you mean." All those working girls, families, sweatshop workers—why would they spend their hard-earned money to see their lives on stage? "But Sally couldn't stop crying when Madame Popesco died of happiness during her son's wedding. How absurd! Who ever heard of someone dying of happiness?"

Reuben laughed. "Sally is a riot. We lived next door to each other when my family first arrived in America. Her name was Sadie then and she had brown hair. Now she comes to the Alliance for drama classes after work."

So she wasn't his girlfriend. "She's pretty enough to be an actress."

"The trouble is she knows it. She's always going to dance halls and the theatre. She spends every cent she earns on clothes."

"Where does she work?" I asked.

"In a garment factory. She lives with her parents. They let her do whatever she wants, as long as she contributes to the rent."

"I wish my parents would let me do what I want."

"No, you don't. I'm afraid Sadie, I mean Sally, will get into trouble."

"How do you mean?"

Reuben blew on his hands. "I keep forgetting you're only fourteen. Those dance halls she likes so much can be dangerous places. The men shower girls with gifts, pretend to court them, and then turn them into streetwalkers."

"Oh!" I covered my mouth with my hand. "How horrible!" I had never given much thought to the women who hung around the street corners or the saloons on Goerck Street. They wore heavy make-up to hide their age. But they must have been young and pretty once.

"And you think something like that could happen to Sally?"

"I hope not. She likes pretty things and doesn't make enough money to buy them all."

We walked the rest of the way in silence. Reuben had given me a lot to think about. I realized that there was more happening around me then I saw going back and forth to school.

"Are you coming home for supper?" I asked Reuben as we approached Goerck Street.

"I'll be back later. I'm going to the Alliance to study and then I have an English class to teach."

"I'll keep the food warm for you." I wished he would eat with us more often. Except for Friday evenings, he almost never came home for supper.

"Thank you, little mother."

"Hey, I'm not anybody's mother!"

"Little sister, then. I had fun. Maybe we can go to a picture sometime."

I watched him walk briskly down the street in the darkening afternoon. It smelled like snow again. I wondered where Lemmel was sleeping tonight.

It had been fun, even though I had to share him with Sally. But what had he meant by *little sister*? Was that how he thought of me? He did act like an older brother to me, explaining things, introducing me to new experiences. At least he didn't like Sally as a girlfriend.

The question was if he liked me. And not as a little sister.

14
Back to School

LEMMEL

The Dodge's "school" wasn't bad. For one thing, it was warm. I headed over when I was done selling my papers. I brought Nickels, too, the kid I had shared a fire with. He was a couple of years younger than me and never made enough money from selling newspapers to buy a night's lodging. The Dodge or his lady friend Mary fed us hot coffee and rolls. He let us sleep in the back room if we didn't have enough money for the Newsboy Lodging.

There was a third kid, the Dodge's assistant. The Dodge called him "Mumbles" because he didn't talk clear, but he hated that name. He called himself "Muscles." I didn't like him much. He was sixteen and always showing off his muscles. He used them on us, too.

"Okay, Louie, come for the wallet," Mumbles called. "Not so fast. Look somewhere else, that's a boy. Now bump into me. Owww, you rotten kid, wanna knock me over or somethin'?"

I reached into his coat pocket. He grabbed my wrist and threw me against the wall.

"Hey, Mumbles, not so hard. Want to break the kid's head? Did he hurt you, Louie?" Mary leaned over me. Her perfume smelled like sweat and roses. She stroked my hair. "I like redheads. You gonna' be one handsome guy when you get big."

"Stop fussin' over the kid and let him work." The Dodge yanked Mary away. She had a blue mark over her eye where he hit her last night when he was drunk. I had heard them fighting in the next room.

"Aww, Dodgie, I didn't mean nothing'."

"Get out of here, already!" The Dodge looked nasty today.

"But Dodgie, it's real cold out. And my head is hurtin' something awful."

"Get out, stupid!" He threw her coat out after her. Mumbles whispered Mary wasn't long for here. He said the Dodge changed his lady friends the way a rich man changed his socks.

Nickels was even slower than me. He was black and blue to prove it. Mumbles and his pinches reminded me of Rebbe Kagan. We practiced until Mumbles took pity on us.

We were going to get something to eat when we passed a gang of little kids skimming along the street like a flock of sparrows. They were heading home for supper, scared their mamas would yell at them for being late. Suddenly one stopped and turned around.

"Lemmel, that you?"

I walked faster.

"Stop, Lemmel, it's me, Shloyme." He ran after me.

"What 'cha want? Leave me alone!"

"When are you coming home? Mama is worried sick about you! Where do you live? Do you sleep in the streets? Is it cold?" He was trotting alongside me, trying to keep up.

"Never!" I shoved him. He lost his balance in the snow and fell on his behind. I kept walking. At the corner I looked back. He was standing under a lamppost crying.

"That your fat little brother?" Mumbles asked.

I nodded. I didn't feel like talking.

"Little beggar only had two cents in his pocket."

"You stole my brother's money?" I flew at Mumbles. We rolled around in the filthy wet snow. I hit him so hard that I couldn't feel him hitting me back.

"Louie, stop! You're killing him!"

Nickels tugged at me. I was sitting on top of Mumbles punching his face. Blood poured out of his nose. I got up and handed him a filthy rag out of my pocket.

"You practically broke my nose, you idiot!"

I waited for him to attack me. I was shaking so hard I could barely stand.

"Look, I didn't mean to take your brother's money." Mumbles wiped his nose and sniveled. "Don't tell the Dodge, okay?"

"Sure." My shakes petered out. I stretched out my hand to help him up. "Let's go eat."

We continued along the street to a joint Mumbles liked. I was hungry. I ordered a steak and a bowl of roast potatoes. I felt good now that I knew Mumbles was scared of me. He was bigger than me, but he was scared of me. He wouldn't treat me like a little kid anymore.

I was cutting into my steak when I remembered how Shloyme had looked standing under the lamppost. And how he would feel when he got home and found his pockets empty. Why had I pushed him so hard? Why hadn't I asked how Mama and Papa were?

"Hey, you gonna eat that or what?" Nickels stared at my steak. He only had money for a bowl of soup.

I pushed it across the table. I didn't feel hungry anymore.

RAIZEL

"I saw him!" Shloyme burst through the door into the apartment.

"How many times do I have to tell you not to be late for supper? Do you want to give me a heart attack?" Mama ladled out a bowl of garlicky bean soup for Shloyme.

"I'm sorry, Mama. I was playing with my friends and suddenly it got dark and I started to run home and I bumped into him!"

"Who?" Papa slowly put down his spoon.

"Lemmel! He was walking down Broadway with this tough-looking kid and. . .hey, my two cents are gone!" His face, already red from the cold and running, got even redder. "They stole my money." Shloyme burst into tears.

"Shloyme!" Mama grasped him by the shoulders. "Stop crying and tell me. Did you talk to him? How did he look? What did he say?"

"He said he's never coming home. And I hope he never does! He pushed me. He's a thief and a bully and I hate him!" Shloyme ran sobbing into the front room.

For a moment we stared at each other.

"Why is Shloyme crying?" Hannah looked from face to face. "When is Lemmel coming home?"

I put a piece of meat into Hannah's soup. "Hush, Hannah, don't upset Mama."

"Haveleh, don't cry." Papa had his arm around Mama's shoulders. "At least we know he is alive. And not far away. That was more than we knew before."

"But why won't he come home? What's happening to him? Stealing money. Knocking his little brother down. I wish we had never come to this cursed country, this America of yours!" Mama refused to be comforted.

Shloyme had fallen asleep on his bed. I took off his wet shoes and pants and tucked him in. Hannah went to bed soon after. Mama was still sobbing in her room when Reuben came home.

"What happened here?" Reuben looked around. Papa sat with Mama in their darkened bedroom. The table was full of half-eaten food. I heated a bowl of soup for Reuben.

"Shloyme saw Lemmel on the street. He pushed him and stole two cents. And said he's never coming home."

Reuben looked at me. "Eat something. You'll feel better." He speared a chunk of herring and put it on my plate.

"Something happened to Lemmel. He would never push his brother, or steal his money before."

"He's become a street urchin," Reuben said. "I worked with kids like that at a camp in the mountains last summer."

"Were they like. . .wild animals?"

"Not animals, but they didn't know right from wrong anymore. They stole food from the kitchen, and took things from other kids. Stealing had become their way to survive."

"But if Lemmel is stealing to stay alive, why doesn't he just come home? Then he won't have to steal anymore."

"You know the answer to that better than I do." Reuben bit into a slice of bread.

I thought about my brother. "Lemmel was always angry at having to go to cheder. Angry that Shloyme was smarter in school. Angry at having to study for his bar mitzvah." I lowered my voice. "He told me he can't read."

"What? Why not?"

"I don't know. He said the words wouldn't stay still on the page, the letters get mixed up, he couldn't remember them, things like that."

"Sounds like excuses to me."

"That's what I thought. But he's smart. He can do math in his head."

"Then he's not working hard enough."

I shook my head. "That's what his teachers said. But he worked hard for his bar mitzvah. He studied for hours on end. I wish Papa had let Lemmel quit school and go to work. Maybe he wouldn't have run away."

"I wish I had, too." Papa set a half-empty glass of tea on the table. "Mama's asleep. That boy is breaking her heart."

"Eat something, Papa." I gave him a fresh bowl of soup. "You're outside in the cold all day."

Cursing Columbus

"I'm used to the cold. Russia was colder than New York. And I prefer being outside to sweating in some filthy shop room."

"So you like being a fat collector, Mr. Altman?" Reuben asked.

"It is the best job I've had since coming to America. I have my own horse. I know how to buy cheap after all those years of being a peddler in the Old Country. And the Irishman is fair with me."

"Did you invite him for dinner, Papa?"

"He's coming on Friday. I hope your Mama doesn't get sick with all this crying."

"I'll help her cook, Papa."

Papa squeezed my arm. "What a good daughter I have. A regular little mother, eh, Reuben?"

I glared at Reuben. He looked down at his plate, but not before I caught him swallowing a smile.

LEMMEL

I was getting better at grafting. Last night Mumbles didn't feel a thing when I lifted his wallet. The Dodge said I still wasn't fast enough, but when it was for real, I would be faster. I don't know what he meant. Mumbles said he would drop by today for a test. Now people were coming home from work. I only had a few papers left.

I spotted Mumbles. He was standing on the corner giving me the nod. I picked up a paper.

"Read all about it! *Thieves steal diamond necklace.* Paper, mister?" I thrust my paper into the face of the man standing in front of me. For a moment he couldn't see me. He handed me a nickel. His wallet bulged out of his coat pocket. I stretched out my hand and . . .

He walked on.

"Wha' happened?" Mumbles shoved my head. "Why didn't you lift his wallet? You chicken or somethin'?"

"I ain't chicken. I'm cold, that's all. My hands are frozen." I rubbed them together. My stomach was doing flip-flops.

"Try again. And don't miss this time or you'll be sorry. You owe the Dodge. And me."

He was right. The Dodge wasn't teaching me out of the goodness of his heart. I wasn't sure there was any goodness in his heart. He threw Mary out. I didn't like Lottie, his new lady. She sniffed at us and never fixed coffee.

A man came hurrying down the street.

"Paper, mister? *Big diamond robbery uptown.*"

He barely slowed down to toss me a nickel and grab a paper. As he passed I flipped his wallet out of his back pocket. In a second Mumbles had pocketed it and moved down the street in the opposite direction. If the man noticed his wallet was gone, I was dead. I braced myself to make a run for it. One minute went by. Two. I couldn't see the man anymore. Five minutes. I took a deep breath. I had been fast, as fast as Harry, as fast as Mumbles. Fear acted like grease, I guessed.

I spotted Mumbles in an alley across the street. He gave me a nod. I started looking for my next graft.

RAIZEL

"The chicken was good, Mr. Clancy?" I put another piece on his plate. He was a big man with sparse blond hair and a round red face. He looked a little like Mr. McGraw, our principal, but he smiled more.

"Excellent, darling. And can I get some more of those fine roast potatoes?"

I passed him the bowl. Mama had outdone herself tonight. She had sent me to the market to buy the best of everything: the plumpest chicken, the firmest potatoes, carrots and raisins for the tzimmis. And for dessert she had made apple cake with walnuts. The moment Mr. Clancy stepped through the door his face lit up from the aroma. Mama kept bustling around putting more food on the table and looking at me to translate for her.

Papa was beaming. He could tell that the Irishman liked the food. We had more to eat tonight than we had eaten in the last month.

"Now let me get this straight. This lovely angel is your daughter Rose. The little one is Hannah, and you must be Shlo, Sho. . .can't quite get the hang of your name, young fellow."

"You can call me Samuel," said Shloyme. "That's my American name."

"And a fine name it is. Straight from the Good Book. And this must be your older son."

For a moment no one said anything.

"I'm Reuben, the boarder."

"My oldest son isn't here tonight." Papa glanced at Mama.

That was the truth.

"Where are you from originally?" Reuben asked.

"Why, Ireland, of course!" Mr. Clancy smiled. "'Tis a fine green place. Sometimes I miss it. But it's a hard place to earn a living. Not that America is easy, but mind my words, young man, if you work hard, nothing can stop you! Why, who would have thought that Tom Clancy from Dingle would own a soap factory and live in a fine uptown house? I only regret that my dear departed wife isn't here to enjoy it with me. She died of the consumption when the boys were still little."

"What a shame," I said. "What do your boys do?"

"Well, they're not so much boys anymore. Johnny is a fireman out in Chicago and Michael runs a pharmacy in New Jersey. I've plenty of grandchildren from Johnny, not that I see them often." He sighed.

"What did he say, Raizel?" Mama asked.

"He told us about his sons. I'll tell you later, Mama."

"This was fine cake, Mrs. Altman. You should open your own bakery. Of course, there's a lot of work in running your own business."

Mama looked at me. "He said he likes your cake and you should open a bakery, Mama."

"And who would clean the house and cook and do the laundry, I'd like to know?"

"Shhh, Mama. He didn't mean anything by it."

"Can I get you a schnapps?" Papa poured two small glasses.

"Don't make a fool of yourself, Binyumin," Mama warned.

"Can I taste it?" Shloyme asked.

"Never too early." Mr. Clancy poured Shloyme a few drops before Papa could stop him.

"*Oy*, it tastes like medicine!" Shloyme ran to the sink for a glass of water.

Mr. Clancy laughed so hard that Papa had to pat him on the back.

Mama and I cleared the table and washed the dishes. We put Hannah and Shloyme to bed. The Sabbath candles had burned out long ago, but Mr. Clancy and Papa remained at the table. The once full bottle was half empty.

Reuben sat with his head in his hands. Every once in a while he started, and I knew he had dozed off. He liked to go to bed early on Friday nights, but with the kitchen full of people, we couldn't put his bed out. Mr. Clancy was telling stories about the men who worked for him.

"A bunch of scoundrels," he was saying. "Always trying to cheat me. You're the first honest man I've met—and a Jew to boot. Who would have thought?"

"Raizel, what is he saying?" Mama looked tired.

"He's talking about his employees. He said Papa is the only honest one among them."

"When do you think he will go home?"

"I don't know, Mama." I stifled a yawn.

Finally Mr. Clancy pushed back his chair. "Well, I must be going and let you folks get some sleep."

"Sure you don't want another drink, Mr. Clancy?" Papa held out the bottle.

"Or a cup of coffee?" I offered.

"No, darling, nothing more for me. Tell your mother she's a wonderful cook and I enjoyed every mouthful. I'll see you on Monday, Ben."

Papa stood up from his chair and fell back down again. Mama bit her lip to hide a smile. Papa walked unsteadily to the door and down the dark stairs with his boss. By the time he returned, I had made Reuben's bed and he was sound asleep.

"He likes you, Papa," I said.

"And he likes his whiskey. *Oy,* what a headache I will have tomorrow."

"Raizel. . ." Mama hesitated. "This was not good."

"Mama, the dinner was excellent."

"It was not good that I cannot speak to our guest. Always having to ask you to translate. I am so ashamed. So you will teach me, yes? And you will not laugh at me when I make mistakes."

"Of course, Mama." I hugged her. "I would love to teach you. We'll start tomorrow."

If Mama learned English, I wouldn't have to accompany her to the doctor. She could do her own shopping. She could even come to school and talk with my teachers.

And maybe, just maybe, she would understand how much I wanted to be a teacher, too.

15
A Night Out

RAIZEL

I was surprised when Sally knocked at our apartment door. How did she know where I lived? She had never been here before.

"Hello, uh. . .Rose. Is Reuben here?"

"No, he won't be home until late."

Sally looked upset.

"Is something wrong?" I was alone in the apartment this Sunday evening, a rare occurrence. Mr. Abrahamson had closed the store early. Mama had taken Hannah and Shloyme to visit Shayna and her new baby. Papa was at a *landsmanshaft* meeting. I was enjoying the quiet to finish my homework and read.

"I was hoping Reuben would come with me." Sally plopped herself into a chair. She was wearing a pink shirtwaist with red roses sewn on the skirt. "My girlfriend Franny got the flu and I know it isn't her fault but she knew how much I was counting on her and. . ."

"You look beautiful," I said. "Are you going to a wedding?"

Sally laughed. "No, I'm going dancing. A man invited me to meet him at this very ritzy dance hall. I've been looking forward to it all week."

"Why do you need Reuben?" I glanced longingly at *Eight Cousins*. I had finished *Rose in Bloom* weeks ago, but had found the first book only last week.

Sally looked at me. "Say, how old are you?"

"Fourteen."

"You act older. Have you ever been to a dance hall?"

"Me? I don't even know how to dance."

"I can teach you. Look, I just need someone to come with me."

"What for?"

Sally took my hand. "This man, he's real smooth. He seems nice and all, but he's more sophisticated than the guys I usually go with and. . . you know."

I didn't. "Tell me again why you need me."

Sally leaned forward. "You must have heard stories about what can happen to young women. Come on, Rose, you can't be that innocent!"

"You mean. . .white slavery?" I was shocked. Everyone had heard stories about men who turned young girls into prostitutes. There were letters about it in the *Bintel Brief* that Papa read to us.

Sally nodded.

"If you suspect this man, don't go! There are plenty of other young men."

Sally shook her blond curls. "Rose, this one is different!" She pulled a pair of soft kid gloves from her pocket. "We only had a cup of coffee and he gave me these. Why, I would have to work for a month to afford them. And last night he sent me a bunch of beautiful red roses! All the men I go out with work in a factory. I know what my life will be if I marry them: work, babies, and more work!" She squeezed my hand so hard I winced. "This is my big chance. He said he'll introduce me to an actor friend of his. Why, I could become a famous actress and have lots of money and. . ."

I admired Sally's ambition. She wanted to become an actress as much as I wanted to be a teacher.

"My parents wouldn't like it. And I have school tomorrow."

Sally made a face. "So? I have work. Come on, Rose, you know what they say about all work and no play. Leave your books and have some fun!"

That sounded like something Reuben would say to me, although he probably didn't mean dance halls.

"Will it be late?"

"We can leave any time. On Sundays, most people leave by midnight. Mondays we're half asleep in the shop. The boss lady has a fit!" Sally giggled. The lace trimming on her sleeves couldn't hide the scars on her hands from the sewing machines.

Wasn't Reuben always saying how I should have more fun? I could have fun with Sally for an hour or two and be back before everyone went to bed. And if I went with Sally to the dance hall, I would prove to Reuben that I was more than just a serious little girl.

I swallowed hard. "Promise we'll only stay only an hour or two? My parents will be frantic."

Sally threw her arms around me. She had her coat on before I had finished writing a note to Mama and Papa that I had gone out with a friend and would be home soon. If I told them the truth, they would just worry. I was worried enough for all of us.

LEMMEL

"You and me make a good team, Nickels. Did I hurt you?" We had done the crying-boy graft. I pushed Nickels down and he bawled his eyes out while I picked pockets.

"Nah." He wiped away a tear. "But next time don't push so hard."

It was one of those gray days when the icy wind blew the papers out of your hands and people were too cold to stop. Even snow was better than this. I wondered when spring would come.

"How much we make?"

I counted the money in the wallet. "Aww, only two dollars. And that guy looked swell."

"That's one dollar for you and one for me." Mumbles appeared out of nowhere.

"Come on, let us keep it. We didn't hardly make enough for supper."

"A deal's a deal." He pocketed the dollar. "Message from the Dodge. He said not to come around tonight. He's got something going on."

"But it's too cold to sleep outside." Nickels looked like he was going to cry again. "This morning they found Skinny and Wilson frozen in an alley like two chunks of meat."

Mumbles sneered. "Then you better get moving and make more money. I'll collect tomorrow. I'm freezing my feet off."

Mumble's feet were wearing warm leather shoes. Our shoes were worn thin and Nickels had holes in his soles. He stuffed old newspapers into them every morning.

"Do you think he knows?" Nickels asked when Mumbles left.

"Probably." When Mumbles wasn't around, we kept the money for ourselves. We needed it more than he did. But it still wasn't enough. In the winter people wore overcoats and it was hard to get at their inside pockets and run away through piles of snow.

"Let's go someplace with lots of people," I said to Nickels. "Unless our luck changes, it's goin' be a long cold night."

RAIZEL

I could hear music even before we reached the dance hall one floor above an old factory. On the cold walk over, I had felt guilty. Mama and Papa would never have let me go if I had asked them. But the music made me feel better. Sally paid our entrance fees and we checked our coats at the door. The hall was fancy, just like Sally said. There were red velvet curtains covering the walls and chandeliers so big they sparkled like a million diamonds. Even the wooden dance floor glowed. I felt like I had entered fairyland.

"Rosie, stop gawking. You look like a kid at Coney Island." Sally held my arm as we strolled around the room.

"Everyone is dressed so elegantly." The women wore skirts of shiny fabric and their pastel shirtwaists were covered with ruffles and flowers. I felt out of place in my old skirt and heavy shoes. I wished I had let Sally rouge my cheeks like she suggested. Anyway my clothes were all wrong.

"Most of them are factory girls, just like me. The shop girls have the pretty things, and so do the secretaries."

"How can factory girls afford such elegant clothes?"

"It's something you learn. I skip lunch and know where to find the really good second-hand stuff. Plus I sew. See, I made these roses." She stroked the silky fabric. "In the spring I'll use them to trim a hat. All the men say I have style. Now if I only had money!"

"Is he here?" We had circled the floor.

"Not yet. Let's dance."

Sally put her arm around my waist and swayed to the music. My feet didn't know what to do with themselves.

"Sorry!" I stepped on Sally's toe.

"It's step together left, then right and twirl. Just relax and let me lead. Don't look at your feet!"

We spun around to the music. Then Sally led us to the center of the floor with a confident smile. We must have looked like an ugly caterpillar dancing with a beautiful butterfly. When the music stopped, three young men rushed up to Sally.

"Can I get you a refreshment?" A tall man with slicked-down hair made a little bow.

"Like to dance, beautiful?" This one had wavy brown hair, a handsome face, and a threadbare jacket.

"Haven't we met before?" The third one was stocky, but had a gold stickpin in his tie.

Sally laughed a high tinkling laugh. "The busy bees are out for honey."

"And you are that indeed!" said Tall One.

"I haven't seen you here before," said Gold Stick Pin.

"I'm teaching my little girlfriend how to dance. I can't possibly abandon her, unless a sweet fellow asks her to dance." Sally fluttered her eyes at Gold Stick Pin.

"Sally, I don't want to dance anymore!" I blurted. "I'll just sit over there and watch."

The men looked relieved.

"Oh no, you won't. You're here to have fun, Rosie." She turned to Handsome. "You'll dance with Rosie, won't you? I'll save the next dance for you." She put out her hand to Gold Stick Pin.

"Lovely lady, your wish is my command." Handsome held out his arm to me. I could tell by his crooked smile that he was less than pleased.

"I don't know how to dance," I said as the music began.

He sighed. "Just try to keep off my feet."

I stumbled as he put his arm around my waist and began to spin around the dance floor. He kept changing directions and dragging me after him.

"Stay off my feet," he hissed.

"I'm trying." I wanted to sink into the floor and disappear. Handsome kept his eyes on Sally and tried to stay close to her. Sally blew him a kiss and smiled at me. I mouthed 'help,' but she twirled away.

"Ouch! Why don't you learn to dance before you come to a dance hall? And stop sniffling or your friend will see you."

"Rosie, is something wrong?" The music had stopped and Sally came up to us.

"I must have stepped on the little lady's toe," Handsome said. He held out his hand to Sally.

""I'm sorry, but this is my dance." A deep voice interrupted us. A burly man dressed in an elegant suit put his arm around Sally.

"The lady promised me this dance." Handsome stood up straighter.

"But I invited the lady here. I'm sorry I'm late, my dear."

Sally's face lit up. "Why hello, Teddy. I thought you had forgotten me. However, I promised this gentleman a dance and I never go back on my word." She fluttered her eyelashes at Handsome.

Teddy's face reddened. He had a long nose and curly brown hair. He wasn't handsome, but there was something proud about his face and the way he carried himself. He looked like he knew what he wanted. And how to get it.

"I'm sure our friend here will understand." His voice had grown cold.

"The lady said she's dancing with me." Handsome was stubborn.

Suddenly Teddy grabbed Handsome's arm and gave it a sharp twist.

"Owww! Wanna break my arm? Who do you think you are?"

"A man who would like to dance with a lady. And if you have a problem with that, we can step outside in the alley."

Handsome looked at Teddy. He must not have liked what he saw because he turned sharply on his heels and, without another word, disappeared into the crowd.

"Now, Teddy, that was a very rude thing to do. I gave him my word." Sally pouted. "I'm not sure I feel like dancing with you at all."

Teddy smiled. "Then let's go have some refreshments."

Sally grabbed my hand. "This is my friend, Rosie. It's her first time in a dance hall."

Teddy made a slight bow. "Well, we'll have to show her a good time, won't we?" The hard face of a moment before was replaced by a smile. When he smiled he was almost handsome, except for a white scar under his eye.

The three of us walked towards the crowded refreshment counter.

"What will you have, ladies?" Teddy gestured at the bar man.

"I'll have a Mamie Taylor, please." Sally said.

"And for this young lady?"

"I don't drink alcohol," I said.

"You must drink something," Sally said. "Otherwise we will be very unpopular around here."

"No, thank you." I needed to look out for Sally and I had heard that alcohol clouded your head.

"I know just the thing," Teddy said. He whispered in the bar man's ear. The man grimaced but nodded. He handed me a cocktail glass just like Sally's.

"It's ginger ale and red syrup, little girl." Teddy took Sally's arm and led her into an alcove filled with an overstuffed green couch. I sat at one end with Sally and Teddy at the other. He flung his arm along the couch back and tickled her neck with his hand. Sally's eyes closed with pleasure like a cat being stroked.

"You are the most beautiful woman here," he said. "And I am not exaggerating."

"That's sweet of you to say, even though I see many more beautiful women. This is a very elegant establishment."

"Ah, but you have something special, an air of purity."

Sally blushed and looked at her scarred hands. For the first time, she seemed to lose her confidence.

"I feel fresh when I'm with you," Teddy continued. "It's not something I say to other women, believe me."

He sounded sincere. Maybe he was a nice person, after all. Then I remembered how he had spoken to Handsome.

"Sally, when are we leaving?" I asked. "My parents will be worried about us." I emphasized 'us.'

Sally took a last sip of her cocktail. "Why, I haven't danced hardly at all."

I guessed Sally was safer dancing than listening to Teddy's sweet talk, although when they actually began, I wasn't sure. I had never seen dancing like that before. Teddy rested his chin on Sally's shoulder and the two spun in place, pivoting in a tight little circle. Then the music changed to something slow and he put his arms around her, pressing her to him until their bodies were so close they could barely move. I was shocked. How could anyone dance in public like that?

"Just look at those two!" A girl not much older than me sat down on the couch. "I've seen tough dancing before, but that tops it all. Whew!" She fanned her face with her hand.

"It's terrible! Why, why she could get, you know. . ."

The girl burst out laughing. "You mean pregnant? Aren't you the innocent! I bet you're still in school."

I blushed and nodded. My friends and I speculated how girls got pregnant. Sitting on a boy's lap was one theory. Dancing like this was something we had never even imagined.

"I used to be like you before I went to work in the shop. You learn real fast there, believe me."

I remembered the shop where I had worked pulling basting threads when we first came to America. Papa had made me sit in the farthest corner. I hadn't understood why at the time. I had watched the young women talking and laughing with each other. The men in the shop would call out to the girls and make them blush.

"Do you like working?"

The girl stared at me like I had gone crazy. "Are you kidding? As soon as I find a young man to marry, I never want to touch a sewing machine again!"

A skinny man strode up, made a slight bow, and they danced into the crowd.

"We're going to have another drink. Would you like one?" Sally held out her hand to me. Her curls stuck to her flushed face. Teddy was nuzzling her neck.

"Sally, we really have to go home!"

Cursing Columbus

"Just one little drink. I'm thirsty from dancing. Then we'll go home, I promise." She grabbed Teddy's hand and pulled him toward the refreshment stand. As they walked off, he glanced back at me. There was something in his look I didn't understand.

Or like.

LEMMEL

"But Mumbles said not to come here tonight." Nickels' teeth were chattering so bad he could barely talk.

"I heard him. But what are we supposed to do? The Lodge is full and we don't want to end up like Skinny and Wilson, do we? Anyway, I got a plan. Know that back room they use for storage?"

"Y-y-yes."

"Well, the window catch is broken. We can sneak in, sleep there and be gone first thing in the morning. No one goes into that room."

We approached the apartment through the back alley.

"Ain't no lights."

"Good. That means Lottie's out."

I tugged at the window. I tugged harder.

"W-w-won't it open?" Nickels sounded scared. He's not tough enough.

"It's stuck. Must be the cold." I looked around the alley until I found a piece of metal. Now the window pried up easy. I gave Nickels a boost. He squirmed in and tumbled to the floor.

"Ouch." He gave me a hand. I climbed inside and closed the window behind me. "It's dark in here."

"Yeah. Let's find something to cover up and go to sleep."

"I'm hungry. Remember those buns Mary used to give us?"

"Forget it. We're not leaving this room. There might be someone else sleeping here. Take this." I passed him a burlap sack.

"Did you hear something?" Nickels huddled against me.

"Just rats." I found an old coat and pulled it over me.

"This is like sleeping with my brother." Nickels wasn't shivering anymore.

"I didn't know you had a brother."

"Mickey. He was older than me. He took care of me after mama died."

"What about your papa?" Nickels had never talked about his family before.

"Never knew him. It was just the two of us."

"So what happened to Mickey?" I was afraid of the answer.

"Donno. We had a shack down by the docks, just the two of us. Mickey was part of a gang. They went out at night and came back with all kinds of stuff like money and jewelry. Then one night last summer he never come back." Nickels was blubbering now.

"Didn't you look for him? What about his gang?"

"They told me to clear out of the shack. That Mickey wasn't never coming back. Since then I don't got nobody."

I thought of Shloyme. What would happen to him if he had to live on the streets? Nickels had no place to go, except an orphan asylum. I had met kids who lived in them before they ran away. They said it was like prison, cold, with never enough to eat. And they beat you. If a kid died, it was one less mouth to feed. They said the streets were better, and they knew.

"Stop crying already. You're too soft. You got to be tough if you want to survive." I shook Nickels roughly.

"I don't want to be tough. I want Mickey." He sobbed even harder. "I want my mama."

I sighed. I hadn't been on the streets long, but I been there long enough. "Okay, get out!" I pushed Nickels away.

"Wh-what?"

I opened the window. "I said, get out! I won't hang around with a crybaby like you."

"But it's cold out there! I'll freeze to death!"

"Yup."

"Louie, you got to let me stay!"

"You can stay if you stop blubbering. I ain't your Mickey and I ain't your mama. Now make up your mind before I throw you out."

Nickels rubbed his eyes. He gulped down a sob. "Okay. I stopped."

I closed the window. Quietly.

"Now go to sleep and quit bothering me."

Nickels didn't answer. He took the burlap sack and curled up with his back to me. In a few minutes I could hear him breathing nice and slow. I couldn't fall asleep. I worried what would happen to a kid like Nickels all alone on the streets. I worried what would happen to me. I wished Nickels was sleeping next to me like before. I wished I was home in bed with Shloyme next to me.

I wished I had an older brother to take care of me.

16
To the Rescue

RAIZEL

The dancers blurred before my eyes. The clock at the end of the hall said ten o'clock. I knew it was time to leave, that Mama would be furious, and that I wouldn't be able to concentrate in school tomorrow. Where was Sally?

I wandered along the edge of the dance floor, peering among the dancers, searching for Sally's blond curls and flower-covered dress. I could see Handsome and Gold Stick Pin, but no sign of Sally and Teddy. I pushed my way through the crowd around the refreshment stand.

"Have you seen my friend with the curly blond hair and roses on her dress?" I asked the busy bar man.

"Girlie, what do you want to drink?"

"Nothing. I'm looking for my friend. She's with a man in a striped shirt and gold cuff links."

The bar man looked like he was about to say something. "Go home, girlie!" I walked around the dance floor once again, peeping into all the alcoves. I checked the crowd of women doing their make-up in the ladies' room. Sally and Teddy were nowhere to be found.

How could Sally do this to me? She had promised we would go home early. Well, now I knew how much her promises were worth! How could Reuben stand having a liar like Sally for a friend? I would just have to walk home by myself.

The freezing wind cut through my coat as I tied my scarf tightly around my head. The dance hall was near the Orchard Street market, so it was over ten blocks to Goerck Street. I thrust my hands into my pockets and began walking home as fast as I could.

LEMMEL

"Louie, you hear something?" Nickels whispered in my ear.

"Shhh!" I heard voices in the next room. Then a thud and the door slamming.

"It's the Dodge and Lottie. Go back to sleep."

"It's cold in here." Nickels huddled against me.

"Not as cold as outside." I shut my eyes again.

RAIZEL

Mama, Papa, and Reuben were sitting half-asleep around the kitchen table.

"Raizel Altman, we were absolutely frantic!" Mama cried when she saw me.

"I'm sorry. I left a note. I didn't plan to be out this late. You see, I went to a dance hall with Sally and. . ."

"What is this dance hall nonsense? Since when does my daughter go to a dance hall?"

I had never seen Papa so mad. "I just wanted to see what it was like. And help Sally out."

"Sally is an old friend of mine from school. She must have come looking for me," Reuben explained.

"But why did you go with this Sally? We don't even know her!" Mama shook her head. "You are always so responsible."

How could I explain to Mama that I was tired of always being the responsible one, that I wanted to have fun sometimes like other girls. I put my arms around her. "I'm sorry, Mama. Sally promised we would be home early."

"Did something happen?" Reuben asked.

"That's why I'm so late. Sally disappeared! She and her boyfriend went to get a drink. She promised to come right back, but then I couldn't find her. I looked and looked, but she must have left so I walked home alone."

"You say she disappeared after she had a drink?" Reuben looked worried.

"I think so. Is something wrong?"

Reuben looked at Papa. "Mr. Altman, do you think. . . ?"

"*Gevalt!*" Papa hit his head with his palm. "Just like in the newspaper. The guy slips something in the girl's drink and takes her away to a brothel!"

"That poor girl! Can't we do something?" Mama wrung her hands.

Reuben stood up. "We have to go to the police."

I looked at Mama and Papa.

"Go, Raizel. You must try and help that poor girl." Papa put his arm on Reuben's shoulder. "You will take good care of Raizel??"

"Of course." Reuben took my hand and pulled me out the door. I forgot how tired and cold I was as I rushed after him.

We raced through the streets, past the noisy saloons, past gaudy women standing under street lamps, past clusters of men talking and arguing. The police station was six blocks away on Sheriff Street.

"Please, we need help," Reuben said to the sergeant at the big wooden desk. I sat down on the bench to catch my breath.

"Lost something, sonny?" The policeman looked sleepy. His blue jacket was unbuttoned.

"Someone. My friend had been abducted from a dance hall!"

The sergeant stared at Reuben. "You mean your girlfriend left with someone else? Don't worry, she'll turn up in the morning."

"You don't understand. Sally went with my friend here to meet a man. Then she had a drink and disappeared."

The policeman called over his shoulder. "O'Hara, got a missing girl for you."

A heavy man strolled out of another room. He stared at Reuben and me. "This here the 'missing' girl?"

Reuben explained all over again. The policeman took us to a smoky little room and began asking me questions.

"What was the name of the dance hall?"

"The Queen's Hall."

"That's not a nice place. I wouldn't let her go there, if I were you," he said to Reuben.

"I'm never going there again!" I promised.

"Now describe the man your friend met. Did you get a name?"

"Just 'Teddy.'"

"Probably not his real name. What did he look like?"

"He was about your height, with brown curly hair, dark eyes and a long nose."

"Fat? Thin? How old was he?"

"Not fat and not thin. He wasn't young, but he wasn't old, either. He wore fancy gold cuff links."

"Did he have a pushed-in nose that looked like it had been broken?"

"No. His nose was straight."

The policeman sighed. "How about a limp? Did he drag his left foot?"

"No. He was a good dancer."

"Tommy! Get in here!" Officer O'Hara yelled. A thin blond man appeared in the doorway. "We're looking for a man, brown hair, not too young, not to old, not too thin, not too fat. Might have abducted a girl."

The man shrugged. "With a description like that, it could be anyone."

"Think hard, little lady. Was there anything distinctive about him?"

I closed my eyes. I remembered Teddy's cold stare when he chased Handsome off. And the funny look he gave me before he disappeared. And I remembered his smile and how it changed his whole face and lit up his eyes and. . ." The scar! He had a white V-shaped scar under his left eye." I looked up hopefully.

"Nathan Dinnerstein's got a scar like that! Didn't know he was pimping. Times must be tough." The thin man looked excited.

"That crook we suspected was mixed up in the horse poisonings last summer?" asked Officer O'Hara. "He's got a place on Ludlow Street."

A few minutes later I found myself sitting in the back of a police wagon with Reuben, heading for Ludlow Street.

"Why do I have to come?" I asked Reuben. I was so tired I could barely keep my head up. Plus I had no desire to see Teddy, or whatever his name was, again.

"Because you might have to identify him." Reuben squeezed my hand inside my pocket. "Your hands are like ice cubes. Give them to me." He rubbed my hands as we rode through the darkened streets in the police wagon. If it hadn't been so cold, I might have enjoyed the ride. The van pulled up in front of a brownstone building. Lights burned in the ground floor apartment.

"You kids stay inside the van. Don't move under any circumstances."

We peered out the window as the two policemen walked up the steps of the building and disappeared inside.

"Why didn't they bring more men?" I asked.

"They said something about a bar brawl. Hey, someone's running away. Wait here!"

"Reuben, the policeman said. . . !" Reuben dashed around the house and disappeared. Against my better judgment, I followed him.

"Stop, you!" Reuben grabbed at someone. "Owww!" The kid kicked Reuben in the leg.

"We didn't do anything, mister." A little kid slipped out of the shadows. "We was just sleeping."

"Awww, get on with you then." Reuben rubbed his leg and the boys disappeared into the night. He limped back to me. "Just a bunch of frightened kids."

"I thought I told you to stay in the van. Come in here!" We followed Officer O'Hara into the apartment. Sally was lying asleep on the couch. Teddy and a woman wearing a green silk bathrobe were sitting on the floor with their hands on their heads. Teddy glared at me.

"Sally, are you all right?" Reuben shook her but she didn't move. "Did you hurt her, you. . . ?"

"Never touched her. Hey, she wanted to come home with me. I didn't plan to bring her but she insisted. As soon as she got here, she fell asleep."

"And what would this be?" The policeman took a tiny bottle from Teddy's jacket pocket." He sniffed it. "Whew! This would put a horse to sleep."

"Right. You're under arrest," said Officer O'Hara. "Put your coat on and come with us."

"What about me? I didn't do anything." The woman in the silk bathrobe smiled at the policemen and licked her red lips.

"Ever seen this woman, girlie? Maybe hanging around the dance hall?"

"No, I've never seen her before. Will Sally be all right?"

"Yeah, until next time. Why these dumb broads get mixed up with scum like this I'll never understand. She'll sleep a long time, that's for sure. Where can we take you kids?"

"We'll take Sally home with us," Reuben said. "Her parents will die of fright if they see her like this."

The policemen carried the sleeping Sally into the van. When we reached Goerck Street, one of them helped Reuben carry her while the other stayed in the van to watch their prisoner.

"You would have to live on the fourth floor," said the policeman gasping for breath.

We laid Sally on Reuben's bed. Mama and I took off her shoes and her fancy dress. "What about her parents?" Mama asked.

"I'll stop by their house in the morning," Reuben said. "Before I go to school."

"What time is it?" I asked.

Reuben looked at his watch. "Two in the morning."

"Reuben, you can sleep with Shloyme," Mama said. "But first both of you will drink a glass of warm milk and honey, you shouldn't catch cold."

"H-how will I ever wake up for school?" My teeth were chattering. I almost fell asleep in the chair waiting for the milk to heat up.

"Shloyme will tell your Miss Norman that you are coming late. Now drink this." Mama put a glass of warm milk in my freezing hands. She bent over and kissed my forehead. "I am going to bed. Good night, children."

We sipped our warm milk. "Do you think he. . .touched Sally?"

Reuben shook his head. "I think she was so sound asleep that he didn't do anything to her. At least I hope not." He gave me a piercing look. "Why did you go with Sally anyway?

"Well," I began. "She was looking for you and needed someone to go with her. I thought you would want me to help her." I met his eyes and took a deep breath. "But I also did it because Sally made it sound like fun. I wanted to have some fun."

"And did you?"

"No. I hated every minute of it." Oh no, now Reuben would think I was a baby.

"I don't like those places either. Girls go to dance halls looking for husbands, while the men are looking for something else. Not that I have anything against dancing. We have dancing classes at the Alliance and sometimes, if I have time, I go to them."

Cursing Columbus

"You?" This was a side of Reuben I didn't know.

"We don't do any of that tough dancing, but dancing is a fun way to meet girls."

"Do you have a. . .girlfriend?"

Reuben laughed. "I have girlfriends, but no girlfriend. I don't have time for a girlfriend. My plan is to marry after I become a doctor. Right now I'm always running between school, my job, and the library. I barely have time to eat and sleep!"

"So I've noticed!" We both laughed. I felt comfortable with Reuben, not like with those men at the dance hall. But not like with an older brother, either.

"Well, I'm going to get a few hours sleep. I hope Shloyme doesn't snore."

I picked up our glasses and put them in the sink. As I walked passed Reuben into the dark bedroom, he reached out and touched my cheek.

"You've got spunk, Rose Altman. Every time I think I know you, you manage to surprise me. That was a brave thing you did today."

"I didn't feel brave."

"You don't have to feel brave to do a brave thing." His hands cradled my face for a long moment. "Good night."

"Good night," I whispered.

I cuddled next to Hannah listening to the gentle in and out of Reuben's breathing, a peaceful ending to a horrible evening.

LEMMEL

"Oh boy, I'm cold. I'm so cold I can't feel my feet anymore!" We huddled around a fire made out of old crates.

"So what do you think, Louie? Why were the cops there?" Nickels danced from one foot to the other.

"I guess the Dodge was up to something rotten."

"Did you think he killed that blond girl the police carried out?"

"Nah, I don't think so." We had hidden in the shadows as soon as that boy stopped chasing us. "But I'm not going back to find out."

"Let's go to sleep next to the fire." Nickels sat down.

"NO!" I kicked him. "We can't go to sleep. The fire will go out and we'll freeze to death like Skinny and Wilson."

Nickels got to his feet. "But I'm tired."

"Go get some more wood for the fire. Wish we had potatoes to roast. Or old bread."

"When will it be morning?"

"How should I know?" The sky was pitch black. Dawn was hours away. "As soon as it gets light, we'll go to that bakery on Second Avenue and buy a roll and a cuppa hot coffee. How does that sound?"

"Good." Nickels wandered away to look for more wood. Finally I had time to think. Because I wasn't sure, but maybe the girl who went into the Dodge's place was Raizel. I didn't recognize her blue scarf and it was dark. But something had reminded me of Raizel. How was Raizel mixed up with the Dodge? And who was that guy I kicked?

How long had it been since I left home? Two months? Three? I'd lost track of time. I pictured everything exactly the same as when I left. But maybe it wasn't. Maybe things were changing at home, just like they had changed for me.

I shivered and moved closer to the flames. I could hear Nickels dragging a crate towards the fire. I had never realized it before. I lived on the streets like the other guys, but I carried my family around inside of me. Because I could run away from home, but I couldn't run away from my family.

17
The Letter

RAIZEL

I opened my eyes to sunlight pouring in the window and Hannah jumping on my stomach. "Oooph, get off me." Why was it so bright in the room? And why was I so tired? Then I remembered.

"Is Sally awake?" I sat up in bed.

"Not yet," Mama answered. "Reuben moved her into the boys' bed so she could sleep quietly."

I looked at the next bed. Sally's blond curls were mashed around her pale face. She moaned in her sleep.

"Do you think she's sick?" I asked Mama.

Mama touched her forehead. "She's cool. Let's try to wake her up."

Together we shook Sally awake. She squinted at us out of half-open eyes.

"Where am I? I don't feel good." She gagged. "I think I'm going to. . ."

Mama pushed an empty chamber pot in front of her. Sally retched and fell back onto the pillow. There were dark circles under her eyes.

"Rose?" Her eyes focused on me in recognition. "How did we get to your house? Ohhh, my head is spinning."

"I'll make you both some tea. Come, Hannah." Mama took the chamber pot and Hannah with her.

I sat on the edge of the bed. "Don't you remember? We went to the dance hall. I wanted to go home but you went to have one last drink. And then you disappeared."

"Oh dear. Did you have to walk home alone? I'm sorry." Sally rubbed her forehead. "I'm so confused. I didn't have that much to drink, did I?"

"That awful Teddy person slipped a drug into your drink."

"What?" Sally sat straight up in bed. "He drugged me? Teddy?"

"His real name is Nathan Dinnerstein. He's a crook. He drugged you and took you home with him."

"A crook? He took me home? Oh no!" Sally pulled the covers up to her face.

"Oh yes. Reuben and I went to the police and they rescued you. We brought you here to sleep."

"But I'm a good girl! I don't do things like that!" Sally clasped her arms around her knees and rocked back and forth. "Rose, do you think he. . .raped me?"

"He said he didn't touch you."

"You were there? Was I dressed? Was I. . .bleeding?" Sally grabbed my shoulders. Her breath smelled like a clogged toilet.

"Ouch, you're hurting me. You were asleep on the couch and Teddy was with his lady friend."

"What have I done? No one will marry me now!" She buried her face in the bedclothes, her body shuddering with sobs.

Mama walked in carrying two glasses of tea. I sipped mine gratefully.

"Come, *meydele*, drink something. You will feel better." Mama stroked Sally's heaving back.

Sally turned to Mama. "I didn't think Teddy was that kind of man, honest I didn't. He was so charming and he promised to help me and. . . what am I going to do? My life is ruined!"

"There, there." Mama rocked Sally back and forth like a baby. "Everything will be all right." Mama looked at me. "Raizel, it's past ten o'clock. Finish your tea and have something to eat."

"Ohhh, I'll be fired from work. And my parents! They'll be out of their minds with worry."

"Reuben promised to stop by your house this morning and tell them," Mama said. "But you should go home yourself."

"How can I go home? I can't face them. Why, he tried to turn me into a streetwalker!" Suddenly she stared at me, her eyes so wide I could see my reflection in them. "You saved me, Rose! You and Reuben rescued me from a fate worse than death! How can I ever thank you?"

I almost laughed. Sally was so dramatic she really should be an actress.

"I feel like I've been born anew! I'll be a good girl like my mother wants. I'll even let her find me a husband."

Mama and I exchanged smiles. Sally had gone from despair to elation in a split second.

"I have to get home! Where's my skirt? Ohhh, my head aches. Thank you so much, Mrs. Altman. Rose saved me! If she hadn't rescued me. . ." Sally shuddered. A few moments later she was dressed and running out the door, but not before she had showered us all with hugs and kisses, even Hannah.

"Where is that smelly lady going?" Hannah asked. "Why was she crying before and laughing now?"

"You're too young to understand," Mama said, stripping the sheets from the boys' bed.

"I am not!" Hannah stamped her foot. "I want to go to school. Look, I can read already." She picked up a library book and read the letters of the alphabet.

"That's wonderful." I gave her a hug. "Where did you learn that?"

"From Mama's lessons," Hannah said. "Now can I go to school?"

"Next year."

"When is next year?"

"After the summer." I buttered a slice of bread.

"But it's winter. I can't wait so long." Hannah began to cry.

"If you want to go to school, you'll have to learn to stop crying,"

I said in my best teacher's voice. "They don't allow babies in school. Anyway, soon it will be spring."

And the baby will be born.

And I will have to quit school.

LEMMEL

"So how much you make?" I asked.

Nickels held out his hand.

"Fifty cents? You could make more begging."

"I didn't sleep last night." Nickels' eyes were red. "I dozed off near a chestnut vendor."

"If you sleep during the day, how you expect to have money for a warm place to sleep at night?" I looked at Nickels in disgust. The kid was too little to be on the streets.

"I'm sorry." Nickels offered me a handful of chestnuts. "How much you got?"

"Not enough for us both to eat and sleep in the Lodge." If it were just me, I could do it. But I was afraid Nickels would freeze to death if he stayed out alone at night. Dumb kid. As soon as it got warmer, I would dump him.

"Maybe we go back to the Dodge's?" Nickels asked hopefully.

"Forget the Dodge. You heard Lottie. The Dodge is history. They're gonna send him up the island for sure." We had been back to his place. Lottie had a bunch of women staying there. She told us to get lost and not come back. She wouldn't even give us a piece of bread.

"What you think happened to Mumbles?" Nickels asked.

"I donno and I don't care. If you like him so much, go tag around with him and leave me alone."

"Uh, uh. I'm sticking with you, Louie. You're the nicest guy I know, after my brother."

I tapped Nickels on the shoulder. "Yeah, well, I won't be nice if we don't get some cash. What say we take a tram uptown? We can warm up while we ride." Uptown people had gold watches and dollars in their pockets. It cost to get there, but maybe we would get lucky.

Or maybe we wouldn't. What I needed was a gang of guys my age or older. Nickels was okay, but he was just too little. I had to watch out for him all the time. I wondered where Tim was. I hadn't seen him in ages. Or Harry. Maybe I could go back to the old neighborhood and check on him. A plan—that much I learned from the Dodge. You needed a plan.

"Hey kid, watch where you're. . .well, look who's here. Louie Boy and Crybaby." Mumbles blocked my path. He looked bad. His hair was filthy and a bruise peeked from behind a layer of dirt on his cheek. He was wearing a second-hand rag instead of his warm winter coat.

"Hey, Mumbles. How's it goin'?"

"'Muscles' to you. Not bad, not bad."

I cocked my head and kept my mouth shut. Mumbles couldn't stand a silence. He always had to be blabbing about something.

"That witch Lottie wouldn't give me my stuff. Or the money the Dodge owed me. She spat in my face and sent one of her thugs to work me over. I told the Dodge she was poison, but he wouldn't listen. If you ask me, she set the police on him."

"Why would she do that?"

"Because she wanted his money and his place, dumbo. She set herself up as a madam." He stepped closer. "So how much you got?"

I backed off. I wasn't splitting the few cents I had with Mumbles.

"Come on, Louie. Cough it up. You owe me half. Hey, we had a deal."

"My deal was with the Dodge, not with you." I looked around for Nickels. The kid had disappeared. Sometimes he was smarter than I thought.

Mumbles grabbed my arm. "You punk." He swat my face hard. "You wouldn't have a cent if it weren't for me. Now hand it over or I'll break every bone in your body."

"You and what army?" I aimed a swift kick at Mumble's crotch. He doubled over. I jumped on his back and pounded his ears with all my might.

"Owwww! Get off me, you midget! I'm gonna kill you!" He grabbed my head and threw me on the pavement. For a moment I couldn't breathe. My back felt like a steamroller had run over it. Mumbles raised his foot in the air to stomp me, tottered, and fell flat on his face.

"Run, Louie!"

I scrambled to my feet and ran after Nickels as fast as I could. Any minute I expected to feel Mumble's hand on my neck. We dodged up and down the back alleys veering left and right so fast I lost track until we suddenly burst into the market. I pulled Nickels into a doorway. We leaned against the wall gasping for breath.

"Th-thanks kid," I said to Nickels as soon as I could talk again. "I owe you one."

"Mickey taught me to hide and look for an op. . .opor. . .I forget the word he used."

"Opportunity." Sometimes I surprised myself. I had learned more in Miss O'Brien's class than I thought. "Was Mumbles following us?"

Nickels shook his head. "I looked back. He was sitting in the snow with blood pouring from his nose." He grinned. "Know what? I think he was crying. Now who's a cry baby?" Nickels danced a little jig.

"Good work. You remind me of David and Goliath."

"I don't know them."

"In the Bible, dummy. David was a kid who fought a giant with nothin' but a slingshot. You must of heard the story."

Nickels shrugged. "Didn't nobody ever tell me stories. Tell it to me, Louie, please."

For a second the crowds faded. Raizel, Shloyme and I were walking in the woods outside Jibatov. We were picking berries for Mama to make preserves for the winter. Sweet preserves full of whole berries that taste like summer no matter how cold it got outside. Shloyme was begging Raizel for a story about a giant.

"Later. Let's see what we can pick up for supper from the carts. If we don't spend money on supper, we might have enough for the Lodgings."

"Pickles!" Nickels clapped his hands.

"Something more filling. How about roasted sweet potatoes?"

Nickels nodded. "And then the story?"

I looked at his dirty eager face. He might be a pain, but he had saved me from Mumbles.

"Yeah, hero, then the story. You deserve it."

RAIZEL

After work I dragged myself up the stairs. My legs felt like stuffed sausages.

"Raizel, set the table. And there's a letter for you."

The postmark was from Belgium. I opened the letter and my heart shriveled. "Oh, Mama!"

"What is it, *meydele?*" Mama sat down beside me.

"Mrs. Goldenberg is dead!" I burst into tears. Mrs. Goldenberg had taken me under her wing when we met on the ocean liner after our deportation from Ellis Island. She had become like a grandmother to me and now I would never see her again! I sobbed onto Mama's shoulder.

"I was afraid of that when the last letter said she was ill. What a shame!"

"Why is Raizel crying?" Papa asked as he walked in from work.

"Mrs. Goldenberg died!" I handed Papa the letter. A piece of paper fluttered out of the envelope.

Papa picked it up. "It's a check for two hundred dollars! And a note from Mr. Goldenberg that his mother wanted you to have it for your

education. I just made my last payment to Mr. Goldenberg last month."
Papa had been paying back the tickets for our second crossing, just as he
had promised.

"I don't want money! I want Mrs. Goldenberg." I couldn't stop
crying.

Mama touched my forehead. "You feel warm. Tonight you go to bed
early. No homework nonsense. Binyumin, the children are next door at
Maria's. Call them for supper, please."

I lay in bed, my head aching and my nose too stuffed to breathe.
I couldn't fall asleep. Mrs. Goldenberg's kind face, her stories of her
poor childhood, her life of luxury in Antwerp, her lack of self-pity at her
blindness—all these had made her special. When she had invited me to
stay in Belgium as her companion and promised to send me to school, I
had been tempted, but my own family was too important to me. She had
understood. She always understood

Shloyme snored in the next bed. I heard Reuben let himself in quietly. Mama spoke to him in a low voice. For a while there was light in
the kitchen as Reuben ate his supper and did his homework. Then the
light went out. Outside I could hear people shouting on the street and
the clip-clop of horses passing.

When I finally fell asleep, my dreams were full of ocean storms.
Sally and I were trapped in a vast dance hall. We ran from door to door
only to find them all locked. Finally I saw Mrs. Goldenberg at the end of
a long corridor. Sally was gone. I followed Mrs. Goldenberg, trying to
catch up with her, but she moved faster and faster, always out of reach,
looking back over her shoulder with her sweet smile, as if in my dream
she had regained her lost sight.

When Mama shook me awake, I still hadn't caught up with her.

18
The Gang's Plan

LEMMEL

Mumbles had to be the last person I wanted in a gang. For one thing, he wasn't smart. For another, he made fun of me and Nickels.

Which was why I almost fell off my chair a week later when he suggested we team up.

"Me work with *you?*" I asked. We were having a cup of coffee. Mumbles was paying. "Why?"

"Because we make a good team, Louie. The Dodge taught me all kinds of stuff. And you're quick and have ideas. We could make a pretty buck."

I took a sip of coffee. I didn't like Mumbles, but he did have experience. And I needed a gang if I was going to survive on the streets. I'd been watching the other newsies. The older guys had their own gangs. They didn't need me. I might not like Mumbles, but I knew him, for better and for worse. I could do worse.

"How's your nose?" Might as well get everything out in the open.

Mumble's nose was red and swollen from his fall. He touched it gingerly. "Don't worry. I ain't mad at you. The brat pushed me."

"The brat comes with me."

"The brat broke my nose."

"The brat is my buddy."

"Aw, come on, Louie. He's a baby. We don't need him. He can't pick pockets worth a damn."

"True. But he's got other uses."

"Like what?" Mumbles looked puzzled.

"He's small. He can get into places you and I can't."

Mumbles cocked his head.

"And he's got those big blue eyes. He stops the suckers in their tracks. They can't resist him."

Mumbles wiped his mouth with his hand. His eyes narrowed. "Okay, but you and me split fifty-fifty."

"What about Nickels?"

"You want him. You pay for him." Mumbles leaned back, a satisfied smile on his face.

"Forty you, sixty me."

"Forty-five me, fifty-five you, and that's final."

"Okay, but we each get an equal vote."

"Vote on what?" Mumbles scratched his head.

"If we can't agree on somethin', then we vote. The three of us gets one vote each and they count equal. That's the American way, Mumbles."

"But I'm the leader of this gang. I'm the oldest."

"You can be the leader. But if we disagree with you, we vote. Even the president of the United States doesn't decide all by himself. The Senate and the House of Representatives get to vote."

Mumbles nodded. "Uh, I guess you're right, Louie. Say, how does a greenhorn like you know so much about America?"

"You said it yourself. I'm smart, Mumbles." Of course, no one in school thought so.

"One more thing. You got to call me 'Muscles' from now on. Nickels, too."

"Sure thing, Muscles." I tried to keep a straight face. "And me, I'm Tough Lou. And Nickels is Nickels, none of this crybaby stuff."

Mumbles, I mean Muscles, nodded his head seriously. He put out a filthy hand for me to shake. I stretched out a filthy hand in return.

Cursing Columbus

RAIZEL

"How are you feeling? Your mama asked me to bring you a cup of tea." Reuben set the tea on a chair next to my bed and leaned against the doorway. I pulled the blanket up to my chin. My hair must look like a dead tree in a windstorm.

"Better. Have you seen Sally?"

"Sure, half a dozen times. I know everything she said to her mother and her mother said to her father and her father said to. . .you get the idea." We laughed. "They're frightened that she's pregnant. They're try-ing to find her a husband."

"No!"

"You're surprised? There are matchmakers in America, just like in the Old Country."

"But I thought American men and women chose each other. Papa read us an article in the *Forward*. The matchmakers claimed they were going out of business."

"So you think matchmakers are outdated?"

"I think people should marry because they're in love."

"Spoken like a true American girl. And where are girls supposed to meet their future husbands? In dance halls?"

I remembered the three men who had pounced on Sally. "At work, maybe, or at the Alliance, or through clubs."

"That's better. But what about men who are too shy to approach a woman, or vice versa?"

"A friend can introduce them." I didn't understand what Reuben was getting at. Didn't he believe in love?

"And people who have a disability like a hare-lip or a lame leg?"

I thought of my friend Dvoyreh back in Jibatov. She had polio as a child and walked with a crutch. Mama told me that she had married a watchmaker. Her father had saved a dowry for her and she was known for her lace making, which sold for large sums. In America, would someone have married her for love?

"I understand what you're saying. But, Reuben, don't you believe in love?"

"Of course I do! I'm just trying to encourage you to use your head. Not everything in America is wonderful and not everything from the Old Country should be discarded. As a modern girl from St. Petersburg, my mother refused the man her parents had chosen and married my father for love. Not that I'm certain she's pleased with her choice these days." He frowned. His mother had written she was very unhappy in Denver.

"And my parents married though a matchmaker and love each other very much."

"See? While marrying for love may be the American way, it doesn't mean other ways are wrong. Now I have to go to work. I'm running a debate tonight, and this was good practice."

After Reuben left, I thought about the fact that I automatically condemned everything from the Old Country. And it wasn't just me. As soon as immigrants stepped off the boat, they tried to prove that they weren't greenhorns. First they ran out to buy American clothes and threw away their old clothes. Husbands forced their wives to take off the wigs they had worn for modesty all their lives. Men stopped going to shul, no longer kept kosher, and worked on the Sabbath. Boys stopped studying Jewish law as soon as they finished their bar mitzvah, and no one wanted to be a yeshiva boy, studying day and night and living on charity. Everyone wanted to strip away the culture they had grown up in and become a part of the new American culture, even if that meant discarding good things, too.

And there was language. From the moment I set foot in school almost four years ago, we had been forbidden to speak a language other than English. If the teachers heard us speaking Yiddish or Italian during recess, they would keep us after school to write 'I will speak only English' on the blackboard a hundred times. Even Shloyme, who had been in America for only six months, spoke English with me. And Hannah babbled to me in English and spoke to Lucia's brothers and sisters in English. Soon she wouldn't remember how to speak Yiddish!

"Here, *meydele*, I brought you something to eat." Mama put a steaming bowl of rice soup on the chair.

"Thank you, Mama."

She touched her lips to my forehead. "I think your fever is down, it should only be gone by tomorrow."

"Mama, I missed you so much when you were still in Jibatov." I had never told Mama that before.

Mama sat down beside me and rested her hands on her ballooning stomach.

"When I was sick I pretended you were taking care of me," I continued. "I envied the other girls whose mamas had come over with them."

"My big girl." Mama hugged me. "It must have been hard for you."

"I love you, Mama." We sat wrapped in each other's arms, the soup cooling on the chair.

"Why are you crying, Mama?" Hannah skipped into the room and stopped short. "Is Raizel sicker?"

"No, little one. I'm crying because. . .because. . .I don't know why." Mama wiped her eyes on her apron and stood up. "We're together again here in America and I have nothing to cry about. . .oh!"

She froze with her hand halfway to her mouth.

I knew what was in her mind. We were together, except for Lemmel. And who knew where he was and if we would ever see him again?

"So where is this gold mine?" I asked Muscles.

"Uptown." We were sitting in Muscle's favorite greasy spoon shoveling in beef stew. As usual I paid for Nickel's dinner. I couldn't stand him watching me eat.

"And how do you know about it?"

Muscles speared a chunk of fatty meat and chewed it slowly. He loved the drama of knowing more than we did. "Connections."

"Have you seen the gold?" Nickels asked.

"Of course I haven't seen it." Muscles made a face at Nickels. "The old lady lives in a fancy apartment uptown. This girl I know used to be her maid. She said the old lady keeps gold spoons and jewelry just for the taking."

"She took some?" I asked.

"You bet she did! She took a gold necklace. The old lady didn't notice until two weeks later. She called the police but they couldn't prove that Nora had snatched it."

I mopped up the watery gravy with a piece of bread. "So how do we get in?"

"Through a back window. It's big enough for Cry. . .Nickels here to crawl through. Then he opens the door for us and—presto, we're inside."

"And the old lady lives alone?"

"Except for the maid. Look, Nora drew me a map of the apartment." He took a crumpled piece of paper from his pocket and spread it on the table.

"This Nora, why's she helping us? What's in it for her?"

"I promised her a fourth of our takings. Besides, she likes me." He patted his oily black hair.

Nickels and me exchanged looks and tried to keep a straight face. Muscles thought all the girls liked him.

"So when we gonna do it, Muscles?" Nickels asked.

"I figure early Sunday morning, around two a.m."

"Saturday night can be noisy." I was thinking of the saloons on Goerck Street.

"Not in that ritzy neighborhood. It'll be as quiet as a grave."

I didn't like the comparison, but I had to hand it to Muscles. It sounded like a good plan.

19
My Brother's Keeper

LEMMEL

We were sneaking down the alley behind the lady's apartment building. Muscles had made us each walk through this afternoon. But it looked different in the dark.

A tin can rattled as loud as a streetcar.

"Shhhh!"

"I didn't do nothin'."

"It's a cat," Nickels whispered. "I c-can see his g-green eyes."

He sounded scared. I wasn't feeling so brave myself. It was one thing to pick a pocket on a crowded street and another to break into a stranger's house in the middle of the night. I wondered if kids went to the same jail as grownups.

"Where's the window?" We should have waited for a night with more moonlight.

"Up here." Muscles and I made stirrups with our hands and Nickels stepped up, just like we practiced.

"I can't get the window open." Nickels tugged so hard he almost fell off.

"Sit on my shoulders and try again." Muscles hoisted him up.

I kept my eyes on the entrance to the alley. I was the lookout. If I saw someone, I whistled two short whistles and ran. Fast.

"Got it!"

"Whew!" Muscles let out his breath. There was a scraping noise as

Nickels crawled through the tiny window. Then a thump as he hit the floor. He tapped on the wall twice.

We waited by the back door. I was sweating in the freezing dark. What if they caught us? What would happen to us?

"Scared, Louie?"

"Nah—you?"

"I done this before, remember?" Muscles always bragged about the jobs he did with the Dodge. I'm not sure I believed him. The Dodge wouldn't waste time robbing some old lady. He would get other guys to do his dirty work. Stupid guys, like Muscles. And me.

Something snapped. The back door opened. Nickels grinned at us.

"Good work!" Muscles patted Nickels' shoulder. We huddled inside. I lighted a candle and passed it to Muscles. Everything was going according to plan.

"Follow me."

We headed up the back stairs past the kitchen. I could smell stale liver and onions. Snores gurgled from the servant's room. Muscles pointed to the stairs going to the second floor. He touched Nickels' shoulder. Nickels sat down on the bottom stair. Now he was the lookout.

I lit another candle and followed Muscles up the stairs. My mind turned off. I thought about putting one foot in front of the other. Quietly.

A stair squeaked. We froze. I could hear my heart beating: boom, boom, boom. Someone was gonna wake up. We had to get outta here.

Muscles started up again. When we reached the second floor, he touched my shoulder. I pressed my back against the wall. I followed the outline of Muscle's thick body as he crept down the hall to the old lady's bedroom. If Nora was right, she would be sound asleep after drinking her nightly glass of port.

Muscles blew out his candle and disappeared into the blackness of the upstairs hall. The silence smelled like dust and lilac perfume. I pictured

Muscles entering the old lady's bedroom and opening the closet door. In my mind I saw him reach behind the fur coats for the jewelry box. His fingers touched metal. He shook the broken lock and opened the lid. In the dark he grabbed a handful of necklaces and stuffed them into his pocket. And another handful. His fingers searched for the diamond ring with a diamond as big as a pigeon egg that Nora had told him about. The ring went into a pouch that he wore around his waist along with the gold coins at the bottom of the box. Then he closed the lid and carefully, quietly pushed the box into the depths of the closet. If we were lucky, she wouldn't notice anything was missing for days. We'd be long gone, spending her money like millionaires, living in a warm hotel, eating roast beef and potatoes every night, and. . .

"Help! Stop, thief!"

RAIZEL

I was finishing my homework after everyone else was in bed when Reuben walked in. I jumped up to warm his dinner.

"Ready for some big news? Sally is getting married!"

"What?" I clapped my hands over my mouth and glanced at the bedroom door. "Tell me all about it," I whispered.

"She asked her parents to find her a husband."

"Who?" I held my breath.

"He's shift manager at a coat factory. And fifteen years older than Sally."

"Oh, dear!" He was almost old enough to be Sally's father.

"She said he earns a steady salary and is saving money to buy a house and move to Brownsville. He comes from the same town that Sally does. Her parents knew him in the Old Country."

"Have you met him?"

"No. I guess I'll meet him at the wedding in two weeks. Sally wants you to come, too."

"Fifteen years older. Doesn't that bother her?"

Reuben shrugged. "She said he brings her gifts when he comes to visit. And he won't let her go dancing or to the theatre."

"But she loves the theatre!"

Reuben sighed. "Rose, Sally's changed. I guess she thought that nothing bad could happen in America. Now she knows better."

"Is she pregnant?"

"I don't know. All she talks about is the wedding and moving to Brownsville. She even looks different. She wears her hair pinned up like a school teacher."

"I know what you mean. She came by last week. She cut off the cloth flowers from her dress and gave them to Hannah to play with." I got up and cleared the table. "Are you staying up to read?"

Reuben rubbed his forehead. "No, I'll get up early. I have an important chemistry exam next week."

"I feel bad about Sally," I said.

He raised an eyebrow. "Why? She's going to marry a nice solid fellow. That's better than running around dance halls and flirting with strange men. It's certainly safer."

How could I explain my feelings? As usual, Reuben saw only the rational side. Sally *was* better off getting married and staying out of trouble. But there was more to it than that. The Sally I had met at the theatre had blazed with ambition. The flame had almost burned her, but without that spark. . .well, without her ambition, Sally's light was gone.

LEMMEL

I tore down the stairs so fast that I tripped over Nickels on the bottom step.

"Wha' happened?" Nickels rubbed his eyes. Asleep! He was *asleep*? "Help! Thief!"

Muscles came thumping down the stairs as the servant's door opened. A huge woman in a white nightgown stared at us, her mouth open in a scream.

"Stop them, Bridget! They stole my jewels!" came the shrill voice.

A tiny woman at the top of the stairs was screaming and waving her arms at us. Strands of hair fluttered around her head like a spider web.

Muscles pushed past us as Bridget grabbed at me. I kicked her ankle and she let go. We ran past the kitchen and down the back hall.

"Open the door!" I yelled

"The lock is stuck!" Muscles pushed against the door with his shoulder. I joined him.

"Owwww!" Nickels crashed into me. "She hit me!"

The door burst open and we tumbled into the alley. I grabbed Nickels' arm and pulled him to his feet as Bridget rushed at us waving a cast iron frying pan in one hand and a butcher's knife in the other. My hand felt wet but I kept running.

"Bridget, catch them! Help, police!"

"Ay, it's cold. I ain't got my shoes on, ma'am."

I almost burst out laughing. She must have stepped in an icy puddle. We ran down the alley to the street and past the house. The front door opened and the old lady started screaming for the police. Lights went on in the window of the house next door. In a minute we'd hear a police siren. I ran down the block cursing our bad luck. Why did she have to wake up? Why did I listen to Muscles, anyway?

"Louie, in here!" Muscles grabbed me and pulled me into a hallway.

"Are you crazy? We got to get away! Where's Nickels?"

"Stop blabbing for a moment. Look at this!" Muscles opened his fist on a huge diamond ring. The gaslight shot sparkles on the wall.

"Wow! Nora wasn't kidding. What else you get?"

"Gold coins and tons of jewelry. We're rich, Louie, we're rich!"

A siren wailed in the distance. I froze. "We got to get out of here. Where's that slowpoke Nickels? I'll kill him!"

I stuck my head out of the doorway. Nickels was two houses behind us, leaning against a street lamp and clutching at his arm.

"That crazy kid! I told you he was no good!" Muscles dashed out and dragged Nickels into the hallway. "You wanna get caught or something?"

"I. . .hurt."

"What the hell?" Muscles looked down at his hands where he had grabbed Nickels' sleeve. "What's all this. . .blood?"

"She cut me. All my blood is running out. Help me!" Nickels swayed and slid to the floor.

"That Bridget must've stuck him with a knife! Did you see what an elephant she was?" Muscles laughed.

"We gotta get Nickels to the hospital!" I grabbed Muscle's arm.

"Not me! I'm getting out of here before the cops arrive." The siren was getting louder.

"Louie, don't. . .leave me." Nickels' voice was barely a whisper.

"It's okay, Louie. The cops will find him and take him to the hospital. Let's move it." Muscles started for the street.

I looked back at Nickels. He was lying on the ground crying softly. Muscles was right. The cops would find him. They'd take him to the hospital and sew him up just like new.

I stooped down. "You gonna' be just fine. Hang on and someone will take you to the hospital, okay, Nicky?"

Nickels whimpered softly, like a wounded puppy.

"I got to go before the cops get here. You understand, don't you?"

"Come onnnn, Louie!" Muscles punched my shoulder.

I got up to leave.

"Don't leave me, Mickey," Nickels pleaded.

What if the cops didn't find him? What if he lay here bleeding to death until morning? He was my friend. He had no one else in the world but me. Nickels was someone's little brother once, like my brother Shloyme. Something from Genesis came back to me: *Am I my brother's keeper?*

I turned to Muscles. "I'm staying."

Muscles shook his head. "I thought you was tough, Louie. I thought I could count on you. You're just a snot-nose like this crybaby here. Well, I've had it with the two of you. Don't come running to me for help!" He spat at my feet and ran into the street. I knelt next to Nickels.

"I'm here, Nicky." I stroked his head. "I ain't leavin' you." The sirens wailed to a stop. I saw light outside the dark doorway. "I'll be back with help."

I took a shaky breath and walked down the sidewalk towards the cops.

20
The Newspaper

RAIZEL

"*Nu*, Raizel, for customers you are too busy?"

I put down the newspaper and looked at Mrs. Marmelstein. "I'm sorry. I didn't see you."

"So now I am invisible?" She shook a pudgy finger at me. "Give me a pound of flour and three eggs." I weighed out the flour and wrapped the eggs. She handed me three cents.

"That's five cents," I said firmly.

"Put it on my bill."

I swallow hard. "Mr. Abrahamson said no more credit."

Mrs. Marmelstein looked like she wanted to throw the eggs in my face. "You tell him I take my business elsewhere!"

"Five cents," I repeated.

"Heartless girl," she muttered as she left.

I went back to my newspaper. Mr. Abrahamson didn't read the *Forward* like Papa, but the more conservative *Yidisher Tageblatt*. We used the old copies for wrapping. A headline had caught my eye:

Thief Saves Friend: I Am My Brother's Keeper

The police arrived at the scene of a robbery last night on Central Park West to discover the thieves waiting for them. The oldest, a boy of fifteen who gave his name as "Tough Louie," had stayed behind to help his friend, a boy of six who was bleeding from a bad cut. When asked by the surprised policemen why he hadn't run away, the older boy repeated: 'I am my brother's keeper' in Hebrew. He was arrested and the wounded boy taken to the hospital. The stolen goods were not recovered and the police suspect that a third thief was involved in the robbery.

I read the article again. And again. My heart was pounding like I had run up five flights of stairs. Could it be? The boy was too old, but Lemmel was big for his age. And his English name was Louis so "Tough Louie" made sense. Plus he knew Hebrew.

I had to tell Papa!

No, Papa would tell Mama and it would be bad for her health. The baby was due soon and she was suffering from swollen legs and shortness of breath. Climbing up and down the stairs left her weak and shaking.

I would ask Reuben.

The important thing was to find out if it was Lemmel.

LEMMEL

I was freezing. I thought it would be warm in jail. "Hey, give me back my blanket!"

I glared at the boy standing over me. He was too big to fight.

"Shut up, kid!" It was the same thing every night. There was no room on the bunks so I slept on the floor. Then some big guy took away my blanket. The first night I tried to stop him. My stomach still ached from his punch.

Even the street was better than this place. At least I could make a fire and get warm. And I had Nickels to talk to. They won't tell me how he is. They said they'll take me to him if I told them where to find

Muscles, only they don't know his name. They called him the "accomplice." I wouldn't squeal on him, even if he did leave us. He was only looking out for himself. He did the smart thing.

I should of run with Muscles. I could be living it up someplace warm, eating roast beef and chocolate cake.

What if Nickels had died and they weren't telling me?

I hated this place.

Tough Louie don't cry.

Not here. Not now.

RAIZEL

"What did you find out?" I asked Reuben the day after I showed him the article.

"Nothing yet. I talked to a few people. One of my teachers has a Jewish friend on the police force."

"There are Jewish policeman?" All the policemen in our neighborhood were Irish.

"A few. In the meantime, shouldn't we tell your papa?"

"No, he'll tell Mama and it will make her sick if it isn't Lemmel." And sick if it was.

"Raizel, she'll have to know eventually," he said softly. "He's in jail."

"But he's just a kid." I couldn't stop the tears.

"He broke into someone's house."

"So we'll get him a lawyer." I raised my face hopefully.

"Lawyers cost money. And good lawyers cost lots of money." Reuben looked around our kitchen, at the scratched table, the rusty stove and splintered cabinets. What could you expect from Goerck Street?

"We'll find a way." I said. "We can't let Lemmel go to jail."

"Okay, kid, let's go through it again." The skinny dark-haired police-man stunk of garlic. At first I thought he was Jewish, but he wasn't. I cursed him in Yiddish and he didn't hit me.

"I want three things from you, punk! Your real name, the name of the accomplice, and how to find him. Tell me that and I'll get you a steak and mashed potatoes. How about it?"

"Get me the steak first and I'll tell you." The food in jail stank: wa-tery soup and potatoes twice a day.

"What do you think I am, a sucker? You're the sucker, punk. Your friend is sitting pretty, spending the stolen money. You think he's wor-rying about you? Not on your life."

He was right. Muscles couldn't care less about me, or about Nickels. But I didn't blame him. That's what you did to survive on the streets. I didn't, and look where it got me.

"What happened to Nickels?" I asked that every day. Maybe one day they'd tell me.

"He your brother?"

I nodded.

"He's real sick. He keeps calling for you. That's how we know your real name is Mickey." The cop put his hand on my shoulder. "Your brother is dying. And his only wish is for you to be there with him."

"So take me to him." I wouldn't cry.

"Of course we will." His voice was soft. "We're not monsters. If you want to see your brother, tell us where to find the accomplice, that's all we ask. Otherwise your brother's death will be on your conscience."

I stared at the wall. If Nicky really were dying, I couldn't help him. And what did the cop mean about my "conshense?" What was a con-shense, anyway?

"You stupid kid. You think you're tough? I'll show you what tough is!" He slapped my cheek. If my hands weren't tied behind my back, I'd show him how tough I was. Another slap! And another. I tasted blood in my mouth. I spat at him.

"Okay, Tony, that's enough." The door opened and the red-faced cop came in.

"This kid makes my blood boil. Give me ten minutes more and I'll make him talk!" Tony was shaking with anger.

Nobody could make me talk.

The Dodge would be proud of me.

RAIZEL

"Explain to me again," Papa said. "Where are we going?"

"To the police lockup at the Tombs, Papa. They have a prisoner who might be Lemmel."

Several days had passed before Reuben's friend got us permission to see the boy they were holding. Last night I caught Papa in the hall and briefly told him about the newspaper. In the morning we had gone to the Irishman to tell him that Papa would miss work this morning.

"That I understood. I don't understand why Lemmel is in jail."

I handed Papa the newspaper clipping. He read it twice. When he looked up, his face was the color of the paper. "A son of mine a thief? For this I came to America?"

"Papa, we don't know for sure it's Lemmel. Let's hope the police made a mistake and he didn't do anything."

The police lockup looked like a white castle decorated with arches and round towers. As we walked down the marble hall, I felt like an insect that had made a wrong turn.

We approached the main desk. "Please, sir, we're looking for Detective Sergeant Rosenberg."

The policeman turned around and yelled, "Harry, where's the kike?"

"*Sergeant* Rosenberg is out," answered a red-faced man. He said "sergeant" as if it tasted bad in his mouth. "What do you want, girlie?"

"Please, sir, we've come to identify a prisoner. He might be a member of our family." I spoke as politely as I could.

"We got lots of prisoners here, girlie. Which one do you want to see?"

"He's a boy of thirteen. He has reddish hair and a long straight nose. His name is Lem. . .Louis Altman."

"Louis. Louie." The policeman's eyes narrowed. "What's he to you?"

"He might be my brother. He ran away from home last November."

"Why'd he run away? Your pop beat him?"

I had to smile. "My papa doesn't hit. He ran away because he didn't want to have a bar mitzvah celebration. You see in the Jewish religion, when a boy reaches the age of thirteen. . ."

"Okay, okay, I don't need a lecture. Your pop understand English?"

"Yes, I know English," Papa said with his thick Yiddish accent.

"Good. So sit down on the bench over there. It may take a while."

"Thank you, sir," I said. "We will wait as long as it takes."

Papa squeezed my fingers. His hand was as icy as mine.

LEMMEL

"This is it, punk. I got no more patience with you." Slap. "Think that hurt? Well, you ain't seen nothing yet."

The cords around my hands were so tight I couldn't feel them anymore. When they untied the rope later in the cell, my hands would hurt like hell.

"You like your new cell?"

Yesterday they moved me into a cell too tiny to lie down in. I spent the night leaning against the wall with my knees up.

"We call it the closet. You don't talk to us, you don't talk to anyone. Get it, punk?" Slap!

"Hey, Tony. Come out here." The red-faced cop stuck his head in the door.

They were gone a few minutes.

"Guess who's here, punk? Your pop and your sister."

I must have looked surprised.

"Got you!" Red-face looked pleased. "I didn't think a street rat like you had a family. But they're here and they want to see their little lost Louie. Your sister is crying and your pop is shaking himself to pieces."

Papa and Raizel were here? How? "I don't got no family. Just Nicky. We're orphans."

"Sure, that Irish guttersnipe is your brother like I'm your uncle." The two cops laughed.

"You want to see them, you give us the name of your accomplice and where to find him. We already know your name: Louis Altman."

RAIZEL

A policeman wearing a big black mustache and blue overcoat walked in hurriedly. He asked the man at the main desk a question. The policeman yawned and pointed in our direction.

"Are you looking for me? I'm Sergeant Rosenberg."

I stood up. "Please, we want to see the boy you're holding. He may be my brother, Louis Altman."

"I'm familiar with the case. He's a tough criminal. For your sake, I hope he's not your brother."

My heart skipped a beat. Lemmel, a tough criminal?

"Lemmel is a good boy. Please, can we see him?" Papa asked.

"Of course." He switched to Yiddish. "But be prepared. The street is a hard place. It changes good boys into something else, even our boys. You know what they say: 'When you lie down to sleep with dogs, you get up with fleas.' Children forget what they learned at home. They start small, stealing coins from the pockets of sleeping drunks. Then they work their way up to pickpocketing. From there it's a short step to robbery. And worse."

"Lemmel would never do that," I protested.

"What's your name, dear?"

"Raizel. Rose."

"Rose, there are bad people out there. They prey on runaway boys and teach them how to rob and steal. Your brother may not have started out bad, but to survive on the streets, well. . .let's just hope that Tough Louie isn't your brother."

We followed Sergeant Rosenberg down a drafty corridor. I wanted the boy to be Lemmel, but if Sergeant Rosenberg were right, then he wouldn't be the Lemmel we knew. Maybe it was better to have a brother who was missing than a brother who was a hardened criminal. At least we had hope.

LEMMEL

"So you won't see them?"

"Nope." They can't help me.

"Have it your way." Red-face untied my hands. "But first clean up."

They took me to a lavatory. The strange boy staring at me from the mirror had long overgrown hair, a bruised face and someone else's eyes. I hadn't seen myself in a mirror since I left home. I scrubbed my face and slicked back my hair.

Cursing Columbus

"Tough Louie thinks he's a pretty boy!" The cops laughed. I followed them into another room with a curtain running down the middle.

"Stand up straight!" Tony kept his hand on my shoulders. He faced me towards the curtain. My legs were shaking. They had forgotten to give me breakfast in the closet this morning. At least I hoped they had just forgotten.

"Stand up, you piece of filth or I'll kick your teeth in."

I stared at the faded black curtain and waited for something to happen.

RAIZEL

"Oh no!" I buried my face in Papa's shoulder. Papa shuddered.

"That him?" Sergeant Rosenberg asked.

Papa looked away from the peephole in the curtain. "Yes, that's my son Lemmel." Suddenly his legs buckled. Sergeant Rosenberg helped him to a chair.

"Can we talk to him?" I couldn't believe how thin he was. "Why does he have all those bruises on his face?"

"The street. I told you it's a rough place. Okay, Tony, take him away!" Sergeant Rosenberg left the room.

He came back a few minutes later with two glasses of tea. "Here, drink this. You'll feel better."

"Thank you." Papa took the glass gratefully.

Sergeant Rosenberg sat down. "Mr. Altman, listen to me and listen well. If it were me, I would walk out of this room, go home, and sit *shiva*."

Papa gasped. "How can you say that? He's my son and he's not dead."

"He was your son. Now he's a thief named Tough Louie. He doesn't want to see you. He won't cooperate with us to find his accomplice. He's one bad boy."

"What will happen to him?" I asked.

"Since he's only thirteen, and not fifteen like we thought, the judge will probably send him to a delinquent home. They call them reform schools. They're supposed to help boys like Louie, but in my experience they just make matters worse. Louie's only been on the streets for a few months. In reform school he'll meet kids who would slit your throat for a nickel. He'll go from bad to worse."

Papa was quiet for a few moments. "What can we do?"

"Empty your savings, get a lawyer, see a loan shark, go into debt, and try to keep him out of jail. And will he be grateful? He'll probably spit in your face."

Papa put down his glass, stood up and held out his hand. "Thank you, Sergeant Rosenberg. I appreciate your help. Come, Raizel."

I followed Papa out the door. "Papa, where are we going?"

"What kind of question is that? You heard the policeman. We are going to get Lemmel a lawyer, the best that money can buy!"

21
An Isle of Tears

RAIZEL

After leaving the police station, we returned to the Lower East Side. I was too upset to go to school, so I accompanied Papa to his *landsleit*, asking for the names of lawyers. We waited until Hannah and Shloyme were in bed to tell Mama.

"A son of mine a thief? *Oy vey iz mir!!* Binyumin, how did we raise such an abomination?" Tears poured down Mama's face.

"It is my fault," Papa said. "I was away from home with my peddling and then here in America. It was not good for Lemmel. He was always a wild boy who needed a firm hand." Papa patted Mama's shoulder.

"G-d help us, Binyumin. What are we going to do?" Mama grimaced and clutched her stomach.

"Mama, come lie down," I said.

"Drink this." Papa put a steaming glass of tea in front of her.

"How can I sleep? How can I eat? My poor baby! Why did we come to this America? A curse on Columbus!"

The door to the apartment opened and Reuben walked in. He stopped when he saw our faces.

"Excuse me, I can come back later."

"*Oy*, the shame, the shame," Mama wailed.

"No, it is alright, Reuben." Papa gestured to a chair. "You are like a member of the family. Raizel told me how you helped find Lemmel."

"So it was Lemmel?" Reuben asked me in a low voice.

"Yes. We spent all afternoon looking for a lawyer."

"A lawyer?" Mama clutched her stomach again. "We barely have money to pay the rent. Where will we find money for a lawyer?"

"The money we will find," Papa said. "For bread you can always find a knife. And now you must lie down. You are worrying me more than Lemmel." He put his arm around Mama's waist and helped her into bed.

"Leave the door open, I shouldn't miss a word," Mama called through her sobs.

"Is Mama sick?" Shloyme shivered in his nightshirt.

"No, she's just tired," I answered. "Go back to bed."

"I can't sleep with everyone talking about Lemmel. What happened?"

I looked at Papa. "The police say Lemmel stole money. They want to put him in jail."

Shloyme wrinkled his forehead. "I didn't tell them, Papa. Honest I didn't."

"I am not talking about the rent money. I am talking about taking money from strangers," Papa said.

"He broke the eighth commandment?"

"Yes, he did," Papa said seriously, although the corners of his mouth twitched at Shloyme's question.

"Can I visit him in jail?" Shloyme asked. "How long will he have to stay there?"

"We don't know. Now go back to sleep and let the grownups talk."

I felt a flush of warmth that Papa had included me among the grownups. I fixed Reuben his supper of potato soup, rye bread and hard-boiled eggs and made us all fresh tea.

"Did you find a lawyer?" Reuben asked between bites.

"We met with a Mr. Saperstein." Papa glanced at me. "What did you think of him, Raizel?"

"I didn't like him. He kept talking about the different ways we could pay him instead of about Lemmel."

Papa nodded. "Moishe, my friend, said he isn't expensive."

"The question is whether he is a good lawyer or not," Reuben said.

"I don't trust him," said Papa. "And if I don't, why should the judge? No, we need someone better."

"I know a good lawyer," said Reuben. "He helped my father when his partner ran out on him. He's from uptown."

"He is Jewish?" Papa asked.

"Yes, a German Jew. I believe he was born in the U.S."

"That's good, Papa. A lawyer who speaks perfect English will make a better impression."

"If he is from uptown, it means. . ." Papa looked worried.

"That he's expensive. But if you explain, maybe he'll help you as a *mitzvah*."

Papa's face turned red.

"I do not take charity! I will find a way to pay him even if I have to go into debt for the next fifty years!"

"But, Binyumin, how will we raise the baby?" Mama called from the bedroom.

"Everything will be all right, Haveleh. I have a good job now. We will manage."

I cradled my glass of tea in my hands. Papa couldn't go into debt. There must be another way.

And then I remembered.

LEMMEL

"You have a good papa," the cop named Sergeant Rosenberg said. "He's getting you a lawyer."

I stared straight ahead. This cop didn't slap me around like the others, but I didn't trust him.

"But even a good lawyer won't be able to help you. Mrs. Smith identified you. You're going to jail."

I looked at my hands. The skin was cracked and raw. After Papa came, they put me in a cell with other boys. But it was still cold.

"You wanna go to jail, tough guy?" He grabbed my chin. "Answer me!"

I shook my head. "No, I wanna see my brudder in the hospital."

"He's not in the hospital anymore."

"Is he. . .dead?"

"Nah. He recovered just fine. I don't know where they sent him. Probably an orphanage upstate."

I let out my breath. Nickels was all right. "Thank you."

"Why do you care about this kid, anyway?" the cop asked. "He's not family."

"He's my friend."

"And the guy who ran out on you was your friend? He left you behind to take the rap. You call that a friend?"

I looked at my hands again. Muscles wasn't my friend. But I wasn't going to squeal on him, either.

The cop sighed. He left and came back with two cups of coffee.

"Okay, Louie. So you want to protect your friend. That's honorable."

I took a sip of the hot sweet liquid.

"But think about your own family."

"I don't need them."

"But they need you. Your pop said he was going to get you the best lawyer that money can buy. You know what that means? Think about it for a minute."

I thought. Papa didn't have enough money for a lawyer. When I left home he didn't even have a job. Where was he going to get the money?

"Tell him I don't need no lawyer."

"He won't listen to me. I told him to sit *shiva* for you, but he wouldn't listen."

"So what can I do?"

"You give us the name of the accomplice. We arrange for the judge to send you to reform school instead of jail. Then you won't need an expensive lawyer."

"Why I should trust a cop's word?"

"Because you got no choice, kid. Mrs. Smith is one important lady in this city. Her late husband was a judge. He had a lot of judge friends. They're gonna send you to prison until you're an old man."

Just my luck Muscles picked a judge's widow.

"So what do you say? You'll get off easy, just a year or two in reform school. Hey, reform school is a lot better than the streets, believe me. And your pop won't go into debt and spend the rest of his life paying off your lawyer."

I didn't want Papa to go into debt because of me. If he went into debt, Raizel would have to leave school. And maybe Shloyme, too. All because of me. I felt awful.

If only we hadn't robbed the old lady. If only I hadn't run away from home.

If only . . .

RAIZEL

I decided not to tell Papa my idea. Not unless I really had to. Better to wait until we finished our meeting with this fancy schmancy lawyer.

"I apologize," said the gray-haired man with the clipped mustache as he shook hands with Papa. "I don't speak Yiddish."

"I speak English," Papa said. "And Raizel, Rose, my daughter, speak very good English. She win Columbus contest. The whole city schools."

Mr. Gray looked puzzled.

"It was a city-wide essay contest. I won honorable mention," I explained.

"That's very nice, dear. Do you like school?"

"I want to be a teacher someday." I glanced at Papa. "That is, if I can finish high school and go to college."

"My wife was a teacher before we married. It's a fine profession for a girl."

"We come about son," Papa said. Clearly he was impatient with American small talk.

"Yes, Reuben spoke to me. He's a good lad."

"Lemmel is thirteen. He ran away from home last fall. And now they say he robbed a rich woman," I said.

"Why did he run away from home?"

I explained about the bar mitzvah and Lemmel's problems in school. Then I handed Mr. Gray the newspaper clipping.

"I don't read Yiddish, Rose." He smiled a tight smile.

"It says here that Lemmel stayed behind with his wounded friend. He wouldn't let him bleed to death. He waited until the police arrived and went to call them."

"Hmmm." Mr. Gray leaned forward. "If this story is true, we might appeal to the judge's sense of mercy. If the boy tried to save his friend that puts a positive light on the case."

"So you will help us?" Papa asked.

"I would very much like to help a fellow Jew, Mr. Altman. I will charge you only half my usual fee. That will be two hundred fifty dollars."

"Two hundred and fifty dollars?" Papa went pale.

"Yes, fees are higher uptown, you know."

"Will we have to pay that even if you lose the case and. . .Lemmel goes to jail?" I asked.

Mr. Gray smiled. "I'm afraid so, little lady. I need to spend time researching the case, preparing my defense, and defending him in court. And if, heaven forbid, we should fail, I will need to prepare an appeal. From my experience, these things can cost five hundred dollars, or more."

Now I understood why Mr. Gray's office had fine oriental rugs and shiny furniture. Papa could never afford two hundred and fifty dollars unless . . .

"It is too dear for me," Papa said. "Perhaps you will recommend a lawyer from the East Side?"

"There are plenty of lawyers down there, although no one I can recommend personally. Most of them don't have the experience with the judicial system that I have, but I'm sure you can find someone less expensive."

"Thank you very much for your time, Mr. Gray," I said. I couldn't keep the disappointment out of my voice.

"I'm sorry I couldn't be of more help, dear. I wish you luck."

"So we return to Mr. Saperstein," Papa said on the way home.

"There must be someone better, Papa."

Papa agreed to ask more people, but we both felt that Mr. Gray was the ideal choice. The court would treat him with respect. He inspired trust and seemed genuinely interested in Lemmel's plight. As we talked I had to bite my tongue to keep from telling Papa my idea.

Because we did have the money.

My money.

The money Mrs. Goldenberg had left me would pay for the lawyer. But after lawyer fees, the money would be gone, and so would my dream of becoming a teacher.

"You can still become a teacher," Reuben said with assurance as we talked that evening. "I know a girl who goes to Hunter College. She works every weekend in a department store to pay her rent. And she works during the summer in a settlement house camp."

"If I can make it to college, then I can work and study at the same time," I agreed. "My problem is finishing high school. I have three more years to go. After the baby is born, I have to get a job."

"You could go to night school."

"But after work I have to help Mama at home. It will take me years and years to finish high school at night." I couldn't keep the tears out of my voice.

"Raizel, don't give up your dream. Only a few years ago you didn't know how to read and write. Now you practically won the city-wide contest. I've seen what working at a sewing machine day in and day out does to girls. It ruins their health and turns them old before their time!"

"I know. My friends who quit school, they planned to go to night school, but after a long day's work, the last thing they wanted was to sit on a hard wooden bench and listen to a teacher droning." I felt like I had no strength left to fight.

"Then don't do it!" Reuben grabbed my hands. "Keep your money. Lemmel made his choices. He chose to run away and to rob that woman. Don't let him ruin your life."

"You mean. . .let Lemmel go to jail?" I felt like Reuben had punched me in the stomach.

"I mean make something of yourself. Twice you crossed the ocean to America. You have the chance of becoming a teacher. Don't throw away your chance!"

"But Lemmel is my brother. Wouldn't you do the same if Susan were in trouble?"

Reuben didn't hesitate. "I wouldn't give up my dream of becoming a doctor."

I stared at him. "Not even for your sister?"

"Raizel, my father is a bankrupt furrier who drinks too much and my mother pretends she's still living in St. Petersburg. I learned a long time ago that I have to look out for myself. When I become a doctor and have enough money, I'll help support my family."

"If you have a family left by then."

Reuben bit his lip. "That's not fair. I love my family. But I am not going to Denver if I can help it. I won't let them stand in the way of my future."

"Then I guess we have different ideas of love," I said quietly. "I couldn't live with myself if my brother went to jail and I could have done something to prevent it."

Reuben flushed. He picked up a stack of books.

"Where are you going?"

"The library is open late," he said. "I have an exam that is more important than sleep." He turned on his heel and strode out the door.

Reuben's anger left a chill in the apartment. Was he right and I should think only of myself and my future? Reuben was smart and I respected his opinions—but I couldn't accept them when it came to putting myself before my family.

I remembered how they had called Ellis Island the Isle of Tears. Well, Manhattan was an Isle of Tears, too—for me, and for my family, and for thousands of other immigrants.

I had promised myself I wouldn't cry anymore, but I couldn't help it. I put my head on the table and cried for Reuben, who would soon be leaving. I cried for Lemmel, who had ruined his life.

And I cried for myself, and my pitiful shattered dreams.

22
The Sacrifice

RAIZEL

"You are sure you want to give up the money you were saving for school?" Papa asked.

"I want you to use the money to hire Mr. Gray."

"This is wonderful!" Mama gave me a hug. "Now we won't have to go into debt."

"It should pay for Mr. Gray's services. But. . ."

I could feel Papa's eyes on me. "I know, Papa. There won't be anything left. I will have to leave school."

"School, shmool! You will find a nice job in a department store and get married." Mama clasped her hands on her belly. "Raizel, you have saved us!"

I tried to smile at Mama. My face felt like a brittle autumn leaf.

Papa rested his hands on my shoulders. "Haveleh, school is very important to Raizel. She is making a big sacrifice for her family."

"But the highest wisdom is kindness." Mama stroked my hair. "Lemmel should only be worthy of it."

LEMMEL

"Tell me why you robbed an old lady." The man opposite me had gray hair and an expensive suit the color of his name. He carefully lit a pipe.

"She's rich. She don't need the money."

"And you do?"

"I got no place to sleep at night. Me and Nickels sleep on the streets. It's cold."

"But you have a home with your parents. They love you very much."

"I don't wanna live at home."

"Why?" Mr. Gray leaned forward like I was about to say something important.

"That's my business."

"No, young man. That is *our* business. The judge will want to know why you ran away from home."

"It ain't his business either."

Mr. Gray sucked on his pipe. The tobacco smelled rich. Someday when I was older, I was going to smoke a pipe. It had more class than cigarettes.

"I don't think you understand the seriousness of the situation you are in, Louis. You stole money from a judge's widow. And you won't give the police the information they need to return the stolen goods."

"I ain't got them."

"But your accomplice does."

"He probably sold them and spent the money already."

"But if they catch him and put him in jail, Mrs. Smith will be satisfied. Justice will be satisfied. The judge will be much easier on you if you help the police."

"What do I care about your justice?"

Mr. Gray took another puff of his pipe. I could see his tie pin was real gold. Papa must be paying him a fortune. I bit my lip.

"Will it help if I tell you why I ran away?"

"Yes. Since you refuse to cooperate with the police, we have to build a case based on your character. Do you know what character is?"

I shook my head. He talked better than anybody I had met, except Miss O'Brien.

"Character is the kind of person you are, Louis."

"So? My character is a thief."

"Ah hah, but an honorable thief! You refused to squeal on your accomplice. And most important, you stayed behind with your young friend to save him. He would have bled to death if you had run away. That will be very important in the judge's eyes."

"So they gonna give me a reward?"

Mr. Gray threw back his head and laughed. His fat belly rumpled under his fancy woolen vest. His gold pocket watch would make easy pickings.

"No reward. But they won't send you to jail and I will do my best to get you into Hawthorne, the new Jewish school for delinquent boys. I am one of the benefactors."

"I don't wanna' go to school. I hate school."

Mr. Gray looked worried. "School is very important, Louis. Your sister Rose understands that."

"For Raizel school is easy."

"And for you school is hard?"

"You bet your life!"

"But you only went a few months before you were suspended. If you had stayed longer, you might have learned to like it."

"I'll never like school!"

"Your papa said you went to *cheder* in the Old Country."

"I hated school there, too."

"Louis, the judge won't like what you are saying about school. It will make a very bad impression."

"Time's up!" The red-faced cop opened the door.

Mr. Gray ignored him. I liked that.

"I want you to think hard about all the things we can tell the judge to impress him with your good character. Think about your attitude toward school and try to change it. I'll see you again next week."

"How long I gotta stay here?"

He turned around with a funny look on his face. I wondered if he had kids my age. Nah, he was too old.

"I'll try to get an early trial date so you don't have to stay here too long. But it may take several months."

Months! I had to stay in this lousy joint for months?

"Move, punk!" Red-face shoved me towards my cell.

At least they stopped slapping me around since I got a lawyer.

RAIZEL

"Can we watch the monkey?" Hannah asked as we walked out of the El station past the park.

A flea-bitten monkey was tipping his hat to an audience of children while the organ grinder played vigorously. Reuben had come home early this Saturday and invited me to the Metropolitan Museum of Art. Hannah had begged to come and Mama had looked at me so pleadingly that I had no choice but to take her. Luckily, Shloyme was at his piano lesson at the Alliance.

"We're going to the museum, remember?"

"But I want to feed the zoo animals. Puh-leeze, Raizel."

I grabbed Hannah's hand and tugged her towards the enormous museum building sitting like a Greek temple atop a mountain of stairs. "You promised to behave like a big girl. Big girls go to the museum!"

"Raizel's mean!" Hannah wailed.

I felt mean. But Reuben had invited me to the museum and that's where I wanted to go.

"We could go to the zoo for just a little while," Reuben said.

"No!" I practically barked at him.

He jumped back in surprise.

"You don't understand," I said. "I always have to take care of Hannah and Shloyme. I never have time to do things that I want to do."

"Well, you don't have to bite my head off."

He turned to Hannah. "Do you know what I'll buy you if you stop crying and act like a big girl?"

"Peanuts?" Hannah asked hopefully.

"A jumbo ice cream cone. Would you like that?"

"I want one right now!"

"Later," Reuben said. "After the museum."

Hannah was cheerful enough as we strolled through the rooms filled with Greek statues and medieval armor. Reuben told her tales from Greek mythology.

"Remember the stories you used to tell on the boat?" Reuben asked. We were resting on a stone bench. "Why don't you tell them anymore?"

I thought a minute. "When I started school, the stories began to fade and seem far away, like. . ."

"Like the Old Country?"

"Yes. They just didn't have the same meaning in America." I sighed. "Why do you ask?"

"I was remembering how sweet and innocent you were on the boat."

"And now I'm not sweet?"

Reuben tilted his chin at Hannah whose eyes were still red from crying. "Sweet isn't a word I would apply right now. You're different. I guess I am, too."

We walked into the hall of European paintings. Reuben hoisted Hannah onto his shoulders so she could see better.

"In what way?" I asked.

"I have my life all planned out. I'm always rushing to school, to work, to the library. Sometimes I feel like I'm running to catch an express train and don't care who I knock over in the process. If I miss the train, I'll be stuck in the station forever."

We stopped in front of a painting of a mother with two daughters.

"Isn't that beautiful!" I couldn't take my eyes off the picture. "I could reach out and stroke their rosy skin."

"Doggie!" Hannah pointed at the black and white dog resting under the feet of the little girls.

"I've been thinking about our conversation last week," Reuben said. "Suddenly I saw myself through your eyes, and I didn't like what I saw."

I touched Reuben's hand. "I know you love your family."

"I do. And as much as I want to stay in New York and go to college, if I have to go to Denver to help support my family, I will. It was wrong of me to judge you."

"I asked for your advice. If you go, I'm going to miss our talks."

"I'm going to miss you, Raizel. I wish. . ."

"I want ice cream!" Hannah kicked her heels against Reuben's chest. "I'm tired of paintings."

"You deserve ice cream," I said. "You've been a good girl."

We each took Hannah's hand. I turned for one more look at the painting. I wanted to remember that simpler world where people had time to be together and love each other. A world I had known which was now only a memory.

LEMMEL

"Well, young man, your trial is in two weeks." Mr. Gray opened his briefcase. "I had to pull strings to get the date moved up, but I was successful."

"Thank you." Anything would be better than this joint. I couldn't stand sitting around all day listening to the other boys brag. From the way they talked, you'd think they were the smartest guys in the city. Well, if they were so smart, why were they here? I wasn't like them. I knew I was stupid.

"Let's see how we can build a case for your fine character, Louis." From Mr. Gray's crooked smile, I could tell he wasn't sure how good my character really was. "We need character witnesses, people who can tell the court what a good boy you are."

"Nickels. He said I'm like his brudder."

"He has been sent to a farm up near Canada. The state won't let me bring him to the city. Do you have any friends or teachers who could speak for you?"

"My friends are all newsies," I said.

"Well, that isn't much help. And your teacher said you were a lazy student who never did the work."

There was that word again.

"I ain't lazy. I wanted to quit school to work, but Papa wouldn't let me."

"And quite right he was. School is the only way to get ahead in America, Louis."

"Sure."

"Why do you hate school so much?" Mr. Gray looked like he was really interested.

"Just because. All the guys hate school."

He puffed his pipe. "Do you know what makes me a good lawyer, Louis?"

"You learned all the laws?"

He laughed until his belly shook. "I certainly know my law, but I also know people. I know when they're not telling me the truth."

I shut my mouth.

Cursing Columbus

"Louis, your papa is paying me a lot of money to help you. If you don't help yourself, then he is throwing his money away—money he needs to help your brother and sisters with their schooling, money for the rent, money. . ."

"I can't read."

"What?" Mr. Gray looked surprised. I surprised myself. Except for Raizel, I never told nobody that before. "You mean you can't read English? But that's what you go to school for."

"I can't read," I repeated. "Not English, not Hebrew, not Yiddish. I'm too dumb." I glared at him.

He leaned back in his chair and frowned. "I find this hard to believe. I spoke with your teacher and your principal, as well as your parents. No one brought up the fact that you can't read."

"So, I'm good at hiding it." I felt like a cockroach crawling on the floor.

Mr. Gray raised his eyebrows. "That's why you didn't want to be bar mitzvahed and ran away?"

"I didn't want everyone to laugh at me—or at Papa." My cheeks were wet. I brushed them angrily.

"What happens when you try to read?" Mr. Gray sounded curious.

"The letters jump around and get mixed up. I can't tell where the letters begin and the page ends. I get all confused."

Mr. Gray took out a piece of paper and wrote something in large letters. "Can you read this?"

It had been months since I tried to read something. L. . .l. . . ou. . . Louis Altman!"

"That's correct. So you can read."

"That's not reading. I'm a good guesser. I see the first letters and guess the rest." The sound of the other kids' laughter filled my ears. "Sometimes I guess right. Most of the time I'm wrong."

"This is interesting, Louis. You're a smart boy."

Me, smart?

"Don't look surprised. If you weren't smart, you wouldn't have been able to hide your problem from your parents and teachers."

"They call me lazy. They say I don't work hard enough." My mouth tasted bitter.

"That must be difficult for you. If you don't go to school, what do you want to do?"

"Work."

"At what?"

"I want to work with my hands. Make things with wood. Or take care of animals. I took care of the horses at the inn in Jibatov sometimes. I liked that."

"Does anyone know that you can't read?"

"Raizel knows. She was helping me prepare for my bar mitzvah."

"Louis, would you be willing to tell the court that you can't read and that's why you ran away from home?"

In front of all those people? "They'll all know how dumb I am. I can't!"

"It may be the most difficult thing you'll have to do in your life. But I think you are brave enough, Louis."

What did bravery have to do with it? "I ain't a coward. I beat up guys twice my size."

"I'm talking about another kind of bravery. Because it's very important to tell the judge the truth. The judge is like me. He will know when you're not telling the truth. The only chance you have is to make him respect you."

"Why he respect me? I'm a thief."

"Don't talk like that, Louis!" I'd never seen Mr. Gray so angry before. "If you give up, we don't have a chance."

"Time's up." Red-face stood at the door. By now he knew Mr. Gray would finish when he was good and ready.

"I've learned some important things about you today, Louis. Before, I thought you were too ignorant to appreciate the importance of school."

"You don't think I'm dumb?" I couldn't believe it.

"Just the opposite. I know how smart you really are. And I want the judge to know too. So you understand how important it is for you to stand up and tell the truth?"

I looked down at the floor. "I can't." My voice sounded little.

"Think about it, Louis. Think hard. Because it may be your only chance."

23
Love and Marriage

RAIZEL

Sally's wedding hall was a large room full of tables covered with white cloth, nothing like the fancy dance hall with its velvet curtains and plump couches. The smell of roast chicken permeated the room and made my mouth water.

Reuben took my coat. Mama had decorated her old skirt with the cloth flowers Sally had given Hannah. Hannah hadn't been happy about parting with them, but I had promised her a surprise from the wedding. Now I wondered what my floppy skirt and blouse would look like in the eyes of Reuben's friends.

"Hey, there's the old bunch!" Reuben waved at a group of boys and girls his age. The girls all wore fancy new shirtwaists. Their eyes traveled up and down my second-hand clothes. A pretty girl with green eyes whispered something behind her hand. "Hi gang, this is Rose. She rescued me from the Denver winter."

"Hello, Rose!" Reuben's friends smiled at me.

The green-eyed girl's smile was the brightest. "Reuben told me all about his little sister, Rose. Why don't you ever come to the Alliance with him?"

"I work after school and Sundays," I said. *Little sister.* "And I help my mother."

"Don't we all!" said a plump girl with curly brown hair. The other girls laughed.

"Have you seen Sally?" asked Green Eyes. "Her dress is really plain."

"She used to dress so well. What a shame. She said that Jake buys all her clothes now. New clothes." The plump girl nodded knowingly.

One of the boys groaned. "Are you going to talk about clothes all night? The *chuppah* is beginning."

The crowd migrated toward a white lace canopy in the center of the room. A tall bearded man stood underneath it.

"Is that Sally's father?" I whispered to Reuben. There was a gale of laughter from the girls.

"That's Jake," said Green Eyes. "I wouldn't marry an older man. I don't know what came over Sally."

"I do." The plump girl tittered behind her hand. "You can tell us, Reuben. Is she pregnant?"

"Kitty, I really don't know."

"So maybe Rosie knows?" Green Eyes put her arm through mine like we were best friends. "Come on, sweetie, you can tell *me*."

"Pearl. . ." Reuben shook his head.

Pearl flushed and lowered her eyes. She let go of my arm. Was she sweet on Reuben? I studied her out of the corner of my eye. She had long black eyelashes and full lips.

A violin began to play as whispers rippled through the crowd.

"There she is!"

Sally walked to the *chuppah* supported by a short man wearing a black yarmulkah on his head. She wore a light blue frock that shimmered in the light. A white veil covered her hair.

"That's an expensive dress," whispered Kitty. "I saw it in an uptown store."

"Expensive but practical. She can wear it anyplace for years," Pearl said. "Do you think she looks fat?"

I stared at Sally's stomach and did a quick calculation. Three months had passed yet her stomach was flat under the silky blue fabric. Perhaps nothing had happened that night.

Reuben glared at Pearl and Kitty. "Stop gossiping."

"Yes, Daddy," Kitty answered. Pearl giggled.

The rabbi stepped up to the *chuppah* and began the wedding ceremony. He droned on in Hebrew, but I barely listened. I was watching Pearl out of the corner of my eye. First her arm touched Reuben's. Slowly her hand found his. He kept his eyes on the *chuppah*. By the time the rabbi had finished and the groom had stomped on the wine glass, she was leaning her head on his shoulder. The violinist began a lively tune and Jake and Sally spun into a dance. For a few moments the guests swayed back and forth clapping their hands. Then Pearl grabbed Reuben's arm and Kitty grabbed Michael's. Suddenly I was alone in the middle of a crowd of dancers. I felt like a three-legged chair. How could Reuben leave me like that?

A group of older women perched on chairs lining the wall. I found a place next to them, swaying back and forth to the music and trying to look like I was enjoying myself. Children frolicked through the crowd. Once a man I didn't know bowed politely and offered me his hand. I smiled and shook my head. I began to wish I were home in bed. Weddings were no fun.

Finally the music stopped.

"Rose, come eat with us." Reuben took my hand and pulled me over to his friends. The table was piled with platters of roast chicken, knishes, potato salad, fruit and cake. Reuben sat next to Pearl. I took the chair next to Kitty.

"I haven't danced so much in ages," Pearl said, draining a glass of soda water. Her cheeks were glowing. "Reuben is improving."

"How can I help it when you won't let me go? Not even for a dance with Rose." Reuben smiled at me.

"Rosie doesn't mind, do you, sweetie?" Pearl bit into a chicken leg.

"How do you all know each other?" I asked, nibbling a spicy potato knish.

Cursing Columbus

"From school and the Alliance. Sally used to drag us to her acting classes. *How now brown cow?*" Kitty and Pearl burst out laughing.

"Do you still go to school?"

"I do," Pearl said. "I'm going to be a teacher." I hated her even more.

"Until you get married." Kitty laughed again. "I work at Lord and Taylor's in the cosmetics department."

"She gets big discounts on lipstick. And powder." Pearl took out a powder box and dusted her nose.

The talk turned to work. Pearl worked on Sundays and was planning to go to Hunter College next year. Her father owned several tenement buildings and could afford to buy her nice clothes and keep her in school. They all talked about the last play they had seen and the movies they wanted to see. I didn't recognize any of the names.

"I hope you're all enjoying yourselves." Sally threw her arms around Reuben and kissed him on the cheek. She smiled at me. "Rose, I'm so glad you came. This is my old bunch. Though I guess I won't have much time for them now that I'm a married woman." She stuck out her hand to reveal a thin band of gold.

"Are you really moving to Brownsville?" Kitty asked.

"Jake found us the nicest apartment! It has three rooms with big windows and our own private bathroom. We're going to buy all new furniture on the installment plan. None of this second-hand junk for my Jake."

Jake walked up and put his big hands around Sally's waist. "Come along, honey. My parents want you to meet all the relatives."

"But, Jakie, I want to spend time with my friends." Sally pouted.

Jake stared at us as if we were a bunch of stray dogs. "Sally, remember what I told you." He turned away.

"Jake thinks my friends are a bad influence," Sally said in a low voice to Reuben. "He expects me to spend the whole day cleaning and cooking and talking to his mother." She sighed. The sparkle had died in her eyes.

"I'm coming, dear." In the middle of the room she turned and waved to us. It felt like she was waving goodbye.

"Well, I never." Kitty sounded more sad than angry.

"That's what she gets for marrying an older man," Pearl said. "Everyone knows how possessive they are. Now I want to dance some more!" She turned a dazzling white smile on Reuben.

I was left alone with Reuben's friends.

We sat eating and drinking the rest of the evening. Kitty consumed quantities of chicken and cake washed down with innumerable glasses of soda.

"I'm too full to dance," she complained to Michael. He asked me, but I felt too clumsy to dance with a stranger. With Reuben it would have been different, but Pearl never released him. When Kitty and Michael got up to leave, they were still dancing.

LEMMEL

"So what I got to do?" Mr. Gray said we needed to practice for the trial.

"First, sit up straight. Clasp your hands. Don't squirm or swing your feet. And don't look directly at the judge. Keep your eyes on the table."

I did like he said. I felt like a bug.

"Now we'll pretend that you're in the witness stand. I'll ask you questions. Speak slowly and clearly and look straight at me. Ready?"

I nodded.

"Louis, did you enter Mrs. Smith's house on the night of March 3rd for the purpose of stealing?"

"I didn't take nothin'."

"Louis, you must tell the truth. Everyone knows you were there to steal."

"Yes."

"Yes, *sir*. Always call me and the other lawyer 'sir.' And call the judge 'your honor.' Understand?"

"Yes. . .sir."

"Why were you stealing, Louis?"

"Because I needed money. I didn't have no place to sleep."

"Were you working?"

"Yes, sir. I was selling papers. But I couldn't make enough money for me and Nickels to eat and sleep. One night we ate. One night we slept in the Newsboys Lodging."

"Who is Nickels?"

"My friend. He was just a little kid. His brudder's dead and he don't have no one to take care of him. So I did."

"What happened to Nickels on the night of March 3rd?"

"This big lady, the maid, cut him with a knife. He was bleeding bad."

"What did you do?"

"I stayed with him until the cops came."

"Don't say 'cops.' Call them 'the police.'"

"Until the police came."

"Could you have run away?"

"Yes, sir."

"Why didn't you?"

"Because I was afraid Nickels would bleed to death. We was hiding in a hallway and maybe the cops. . .I mean the police, couldn't find him and he died."

"So you took it upon yourself to remain with him while your accomplice ran away?"

"I don't understand. Sir."

"You accepted the responsibility."

"Yeah, I did." *And look where it had gotten me.* "I'm hungry."

"Here, you can have this." Mr. Gray opened his briefcase. "My wife made it."

I took a bite of the sandwich. It had thick slices of roast beef inside. "Thank you." I gobbled it down. Mr. Gray handed me an apple.

"Next time I'll ask her to make two." He smiled at me. I had the feeling he had given me his lunch. Well, he had money to buy another. But I liked him just the same.

"I'm ready." I sat up straight, folded my hands in my lap and looked at the table. Mr. Gray laughed.

"You're a good pupil, Louis. Now I'll pretend to be the prosecuting attorney. He's not going to be nice so I won't be nice either. Ready?"

I took a deep breath. "Yes, sir."

RAIZEL

"Oh, Reuben, just one more dance." Pearl pulled at Reuben's arm as he approached our now-empty table.

"It's late. I have to take Rose home." Reuben sounded annoyed.

"You never have any fun." Pearl pouted. "Anyway, you'll take me home too, won't you? That pig Kitty left without me and I'm afraid to walk home alone after midnight." She looked pleadingly at Reuben.

"But you live in the opposite direction. Why didn't you leave with Kitty?" Reuben sighed.

"Why? Because I was dancing with you, of course." Pearl laughed and planted a kiss on Reuben's cheek. Then she ducked her head and glanced up from behind her long lashes.

"Well, come along then, ladies. We're going for an evening stroll."

Pearl lived on Houston Street. When we got there, I sat down on the cold steps.

"Up past your bedtime, little Rosie?" Pearl asked. She took Reuben's hands. "I had a lovely evening," she said in a soft voice.

"So did I. Good night, Pearl."

"Reuben. . ." Pearl leaned towards him with her eyes half-closed. In another second their lips would meet. I wanted to sink into the stairs and die.

Abruptly Reuben turned and offered me his hand.

"G'night, Pearl," I called. She watched us go with a half smile on her face.

We walked in silence for a while. "Did you have a good time to-night?" Reuben asked.

"I enjoyed meeting your friends," I said. I had had a horrible time.

"Kitty has a great sense of humor."

"Pearl seems to like you." Oh no, I must sound jealous.

"Pearl is husband-hunting."

"But she wants to go to college and become a teacher."

"That's what she says, but a husband is what she wants."

We crossed the street. "I think she wants you."

Reuben stuffed his hands into his pockets. "I'm not planning to marry until I've become a doctor. If Pearl is still single by then, who knows?"

I stumbled. "So you like her?"

"She's fun to be with. I think she'd make a good doctor's wife."

Reuben had it all planned out, as usual.

"But by then she'll probably be married to a rich lawyer," Reuben continued.

"She's beautiful."

"Yes, she is."

Even though it was after midnight the usual crowd of painted wom-en and drunken men were lounging under the street lamp at the corner of Goerck Street. I moved closer to Reuben.

"You didn't have much fun tonight, did you?" Reuben asked softly.

"I didn't know anybody. And I don't know how to dance." Reuben opened the front door of our building and we plodded up the stairs.

"You should learn to have more fun."

"I work and study and take care of my little brother and sister. When do I have time for fun?"

"Rose, stop it. You're too young to be bitter."

Anger boiled up from a dark place inside me. "You stop it! I don't have a rich father to put me through school and buy me dresses like pretty Pearl. In a few weeks the baby will arrive and I'll have to go to work so that we have enough to eat. If that sounds like fun, well. . ." I was crying too hard to continue.

I opened the door to the apartment, slipped off my shoes, and without another word to Reuben, ran into the front room. Through my sobs, I could hear him getting ready for bed. Wasn't it enough that he had danced with Pearl all evening? Did he have to criticize me too? Let him marry Pearl and see what kind of life he had. I hated him!

And I hated my life.

24
On Trial

RAIZEL

Mr. Gray wanted the entire family at the trial, even Hannah. He said it would make a good impression on the judge. We got up early and put on our best clothes. But halfway down the stairs, Mama suddenly doubled over.

"Owww!" She clutched her stomach. "I cannot go."

"Mama, is the baby coming?" *Please not now.*

"I don't think so." Mama rubbed her stomach. "But it hurts my legs to walk down the stairs. And I don't think I can ride the streetcar." She was gasping for breath.

Papa turned to me. "Take the little ones and wait on the stoop while I put Mama to bed. All this tension is too much for a woman in her condition. She has not slept for days."

Mama's stomach was so enormous I didn't see how she could sleep, even without her worries about Lemmel.

When Papa finally came down the stairs, we dashed for the streetcar.

LEMMEL

I was wearing the shirt and pants that Mama sent and new shoes that Mr. Gray bought. He even paid a barber to give me a haircut so I would look "presentable," whatever that was.

I hadn't slept good last night, though. The boy next to me, Ryan, had nightmares and cried for his mama. Sometimes the other guys hit him and he cried even more. He told me he only stole a loaf of bread. He said his father left and his mama had seven kids to feed so she made him steal. I didn't believe him. I didn't trust anything they told me in here.

"Good morning, Louis." Mr. Gray put his arm around my shoulder. "Are you nervous?"

"No, I'm scared."

He laughed. I didn't mind when he laughed at me. He wasn't laughing from meanness, but because something I said struck him funny.

"It's natural to be scared. I'm scared, too."

"You?" I'm the one who was going to jail.

"Every time I walk through those doors, I feel like Adolf Gruenbaum, straight off the boat from Germany."

"I thought you was born in America." We were walking down a long corridor.

"No, I came over when I was around your age. My father died and my mother sent me to live with her brother. I never saw her again."

"You was all alone?"

"Yes. And the worst part was that my uncle no longer lived in New York, as I discovered when I went looking for him. He had moved to Pittsburgh, but I didn't find that out until months later."

"So you lived on the streets?" I couldn't believe it.

"Fortunately, I didn't have to. I went to the synagogue and was 'adopted' by a man from Berlin. He and his wife took me in. They had no children and treated me like a son. I was very lucky, and I try never to forget it."

He pushed open a set of heavy wooden doors. There were rows of benches and a high desk at the front of the room. The benches were empty except for an elderly lady wearing a brown fur coat and pearl earrings. I didn't recognize her, but guessed she was the woman I'd robbed.

Cursing Columbus

A large woman with a rough face was sitting next to her. They both glared at me.

"Where's my family?" I asked Mr. Gray as we sat down at a long table.

"They'll be here." He took out his gold watch. A man strode down the aisle and bowed slightly to Mr. Gray. "That's Mr. Adams, the prosecutor. Remember what I told you about him?"

Mr. Gray said to give him short answers and whatever I do, not get angry. Otherwise he would tear me to pieces. I didn't want to be teared to pieces.

The side door opened and a short gray-haired man in a black robe walked in. Everyone stood up. Before I sat down, I looked around again. They weren't here. If they cared, they would be here.

"Mr. Gray, please make your opening remarks," the judge ordered. Mr. Gray got up, buttoned his suit jacket, and began to talk about the hardships of immigration life. He talked about our family and the long separation from Papa, then about our reunion and Papa losing his job. I listened, but it sounded like he was talking about some other boy named Louis and some other family. Then he told the court about Nickels and how I wouldn't leave him.

Suddenly the doors opened with a thud. Everyone turned around.

Papa, Raizel, Shloyme and Hannah tumbled into the courtroom. They slid onto a bench in back of me. But where was Mama?

"Order in the court!" The judge rapped his wooden hammer. "Who are these people?"

"They are the family of the defendant, your Honor," answered Mr. Gray.

"One would think that they could make the effort to get here on time. Please continue."

I didn't like the judge. He looked like he had been sucking lemons.

After Mr. Gray, the judge called Mr. Adams, the prosecutor. He smoothed down his hair and said I was a thief who had robbed a helpless old lady. He described how I snuck into her bedroom and how she was afraid for her life and could have died of a heart attack. Then he said I stole the jewelry her husband gave her and that I refused to cooperate with the police to get her things back. He called me a hardened criminal and a danger to society and said I should be put away before I murder people. I listened to every word, but he wasn't talking about me, either.

"I call Louis Altman to the stand."

RAIZEL

The bruises on Lemmel's face had healed, but he was still too thin. Mama would cry if she saw him. I was worried. What if the baby came when there was no one home to help her? We shouldn't have left her alone.

"Why is Lemmel acting so funny?" Shloyme whispered. "He keeps his head down and doesn't look at us."

"I don't know." Lemmel wasn't acting like himself. Mr. Gray asked questions about why he robbed the house and why he wouldn't leave his friend to die. I could barely hear his answers. Then Mr. Gray finished and the prosecutor got up. Right away I didn't like him. He had a pointy nose like a fox.

"Well, Louis, Mr. Gray would have us think that you are a hero who sacrificed himself to save his friend. Are you a hero, Louis?"

"No, sir."

"What are you?"

"Objection!" Mr. Gray jumped to his feet.

"Overruled. Answer the question, boy." The judge frowned.

"A thief, sir."

"Yes, you certainly are," Mr. Adams continued. "And what do we do with thieves, Louis?"

"Send them to prison, sir."

"That is correct. Can you give me a good reason why we shouldn't send you to prison, Louis?"

Lemmel looked confused. He squirmed in his chair and glanced at us.

"Answer the question, boy."

"Because my family will be sad. Especially my mother."

"Your family will be sad, Louis? Your mother didn't even come to court today."

Mr. Gray stood up. "Your Honor, the defendant's mother was not physically able to travel to the courtroom."

"You say your family will be sad. Isn't it true that for five months your family had no idea where you were?"

"Yes, sir."

"Isn't it true that your family's happiness was of little consequence to you?"

"I don't understand the question, sir."

"Never mind. I think the court understands."

"Can I say something, sir?" Lemmel looked at the judge. Papa leaned forward in his seat.

"Yes, you may, boy."

"I'm sorry for what I done. I didn't mean to steal, only Nickels and me was hungry and cold and we couldn't make enough money selling papers. It was the first time I done it and I won't do it again."

"Very touching, your Honor," said Mr. Adams with a sneer. "But far from the truth. You see, I have information that Louis Altman is a confirmed pickpocket. In fact he learned from the notorious criminal Nathan Dinnerstein, as did his young friend, Michael Kelly."

"Objection! This has no bearing on the crime in question." Mr. Gray looked confused.

I held my breath. Nathan Dinnerstein was the name of the man who had abducted Sally! What was Lemmel's connection with him?

"It has bearing on the accused's character," Mr. Adams continued. "This is no innocent boy who made one small mistake. Louis Altman is a hardened criminal who was suspended from public school for cheating, ran away from home, and learned the pickpocketing trade from a master. I had the 'pleasure' of speaking with Nathan Dinnerstein before he was sent away to Sing Sing. He told me all about Louis Altman, his very able pupil."

"Bad, very bad," said Mr. Gray to Papa during the lunch recess. "This business with the pickpocketing school is new to me. Louis said nothing about it."

Papa looked miserable. "I did not know." He shook his head. "So there is no hope?"

"There is always hope. I'm going to put Rose on the stand after I cross-examine Louis."

"Me?" My heart plunged into my shoes. "What can I do?"

"Just tell the truth, my dear," said Mr. Gray. "Now I think I'll have a chat with our young pickpocket."

25
Nothing But the Truth

LEMMEL

Mr. Gray was furious. He said I hadn't been telling him the whole truth. But he never asked about the Dodge, so why should I tell him?

Why did the Dodge have to rat on me? I never done nothing to him.

"They probably promised him leniency in return for his testimony," Mr. Gray explained.

"Huh?"

"They took time off his sentence."

And put it on mine.

RAIZEL

After the recess, Mr. Gray put Lemmel on the witness stand again.

"Louis, did you take part in the pickpocketing school run by Nathan Dinnerstein?" Mr. Gray asked.

"Yes, sir."

"Why?"

"Because I couldn't make enough money selling newspapers."

"Did you know pickpocketing was a crime?"

"Yes, sir. But I only took from rich people. They got plenty."

"He's a dirty thief!" The woman in the fur coat shrieked at the judge. "He should be locked up!"

"Order in the court." The judge banged his gavel. "Please sit down, ma'am."

"Louis, what do you know about Nathan Dinnerstein?"

"He's a crook. He taught me to graft and I paid him a percentage."

"Your honor, I would like to point out that Nathan Dinnerstein was most certainly involved in the heinous horse poisonings on the East Side last summer. He is now in Sing Sing because he was caught abducting a young woman with intent to sell her into prostitution."

"Where is this leading?" the judge asked.

"My client Louis was young and fell under the influence of a dastardly criminal who had no compunctions about making a deal with the district attorney in exchange for supplying negative evidence against him. This clearly shows what a terrible impact the streets have on boys of a tender age."

"Keep it short, Mr. Gray."

"Your Honor, I greatly fear what will happen to my client if he is incarcerated in jail far from the positive influence of his family."

"Objection!"

"Sustained. Save it for your closing remarks, Mr. Gray," said the judge.

Mr. Adams rose to cross-examine Lemmel.

"Young man, you knowingly entered this so-called 'school' in order to learn a dishonest trade?"

"I don't understand the question, sir."

"You went to learn to be a pickpocket?"

"Yes, sir." Lemmel hung his head.

"That brings me to the next question. Louis, why did you run away from home?"

Lemmel glanced at us and ducked his head again.

"Please instruct the defendant to answer."

"Louis, you must answer the question, understand?" The judge leaned towards him.

"Yes, your honor. I. . .I didn't want to go to school."

"Did you parents beat you?" asked Mr. Adams.

"No, sir."

"Did they give you enough to eat?"

"Yes, sir."

"So you left a good home and family because you were too lazy to go to school?"

"I'm not lazy!" Lemmel glared at Mr. Adams.

"That's what you say. I have affidavits from your teacher and principal stating that you did poorly in school because you didn't work hard enough. You copied your little brother's composition. Even before you left home, you were a cheat and a liar."

"Objection!"

"Overruled."

Mr. Adams smiled. "You are dismissed."

Mr. Gray whispered something to Lemmel, who shook his head. Things looked bad. The prosecutor had made a strong case against Lemmel. He had broken the law more than once.

"The defense calls Rose Altman."

I started. Hannah had fallen asleep on my shoulder. Papa lifted her into his lap.

"State your full name, age, and relationship to the defendant."

"Rose Altman, age 14. I am Louis' sister, sir."

"Rose, tell us about your brother."

"Louis is a good boy. He helped Mama when she was alone. Papa and I came to America four years ago. The rest of the family came last September," I explained to the judge.

"Are you a good student, Rose?" Mr. Gray asked.

"Yes, sir. I want to be a teacher when I grow up."

"Objection! This has no relevance to the case at hand."

"Your honor, I ask for the court's leniency. I wish to demonstrate something very important about the defendant's character."

"You may proceed, Mr. Gray."

"Rose, was Louis a good student?"

"No. He never liked school, but he's not lazy."

"Why do you say that?"

"He studied for his bar mitzvah for hours and hours. I tried to help him but. . .I couldn't."

"And why was that, Rose?"

Lemmel was staring down at the table. "He had trouble reading, sir."

"Did he tell you that?"

"Yes. He told me the letters jump around."

"Objection! This is ridiculous, your honor. The boy is a confirmed liar." Mr. Adams looked bored.

"Mr. Gray?" The judge tapped his fingers on the polished surface of his lectern.

"I request the court's leniency for one more minute. Rose, did you believe this was true?"

"Yes, I did, sir. I tried to help Lemmel learn to read, but he couldn't keep the letters straight, no matter how much he tried. It was strange."

"Why do you say that, Rose?"

"Well, I learned how to read after only a few weeks at school. I know Louis isn't dumb. He can add figures in his head better than I can. So he should have been able to learn, but he couldn't."

Mr. Gray nodded. "Your honor, I believe that the defendant suffers from some kind of reading inability. Just as some people are unable to hear, some are unable to walk, and others unable to see, so my client is unable to read. I have consulted with several experienced teachers. All say they have seen students who, no matter how hard they tried, just could not learn to read. All these students left school at an early age."

"What are you saying, Mr. Gray?" The judge looked puzzled.

"I contend that the defendant was unable to succeed in school be-cause he was not capable of learning how to read, or perhaps I should

Cursing Columbus

say, the school was not capable of teaching him. He copied his brother's composition in a desperate attempt to be thought a good student. And he ran away from home because he was unable to prepare for his bar mitzvah and did not want to disgrace himself and his parents."

The judge looked at Lemmel. "Boy, is this true?"

Lemmel looked up. Tears were streaming down his face. "Yes, your honor. I just want to go to work. I'm a good worker. I won't steal anymore, I promise."

The judge wrote something on a pad of paper. "Your witness, Mr. Adams."

The courtroom seemed to grow colder.

"Rose, would your father have beaten Louis or kicked him out of the house for not knowing how to read?"

"No sir, definitely not!"

"Thank you. That will be all."

"I will hear closing arguments tomorrow." The judge banged on his lectern. "Court dismissed."

Before the guard took Lemmel away, he called to me. "Raizel, is Mama alright?"

"Mama's going to have a baby. She isn't feeling well."

He looked shocked. I had forgotten that he had been gone so long. "Will she come tomorrow?" The guard jerked him roughly away.

"I don't know. Don't worry."

For a moment, I saw in Lemmel's face the boy who had loved to climb trees and pet horses, the boy who had pretended he was too old to listen to my stories. Then the moment passed, and he looked like a street rat, hard and cold.

Mr. Gray was talking to Papa. "I just don't know. I've never had a case like this before."

"But vat can the judge do? Lemmel stole from that woman. He broke the law."

"Yes, that's true, Mr. Altman. But the judge has a certain amount of leeway in terms of sentencing. This is Louis' first offense and he stayed behind to save his friend. I've also shown that there were mitigating circumstances that caused him to run away from home."

Papa looked confused. "Tomorrow you vant I should bring the whole family?"

"That's not necessary. But you should come, Mr. Altman. Now, if you don't mind, I need to prepare my closing argument." He chucked Hannah under the chin. "I believe you're going to be as pretty as your big sister Rose." Hannah buried her face in Papa's coat.

"Of course I come tomorrow. What kind of father does he think I am?" We were riding back home in the crowded streetcar.

"But what a *dummkof* I was," Papa continued. "Why did Lemmel not tell me he could not read?"

"I think Lemmel was ashamed to tell you, Papa. He was afraid everyone would think he was stupid."

"He is stupid," said Shloyme. "I can read and I'm only six!"

"Shloyme," Papa said sternly. "You must never call your brother stupid. It is like your talent for playing the piano. I cannot play the piano, but does this mean that I am stupid?"

"Of course not, Papa."

"Just because Lemmel cannot read, does not mean he is stupid. So you do not call him that again. Understand?"

"Yes, but the other kids will call him stupid."

"It is not important what other people say. We know the truth."

I clutched the strap as the streetcar made a turn. If only it were that easy.

The streetcar jerked and swayed down the crowded streets. It was taking us so long to get home. Anything could have happened to Mama.

Cursing Columbus

26
In the Wilderness

RAIZEL

As we rounded the corner of Goerck Street, Papa broke into a run. I followed dragging Hannah by the hand.

"Raizel, wait for me!" Hannah howled as we reached the entrance to our home.

I pounded up the stairs. Neighbors poked their heads out the doors. On the fourth floor, I almost fell over Lucia and Roberto playing on the landing.

"Rosie, guess what?" Lucia called as I burst into our apartment.

The kitchen was empty. Suddenly I heard a thin wail from the back bedroom. Papa came out holding a tiny bundle in his arms and a big smile on his face.

"Raizel, meet your new sister."

"Is Mama alright?" I brushed past him. In the gloom I could see Mama propped up on a pillow. Her face looked drawn. She opened her eyes as I walked in and held out her hand to me.

"Mama, how do you feel?" There was a glass of water on the night table. I gave her a sip.

"Like a woman who just had her fifth baby. Did you see her?"

"Not yet."

"She looks just like my father Shimon, may he rest in peace. The same olive skin and dark eyes. I'm going to call her Sima, after him. Where is Lemmel? Did he come home with you?"

I kissed Mama's forehead. "Mama, he's in jail. You know that."

"I had a dream that he came home in time for Passover next week." She brushed away a tear. "How was it?"

"It was. . .hard. The trial continues tomorrow."

"They won't send him to jail, will they?" She squeezed my hand. "Tell me the truth."

"No one knows, Mama. Lemmel asked about you. He was worried when you didn't come."

"For months he doesn't worry about his family and now he worries?" A touch of color bloomed in Mama's cheeks.

"Shall I fix you a cup of tea and something to eat?"

"Yah, I'm hungry. Having a baby is hard work."

I sat with Mama while she ate a soft-boiled egg and tea. She told me how the labor pains had started shortly after we left. She couldn't get up from the bed so she banged on the wall until Maria came. Maria ran for a midwife in the next building. Together the two delivered the baby. My new sister.

"But why didn't they call the doctor, Mama? That's the way it's done in America."

"Doctor, shmactor. You think I had a doctor when you were born, or Shloyme or Hannah? If I had waited for a doctor in Jibatov, I would have grown a beard!"

I laughed. Hannah lay next to Mama on the bed, sucking her thumb. Papa was walking the baby so Mama could have a few minutes to eat.

"Where's Shloyme?" I asked.

"Downstairs," Papa said. "I told him he could play outside until supper."

Supper was my job. "Papa, I'm going to the store."

I met Reuben on the landing. We had barely spoken since Sally's wedding last week.

"Mama had her baby! I'm going to buy food for supper," I said.

"*Mazel Tov!* I want to hear what happened at the trial. I'll put my books away and walk you to the store."

On the way, I told Reuben about the trial. When I came to the part about Nathan Dinnerstein and the pickpocketing school, he stopped short.

"What's the matter?"

"Remember when we went to look for Sally and I ran after some boys? The older one had red hair and freckles."

"Lemmel!"

Reuben nodded. "If only I had held on to him..."

"This never would have happened." I felt sick.

"I'm sorry, Raizel." Reuben put his arms around me. I buried my face in his coat. "I'm so sorry."

LEMMEL

They put me alone in a cell. I sat with my knees up, thinking.

I thought about how Papa looked when Raizel explained about my reading. I watched him. He was crying.

He wasn't mad.

Why did I think he would be mad?

Why did I run away?

I was so dumb.

Mama would have yelled that I was a disgrace to the family and chased me with a broom like she did back in Jibatov.

So what? I had got hit plenty on the streets, and in jail. I wasn't afraid to take a beating.

Afraid. I was afraid of what Papa would think of me. Afraid of Mama's disappointment. Afraid that people would laugh and call me dumb.

I ran away because I was a coward. Lemmel, the coward.

I didn't want to go to jail or reform school. I wanted to go home to my real life. Find a job. Help Papa support the family. Hang out with my friends. Let Mama take care of me.

Be a kid again.

RAIZEL

Papa and I arrived at the courtroom just as they brought in Lemmel. Shloyme had gone to school. Hannah refused to leave Mama. She wouldn't even look at the baby. Mama said she'd get over being jealous, that Hannah had been the baby for so long, it was hard for her to accept a new baby.

Papa spoke briefly to Mr. Gray.

"Good morning, your honor." Mr. Gray addressed the judge. "Mr. Altman just informed me that his wife gave birth to a baby girl yesterday. May we have a minute with my client?"

I rushed over to Lemmel. "Mama's fine. We have a baby sister named Sima Leah! Mama sends her love and wishes she could be here."

Lemmel looked stunned and then happy. "Will they let me out of jail to see her?"

Papa gave Lemmel a hug. "Be strong, no matter what happens. Everything will be all right."

Lemmel nodded and ducked his head.

"Mr. Gray, may we begin?" The judge seemed annoyed this morning. Mr. Adams glanced around the almost-empty courtroom. He looked very sure of himself. "I will hear closing arguments."

Mr. Gray spoke about our family and the hardships we had endured to come to America. He told the court about Papa's job and my participation in the Columbus contest. He made it sound like we were the best family in the world. Then he spoke about Lemmel, his problems in school, and how in a moment of foolishness, he had run away and fallen under the influence of the street. He talked about Lemmel's bravery and loyalty in remaining behind to save his friend and how he knew right from wrong and had learned his lesson.

"So I ask the court for leniency. Louis is a child and made the mistakes of a child. I beg the court to send him home to the custody of his family, where he will once more learn to walk the path of righteousness and become a fine upstanding citizen. I have known many criminals in my long career, your honor, and I can honestly say that Louis Altman is not one of them. He is a boy who went wrong. Let us give him a chance to return to society. It is a heavy responsibility for Louis, but I believe he can live up to it. Although he committed a crime, he is a good person and, with the court's help, will become an upstanding citizen of whom this country can be proud! Thank you."

I felt like applauding. Mr. Gray had given a stirring speech. No matter what the outcome of the trial, no matter what the judge decided, I knew I had made the right decision in giving up my money and my dreams. No one could have done a better job than Mr. Gray, and I would always be grateful to him.

Mr. Adams stood up holding a newspaper in his hand. "Your Honor, last night a gang of street rats broke into the home of a family on Park Avenue, stole their silver, and beat the gentleman of the house when he woke up and tried to stop him. That blameless citizen now lies in a coma in the hospital, and his wife and children sit crying by his bedside." He threw down the newspaper and pointed at Lemmel. "I ask your Honor, how long can this go on? How long will it take before honest citizens can sleep in their beds without fear? Only last month, the department of welfare published a report stating that over 20,000 homeless boys roam the streets of New York City, with more arriving every day. Our great city had been invaded by the rabble and detritus of the world. Honest

Americans huddle behind locked doors while hoards of foreigners, people who do not even take the trouble to learn our language, swarm the streets, eating our bread and stealing our livelihoods."

He took out a white handkerchief and wiped his forehead.

"What is he saying about Lemmel? I do not understand," Papa whispered.

"He's not talking about Lemmel." I was shivering, and not from cold.

"You may well ask what this has to do with the accused, Louis Altman." Mr. Adams strode to the center of the courtroom. "America welcomed this illiterate immigrant only nine months ago and sent him to a school where he was taught English and given every opportunity. And what did he do?" Mr. Adams looked like he wanted to toss Lemmel in the garbage. "He ran away from home, became the protégée of a known criminal, and committed innumerable crimes until he was finally caught stealing from a helpless old lady.

"My colleague would have us believe that Louis Altman is a child who made a simple mistake, but I say differently! Would you want this so-called child sneaking into your bedroom in the still of night? Would you want to end up like that poor father gasping out his life in the hospital at this very moment?

"Your Honor, when will Americans once again sleep at night free of fear? I will tell you. Only when we say 'stop' to the deluge of destitute immigrants who are flooding our golden gates. Louis Altman is no more than a drop in the filthy bucket of crime, but we must plug that leak before it becomes a torrent." He picked up the paper again. "What will tomorrow's headline be, your Honor? Another family robbed and beaten and their breadwinner killed, or praise for a wise court that understands the importance of making an example of the accused and sending the tremor of fear into the criminals of this city. Let Louis Altman be a lesson to them! Send him away to prison for the maximum sentence! Thank you."

Cursing Columbus

I was furious at Mr. Adams. I wanted to jump over the banister and beat his smug face with my bare hands. What did he know about the life of an immigrant? How could he be so cold-hearted, so full of hatred? How many people like Mr. Adams were there in America?

It was then I noticed a reporter sitting in the back of the courtroom scribbling frantically. He hadn't been there yesterday.

"Did you see the newspaperman?" I asked Mr. Gray afterwards in the corridor. The judge had dismissed the court for a recess until he reached his verdict.

He nodded. "Adams probably invited him. The man is a nativist riding the anti-immigration wave," he continued. "He obviously has political ambitions and is using this case to enter the public consciousness."

Papa shuddered. "So what will be?"

"If I only knew." Mr. Gray attempted a smile. "I'll see you later. We have until four o'clock before the judge returns his verdict."

"Mr. Gray gave a wonderful speech," I said. "I wish I had written it down."

Papa met my eyes.

"No, I don't regret it, Papa, no matter what happens. Mr. Gray was right about Lemmel. He's changed. I wasn't sure when we first saw him, but now I am."

"I only hope the judge will give him the chance to prove you right."

LEMMEL

Mrs. Gray had sent me roast chicken for lunch. It smelled delicious, but when I took a bite, my stomach turned over.

Mr. Gray said Hawthorne was a good place where I could learn to work with my hands and be with other Jewish boys. Only now it was full. Who knew where the judge would send me? It couldn't be worse than jail.

But it wasn't home. I wanted to go home. I wanted to see Mama and the baby. I wanted to play with my friends again. They would be grown up by the time I got out. Everyone would have forgotten me except Mama and Papa, if they were still alive. I wiped my eyes on my sleeve.

Mr. Adams talked about that man in the hospital like I had done it. I never hit nobody. Funny, I thought they only hated Jews in Russia. The boys there called us "Zhids" and pulled our side curls, until I cut mine off. It hadn't helped. When I got bigger, I beat them up, but there was always a bigger boy coming after me.

I remembered how people wrote to their relatives in Jibatov about America, where the streets were paved with gold. On Goerck Street they were paved with garbage and saloons and drunks sleeping in the alleys, whores on the corner and people evicted and begging on the streets. Why didn't that Mr. Adams talk about how immigrants had no money to feed their babies or pay for medicine? How kids had no place to play but on the streets?

Sometimes it seemed like my life in Jibatov had been a dream. I had walked in the woods and picked apples and cherries off the trees. I swam in clear clean water, not the muck of the East River. We had our own little house without noisy neighbors poking around all day. There were . . .

"Get a move on, punk." Red-face opened the cell door. "Time to get what you deserve. I hope that judge sends you up the river for the rest of your life."

Cursing Columbus

27
The Promised Land

RAIZEL

The reporter was gone when we returned to the courtroom. Clearly nobody cared about Lemmel's fate except us. I thought of the homeless boys with no family. No matter what happened, Lemmel was one of the lucky ones.

"I have reviewed all the evidence and listened carefully to the closing arguments," the judge began. "It is clear in my mind that the accused, Louis Altman, committed the crime in question. He also refused to cooperate with the police to enable them to retrieve the stolen goods."

I glanced at Mr. Adams. He was leaning back in his seat, his hands clasped behind his head.

"According to the letter of the law, the maximum penalty for a first offense is two years. However, I am governed not by the letter of the law alone, but by the spirit of the law. While the law recommends two years, it does not require me to invoke the maximum penalty. I have listened closely to Mr. Gray, and to Louis and his sister. They have convinced me that Louis, while he made serious mistakes, is a decent person at heart. He may even be a noble person."

Mr. Adams leaned forward suddenly. I caught my breath.

"I was impressed by Louis' decision to remain with his wounded friend. It was clear to me, as it was clear to Louis, that his friend would have bled to death if he had run away. At the same time, Louis knew full well that by remaining with his friend, he was delivering himself into the hands of the police. It took a brave heart to make that decision, and I, for one, respect a brave heart.

"Therefore, while I find Louis Altman guilty of robbery and sentence him to two years in prison, I am suspending that sentence and remanding him to the custody of his parents. Louis, stand up. Do you understand what I am saying?"

"N-no, your Honor."

"You are free to go home, Louis. But, if you commit another crime, any crime at all, you will be arrested and your suspended sentence will be added to your new sentence. You will live with a sword hanging over your head, Louis, but you will decide whether that sword will fall. I also remand you to the supervision of the Department of Corrections. Until you reach the age of eighteen, you will report to your local police station once a month, and you are forbidden to leave the state of New York. Is that understood?"

"I can go home?"

"Yes, you may. And from now on, Louis, you will do as your father says and always, but always, be a good boy. I have put my trust in you. Don't betray that trust."

"I promise, your Honor."

Papa turned to me. "Did I understand right? Is this a dream?"

"It's Mama's dream! Lemmel is free to go home!" I threw my arms around Papa. Suddenly Lemmel was there, hugging us and crying and laughing at the same time.

"Well, well." Mr. Gray's grin lifted his whole face. "I am speechless. The judge surprised even an old warhorse like me. A suspended sentence. Louis, you are one lucky boy."

"Thank you, Mr. Gray." Lemmel pumped his hand up and down. "Thank you for everything you done for me."

"You understand that you must behave yourself? If the police so much as catch you breaking a window or beating up another boy, they will throw you in jail for two years."

Lemmel nodded. "Yes, I understand."

Mr. Gray shook Papa's hand warmly. "I shall send you my bill. I think you will be pleasantly surprised at how low it is. I don't know when I have felt so satisfied with the outcome of a case. And Louis..." He put his arms around Lemmel and gave him a hug. "This is the last time I plan to represent you, understand?"

We laughed. Lemmel looked around the courtroom as if he couldn't believe he was free to leave. Then we walked out together into the late afternoon sunshine.

LEMMEL

"Why is this night different from all other nights?" Papa read the four questions of the Passover Seder. Shloyme, as the youngest son, recited the familiar answers.

"Because on every other night we eat leavened and unleavened bread. On this night we eat only matzoh," Shloyme chanted.

Then Papa surprised me. He asked the question a fifth time and winked at Shloyme.

Shloyme didn't hesitate a second. "Because on this night Lemmel has come home to us!" Everyone stopped singing and hugged me. I was black and blue from hugs. I think Mama had given me a hug for every day I was gone.

I didn't realize they had missed me so much.

All the men at the Seder took turns reading the story of Moses leading the Israelites out of Egypt into the Promised Land: Papa, Mendel, Mr. Abrahamson, Raizel's boss, and Reuben, our boarder. Papa skipped over me, but no one seemed to notice. We were all sitting in the front room using the beds as benches. Papa had made a long table out of old doors. Covered with clean white sheets, the table looked festive.

Not like Uncle Nahum's house back in Jibatov, but nicer than I had expected.

They read the story of Pharaoh's daughter finding baby Moses in the bulrushes. I looked at our new baby. She was skinny and cried a lot, but there was something about her I liked. She looked me straight in the eye. She had American spunk.

Now the grownup Moses was wandering in the desert. It reminded me of my wanderings around New York. Moses found the burning bush and knew what he had to do: free his people.

What was I going to do?

Papa had sent me back to school, but Mr. McGraw said that because I'd be fourteen next fall, I didn't have to come back. He suggested I take night school classes. Raizel said she would try to teach me.

Papa wanted me to learn a trade. I told him I wanted to be a carpenter or take care of animals, but he said he never heard of a Jewish carpenter in America, and they didn't have any animals to take care of in New York City, except in the zoo. I had had enough of cages.

Papa said he would talk with his boss, Mr. Clancy, the big Irishman sitting next to Raizel at the end of the table. Mama wasn't pleased when Papa invited him. She said he would eat too much, but she finally agreed.

We reached my favorite part of the Seder. The Egyptians were suffering from the ten plagues, their punishment for not releasing the Hebrew slaves. We shook a drop of sweet wine on our plates for each plague.

If I were still on the streets, I wouldn't even know it was Passover. Well, maybe I would see people buying extra food at the market. They would be loaded down too much to chase me when I stole their money.

I didn't do that anymore.

The gang welcomed me back. They acted like I was some kind of hero for being in jail and living on the streets. They wanted me to be their leader, but their games bored me. They thought they were tough, but they were just silly kids. And I wasn't allowed to break windows or fight with anybody, so it wasn't much fun. When I had a job, I wouldn't have time for games. Well, maybe a game of stick ball on Sunday.

Finally the Israelites were leaving Egypt for the Promised Land. Raizel explained to Mr. Clancy how America was the Promised Land for us. He said it was the Promised Land for the Irish, too.

"I'm hungry, Mama," Hannah complained.

"Shhh, eat a hardboiled egg."

Hannah stuffed an egg into her mouth. Shloyme was nibbling matzoh, but I could wait. The Israelites were wandering in the desert after the miraculous parting of the Red Sea and the drowning of Pharaoh's army. It wouldn't be long before we reached the promised land of dinner.

Now Mama and Raizel and Shayna were running back and forth carrying platters of food. Mr. Clancy clapped his hands every time they set a plate on the table. Even Mr. Abrahamson, whose wife had died this winter, wore a smile on his face. The table was bursting with platters of chicken soup and matzoh balls, beef brisket, roast chicken, roast potatoes, carrot tzimmis, and applesauce, as well as matzoh. I looked at all the food and suddenly I couldn't eat. I wondered where Nickels was and whether they were feeding him enough. Funny. He felt more like my brother than Shloyme did.

"Eat, Lemmel." Mama put a thick slice of brisket and a helping of potatoes on my plate.

Everyone was looking at me. I wanted to tell them about the homeless boys on the street who never had enough to eat. About the boys who didn't wake up on cold mornings. About the children who had no place to call home and no one who cared about them. But I didn't want to ruin the happiness of the holiday. There were some things I would never be able to talk about.

I pushed a piece of brisket into my mouth. "Mmmm, delicious!" Mama beamed at me.

After we finished eating, the singing began. Papa poured everyone a fourth glass of wine and set a traditional glass for the Prophet Elijah. Hannah ran to open the door for him and Lucia and her brother tumbled into the room.

"Come in, come in," Mama called, and fixed them plates of leftovers.

When I was little, I used to believe Elijah really visited on Passover. I would check to see if the wine level in his cup was lower. Now Shloyme measured the cup with his eyes.

"He was here! He was here!" Shloyme cried.

Before, I would have laughed at him for being such a baby and he would have cried. But I let him believe. Little kids should be happy as long as they can.

Papa nodded his head at Shloyme. He and Hannah raced through the apartment searching for the *Afikomen* that Papa had hid. It was just a plain piece of matzoh, but whoever found it got a gift. I remembered one year in Uncle Nahum's house when he gave me a silver coin in exchange. I had never had so much money in my life.

"We found it!" Hannah ran in holding the matzoh wrapped in a white napkin. "It was in the baby's crib." Papa gave them each a nickel. They sat down chattering about how they would spend their fortunes.

After the singing, Mama, Shayna and Raizel cleared the table. Reuben tried to help, but Mama made him sit down with the men folk.

"Lemmel, listen to what Mr. Clancy has to say!" Papa called me over.

"I hear you're looking for a job, lad," said Mr. Clancy. "Well, take my advice and go back to school. That's the way to get ahead in America."

I looked at Papa.

"Louis is smart, but he doesn't like school," Papa explained.

"I can do arithmetic in my head," I said.

"Eleven plus forty-five." Mr. Clancy leaned forward.

"Fifty-six."

"Twelve times twenty-one."

I did the math in my head. "Two hundred and fifty two."

"Good! Ten percent of twenty-five."

I shook my head. "What is this 'percent'?"

"No matter, you'll learn. You have a good head, boy." He looked at Papa. "I have a friend who owns a warehouse. I'll see if he could use a stock boy. And I'll make sure he pays a fair wage."

"Please, what does a stock boy do?" I asked.

"You count the goods as they come in, put them on the shelves, make sure nothing runs out. It's not easy work, but if you're like your papa, you're not afraid of hard work."

"Sir, are there horses?"

Mr. Clancy laughed. "So you like horses, too? Horses are going out of fashion these days, but there are still a few around. Perhaps you can help out in my stables after work. I can't pay much, but you could earn an extra dollar or so a week. Would you like that?"

"Oh yes!"

"I've never seen a boy so eager to work." Mr. Clancy laughed again. "Well, Ben, I must be going. I'll just thank the missus for a wonderful dinner." He went into the kitchen where Mama was putting away the food while Raizel washed the dishes. I could see Mama talking to him and giving him a package of food to take home. I didn't know Mama had learned English! I wondered what else had changed around here that I didn't know about.

When I first came home I thought everything would be exactly the same, but it wasn't. There was the new baby, the boarder, Papa's job. And Raizel. I had asked her why she looked unhappy. She wouldn't tell me. She said she didn't want to ruin my homecoming with her problems.

RAIZEL

Every muscle in my body ached. For the past week I had done nothing but clean the house for Passover, shop, help Mama cook, and now clean up after the Seder. But I wasn't too tired to go downstairs when Reuben invited me.

It was late. The guests had left and everyone else had gone to bed. We sat down on the front stoop. Even on Goerck Street, the air smelled like spring.

"Guess what?" I grabbed Reuben's arm. "Papa said Mr. Clancy is going to help Lemmel find a job. And he gave Papa a raise."

"Raizel, that's great news!"

"No, you don't understand! Papa did some calculations. If I continue my job at the store and Lemmel makes enough money, I might not have to quit school! He said we'll see how things are in September. So there's a chance I can finish high school."

"That's wonderful!" But his voice didn't sound happy. "And now I have to tell you my news. I've decided to move to Denver after all."

"But your studies! You said. . ."

"I had a letter from Mother. Father lost his job again. Mother thinks he may be drinking. She begged me to come."

"Reuben, you're not giving up your dream of becoming a doctor?"

"I read there's a medical school in Denver. I'll need to work for a while and help my family but. . ."

For all his planning, it sounded like Reuben had to choose between his family and becoming a doctor after all. I wondered which he would choose.

"Will you write me?" I tried to keep the tears out of my voice.

"Of course." He kissed the top of my head. "You're my best friend. I can't talk to anyone the way I can talk to you. And who knows? If you're still single by the time I finish medical school, then I just might come back to New York and marry you."

Marry me? Was Reuben teasing? In the shadows from the gas light, I could barely make out his eyes. "I'm sorry. . .what did you say?"

Reuben cupped my cheek in his hand. "I said marry you. I love you, Raizel Altman."

I let my breath out ever so slowly. "And I love you," I said. "I always have."

I leaned my head on his shoulder. Reuben loved me. Nothing could take away tonight's happiness. Not the parting. Not the years of hard work and study that lay ahead of us. True, Goerck Street wasn't paved with gold and the immigrants' dream of instant happiness was just that, a dream, but I wasn't going to waste my time cursing Columbus. I had better things to do.

"Let's go to Central Park tomorrow," Reuben said. "I hear the daffodils are in bloom."

"I'll have to take Hannah. And Shloyme will want to come."

"You think I don't know that? The front stoop is the only place I can be alone with you."

A couple strolling arm in arm plopped down on the bottom step. Reuben and I burst out laughing.

"Shall we walk?" Reuben asked.

"I'm too tired."

"I'm going to miss you, Raizel." He kissed my cheek. "I don't want to lose you."

"We lost each other before," I reminded him. "And found each other. Let's make a promise that no matter what happens, we won't lose each other again."

And so we did.

Afterword

Unlike *Double Crossing*, which was based on the true events of my grandfather's rejection at Ellis Island, the story in *Cursing Columbus* is fiction. But this story, too, weaves in wisps of fact. My aunt Rose, Raizel, did become a teacher and eventually married a doctor. My uncle Shalom, Shloyme, was a superb musician and founder of the music department at Gratz College in Philadelphia. My uncle Louie, Lemmel, was the only one of his five siblings who did not attend college, but his learning disability and street adventures have no basis in biography. (The background of the newsies, petty crime, the pickpocketing school, and the dance hall abduction are historically accurate, however.) My mother Hannah used to complain that she had to take care of her baby sister, Sima, after school, but the two were best friends until they died. And my grandfather worked as a fat collector and later inherited the business from his Irish boss.

My depiction of their life on the Lower East Side is based on historical research and the stories of my mother. When I was growing up, my favorite book was *All of a Kind Family* by Sydney Taylor. A good balance to the rosy picture of Jewish life on the Lower East Side painted in that series are the fascinating, often heartbreaking, memoirs written by Jewish immigrants at the turn of the last century.

I would like to thank the helpful people at the Tenement Museum on the Lower East Side. Their fascinating tours through the reconstructed tenement apartments at 97 Orchard Street furnished a sense of place for my story.

I highly recommend the following books for anyone seeking to learn more about Jewish life on the Lower East Side a century ago:

Brumberg, Stephan F. *Going to America, Going to School: The Jewish Immigrant Public School Encounter in Turn-of-the-Century New York City*. New York: Praeger Publishers, 1986.

Cohen, Rose. *Out of the Shadow: A Russian Jewish Girlhood on the Lower East Side.* (1918) New York: Cornell University Press, 1995. (memoir)

Diner, Hasia R. *Lower East Side Memories: A Jewish Place in America*. New Jersey: Princeton University Press, 2000.

Gilfolye, Timothy J. "Street Rats and Guttersnipes: Child Pickpockets and Street Culture in New York City 1850-1900." *Journal of Social History*. Vol. 37, 2004.

Hapgood, Hutchins. *The Spirit of the Ghetto: Studies of the Jewish Quarter of New York*. Ill. Jacob Epstein. Notes: Harry Golden. (1902), New York: Schocken, 1972.

Howe, Irving. *World of Our Fathers: The Journey of the East European Jews to America and the Life They Found and Made*. New York: Simon and Schuster, 1976.

Joselit, Jenna Weissman. *Our Gang: Jewish Crime and the New York Jewish Community, 1900-40*. Bloomington: Indiana University Press, 1983.

Metzker, Isaac, ed. *A Bintel Brief: Sixty Years of Letters from the Lower East Side to the Jewish Daily Forward*. New York: Schoken, 1971.

Peiss, Kathy. *Cheap Amusements: Working Women and Leisure in Turn-of-the-Century New York*. Philadelphia: Temple University Press, 1986.

Riis, Jacob A. *How the Other Half Lives. Studies Among the Tenements of New York*. (1890). KS: Digireads.com, 2005.

Rockaway, Robert A. *Words of the Uprooted: Jewish Immigrants in Early Twentieth-Century America*. Ithaca, New York: Cornell University Press, 1998.

Spewack, Bella. *Streets: A Memoir of the Lower East Side*. New York: The Feminist Press, 1995. (memoir)

Weinberg, Sydney Stahl. *The World of Our Mothers: The Lives of Jewish Immigrant Women*. Chapel Hill, NC: University of North Carolina Press, 1988.

Yezierska, Anzia. *Bread Givers*. Intro. by Alice Kessler-Harris. (1925) NY: Persea, 2003. (novel)

Glossary

bar mitzvah	Religious ceremony held for Jewish males at age thirteen to mark their obligation to observe the religious commandments. It is the first time the boy reads from the weekly Torah portion in front of the congregation.
Bobbe	Grandmother.
challah	Bread baked in the shape of a braid for the Sabbath and holidays.
cheder	School where boys learned to read and write Hebrew and studied religious teachings.
chuppah	The canopy a couple stands under for the Jewish marriage ceremony.
dummkof	Stupid person.
farfel	Small pieces of noodle.
gonif	Thief.
kiddush	Blessing over the wine.
kugel	Sweet or salty casserole usually made of noodles or potatoes.
landsleit	Compatriots, countrymen.
landsmanshaft	A self-help organization made up of immigrants originally from the same town or region of Europe.

maideleh	"little girl"—term of endearment.
mitzvah	1) good deed 2) religious commandment.
Rebbe	Rabbi.
Rosh Hashana	Jewish New Year (usually observed in early fall.)
seder	A ritual meal accompanied by the reading of the Biblical story of the Exodus from Egypt. The celebration emphasizes the transition from slavery to freedom. Held at home on the evening of the Passover holiday, it falls in the early spring.
shiva	The seven days of ritual mourning observed by the immediate family following a death.
shul	Synagogue.
tzimmis	Carrots cooked in a sweet sauce (Raisins, apples, sweet potatoes, or apricots are optional ingredients.)
Yontif	Literally "good day" —a holiday greeting.